BREAK INSIDE

KAREN RENEE

ISBN: 978-1-957194-42-4

Paperback ISBN: 978-1-957194-49-3

Cover Model: Draven

Photographer: CJC Photography

Design: Bee at Bitter Sage Designs

Author's Note

THE RIOT MC
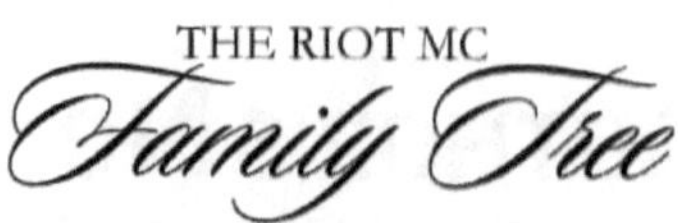

PARENTS	CHILDREN
HENRY "VOLT" ADLER JACKIE ADLER	SIMONE BOBBY
CAL "CALLOUS" ROBERTSON MALLORY ROBERTSON	ALEXANDRA
HOMER "ROLL" ROLLAND TRIXIE ROLLAND	RAFFERTY (ROAD NAME: BLUFF) JASMINE
CARY "VAMP" SULLIVAN LORRAINE SULLIVAN	GABRIELLA
GAGE "GAMBLE" GARRISON VICTORIA GARRISON	KILLIAN (ROAD NAME: RICOCHET) RYAN (ROAD NAME: NICKEL) MICKAYLA

Playlist

DANG by Rainbow Kitten Surprise
NEW HOUSE by Toro y Moi
IF TROUBLE WAS MONEY (LIVE) by Gary Clark Jr.
ROAD 2 HER/HOME by Ottmar Liebert
MISSISSIPPI GODDAM by Nina Simone
RIGHT TO COMPLAIN by Trombone Shorty
AIN'T MESSIN 'ROUND by Gary Clark Jr.
TONIGHT, TONIGHT by Stephen Wilson Jr.
I'M IN LOVE WITH YOU by The 1975
I JUST MIGHT by Bruno Mars
THE TWIST by Chubby Checker
OCEAN EYES by Billie Eilish
MORSE by Nightmares On Wax
2 by squeezyX

CHAPTER 1

IT'S PRIVATE

IVY

AFTER MONTHS OF SEARCHING old records, Internet-digging, and even a failed roadtrip that my friend Chad wouldn't let me forget, I sat outside a new neighborhood bar called 'On a Lark', determined to find my biological dad.

The neon 'Open' sign wasn't lit, but I'd watched at least four couples walk through the doors, and they'd yet to come out. Rumor had it there was a soft launch going on, and another rumor said the bar's name tied back to the man in charge.

Lark.

The same motorcycle club road name attributed to the man I was looking for: a sperm donor Mom had chosen over twenty years ago.

I inhaled slow and deep to calm my nerves. There were seven motorcycles in the parking lot. The last couple I'd watch go inside the bar had arrived on a bike. I'd never been to a biker bar. I'd watched a few movies and a long-running TV series about bikers, and even if those weren't entirely accurate (and I suspected they weren't) I knew this could go the wrong way. Especially since I was here alone.

A shiny, bright blue Ford F-150 pulled into the lot and parked two spots over from my car. Part of me was relieved at that because the side mirrors jutted out from the cab much farther than necessary. Three men got out of the truck, two of them loud and obnoxious.

I kept my gaze pinned to my phone in my hand hoping they wouldn't notice me inside my car.

My head jerked up at a metallic bang coming from my hood. I locked eyes with a white man in his twenties wearing a black baseball hat with the bill facing backwards.

He laughed and grinned at one of the other men. "Scared the shit out of her."

Chad's words from earlier in the day raced through my mind.

Why are you doing this?

That was the million-dollar question.

I'd told him I didn't know, but that wasn't entirely true.

Over the years, Mom had off-handedly said she'd love to meet the man who helped make me who I was.

I'd stopped telling her that *he* wasn't the man who made me who I was since that would require his presence in our lives.

Still, for some reason, ten months ago her words-slash-request had taken root in my head, and I couldn't let it go.

I wanted to meet him, too.

Even more, I wanted *Mom* to meet him.

Yeah, the jerk banging on my vehicle hadn't scared me. The prospect of walking into that bar and coming face to face with Lark scared me, but if Mom had taught me anything it was to face my fears with my chin held high.

So, I tucked my keys in my pocket, grabbed my purse, and faced reality.

Three paces into the bar, I stopped short, for two reasons.

One, the set-up was wrong. I expected to open the door and wander to the actual *bar*. Instead, I found myself inside a small room with a glass-case that doubled as a counter and held a variety of t-shirts.

Two, the man behind the counter with his leather vest, bulging biceps, light brown hair and alert blue eyes riled my nerves more than any group of rowdy rednecks ever could.

I swallowed and pushed through my frazzled nerves.

"Hi. Is there a cover charge to get in?"

One of his eyebrows rose ever-so-slightly. "Why would you think there's a cover?"

I hadn't expected that. Answering a question with a question had to rank as one of my least favorite conversational gambits.

Worse, this made me a hypocrite since I was rather adept at it myself, working as a Realtor.

Before I could answer, another man entered the small room. A man who was clearly his brother since he looked identical to the man in front of me. Only he had an air about him that screamed troublemaker, and made it clear his brother was the good one.

What in the world had I gotten myself into?

The two of them had a brief conversation, but I'd been so blindsided I'd tuned them out.

You know the cartoons that show the good angel and the bad angel? These men were twins, that much was clear. What was also clear was that they appeared to embody good and bad.

Yeah... I wasn't a girl who went for threesomes, but I had a sudden urge to be sandwiched between these two.

"I don't think I like that look on her face," the good one said.

"I *know* I don't," the edgier, 'bad' one said.

I shook myself out of my reverie. "I'm looking for Lark. Is he around?"

"Why?" the bad one asked.

"It's private."

"So is his location."

He was lying. I knew it, but I wasn't going to cave.

With a glance toward the doorway, I saw they weren't busy. I shifted my gaze to the good twin. "What time do you close?"

"In an hour," the 'bad' twin said.

I glared at him. "I was speaking to your twin."

I'd never seen an evil smirk, but this man's was downright diabolical. "Triplet."

"Good Lord... three of you," I breathed, wondering if the third brother would be 'just right' between the two of them.

A flirty, feminine laugh filled the air. "Killian! Don't scare the girl that way."

A woman entered the room and slugged Killian – the bad twin – in the bicep. Immediately, I knew she was their triplet sister. She was striking.

"What do you want with Lark?" she asked.

I smiled. "Like I told Killian, it's private. I'll come back another time."

Before I could turn on my heel, the 'good' twin said, "You'll still have to go through me or Killian, so your privacy won't matter then, either."

His tone sounded angry, it was so tight. My eyes darted to Killian and back to him. Maybe he wasn't so 'good' after all.

"Seriously, Ryan? You just have to pile on when Kill does."

I smiled at the unnamed sister. "Have a nice evening."

"I'm Mick, and not to pile on... *further*, but you'll still have to tell one of us before you get to Lark."

With a chin lift, I said, "I'll cross that bridge when I get there."

***

"Did you find him? Is it done?" Chad asked.

Lying in my bed, in the dark with my cell phone to my ear, I said, "No."

"His name's on the business, Ivy. 'On a Lark Bar & Grille,' how could you *not* find him?"

I sighed. "I said it wasn't done. He has triplets who keep people away from him."

There was a long pause on the line and I wondered if Chad were smoking.

"You're telling me he donated his sperm *and* he had triplets with somebody?"

"I sure as hell hope not," I blurted.

"What? Why? All you've *ever* wanted was siblings."

I chuckled. "Yeah, but not with a side effect of insta-lust. Those two were so hot, I had immediate visions of being between them. If we're related... that's just gross."

"Being between three men is gross period, Ivy. Not to mention cumbersome."

I laughed. "No, Chad. These triplets are two men and a woman. Even though I don't swing that way, I'd be interested in her. Though... not if we're related."

"Oh," he muttered. "Still. Why would he donate sperm if he already had kids?"

I contemplated that. "If I'm lucky, I'll find out. It just won't happen any time soon."

"Why not?"

After a rueful chuckle, I took a deep breath. "Let's just say, I'm determined to corner this man without either of these three people playing gate-keeper. That's gonna take a while."

Chapter 2

Are You Over Your Snit?

Ryan

I should have looked away, but that woman had a pull on me and I couldn't tear my eyes away from the sight of her lush round ass swaying as she walked out the door. Something deep inside me said she was another one of Lark's conquests, and I suspected she was pregnant to boot, which irritated me.

"How long do we have to do this shit for Lark?" I asked a moment after the door closed.

Killian shoved my shoulder. "We're prospects. We do whatever the brothers tell us to for as long as it takes."

I sighed. "What about Mick? She's not a prospect. And Lark should handle his own shit."

"Why are you so mad?" Killian asked.

My lips quirked and I shrugged, then faced my brother. "It's fucked up. Telling women Lark's not around. Why he sleeps with women half his age—"

"You don't know that he slept with her," Killian said, shaking his head.

A bitter laugh crept out of me. "I'm pretty sure she's pregnant – and it pisses me off."

Mickayla put a hand on the edge of the glass counter-top and used her other hand to flick her mass of wavy hair behind her shoulder. "Did she *say* she was pregnant?"

I shook my head.

My sister tilted her head, looking so much like Mom it wasn't funny. "Then you don't *know* anything. Stop assuming, Ry. It isn't like you."

I couldn't stop myself from arguing. "It isn't like me, but my gut instincts are rarely wrong."

Mick let go of the counter and leaned toward me. "You aren't a woman, so please, do us both a favor here, and listen to me. Your gut can be, and very likely *is*, wrong about her pregnancy status. She was cute and curvy – just how you like your women—"

"Mick," I started.

She shook her head. "Oh, no, Ry, you earned this. Just because a woman has curves doesn't mean she's pregnant. Hell, I get bloated around that time of the month and let me tell you, it sucks."

I'd heard more than my fair share about my sister's cycle, and I didn't want to court more of that.

"Mick, she said it was private. What else could she need from Lark? She's younger than us."

"Did you card her?" she asked.

I slid my eyes to the side. "No."

Killian chuckled. "Yeah, I'm thinking she's our age or older. She just drove by, and there's a picture of her on her car. Ivy Brummis and her phone number. Looks like she sells real estate." He turned his head toward me. "How many women younger than us do you know driving around with a car magnet for that sort of business?"

Mick shot me a knowing look. "Listen, Lark wanting us to keep people away from him isn't that difficult, and to be fair, it lets him focus on more important shit. Speaking of important shit, the same group of jerks from the other night came in before her. I'm going to work the bar, so we don't have another scene like before."

"You mean last night," I muttered.

She raised her chin defiantly. "Anyway, be on your toes. We don't need a bar fight tonight. Or any night, really."

Killian clamped a hand on my shoulder. "Hit the walk-in fridge. We need kegs lined up, and it'll give you a chance to cool off. Hell, Raff's here with Alexandra. Chat with them, get your mind off shit."

I followed my sister into the main barroom and prowled to the walk-in fridge. Once I was relatively cooled off, I went behind the bar. On the customer side, Mickayla was chatting with Rafferty and Alexandra. Rafferty was also prospecting with the Riot MC and, like me and Killian, his dad was a patched member. Alexandra was Cal's daughter and he was the Sergeant-at-Arms for the Jacksonville chapter.

I stopped in front of Rafferty. "Another?"

"Sure," he said.

I felt my sister's eyes on me while I pulled a bottle of Blue Moon from the cooler.

"Are you over your snit?" she asked.

I put the beer in front of Rafferty, and turned toward Mick. "Not a snit. Like I said, I don't trust her."

"How come?" Alexandra asked.

I rested both of my hands on the bar at an angle and leaned toward Alexandra. "Instinct. She's my age, maybe a little younger. A woman like her shouldn't be strolling in here, asking about Lark."

"Why not?" Alexandra asked.

"Lex," Rafferty said in a warning tone.

Alexandra turned to Rafferty. "It's a valid question. Why can't anyone come in here and ask to talk to Lark?"

"Why couldn't she tell me what she wanted with him?" I asked.

That had *to be what rubbed me the wrong way.*

Granted, it probably wasn't my business, but at the same time, that's the position Lark put me in by insisting that I play gatekeeper with anyone asking after him.

Alexandra turned her hands up on the bar. "I'm just saying, it's a daunting task to go anywhere looking for someone. It's even worse when it's a biker bar and you *aren't* part of our culture. I didn't hear what she said, but from the way she held herself – I don't think she's ever met a biker."

I leaned back and crossed my arms on my chest. "That might be true, but even if this were a mom-and-pop shop, and someone asked *why* she was looking for someone, saying it's private isn't going to cut it."

Mickayla shook her head. "I don't know about that, but where is Lark? Did you tell him about this?"

I hadn't and part of me wanted to keep it from him, for some fucked-up reason.

I shook my head. "No. I went to the keg room to cool off. I don't know why that woman made me mad, but she did. You can let Lark know that a woman who's probably thirty years younger than him is looking for him."

Mickayla narrowed her eyes at me. "She's not thirty years younger than him. She looks like she's twenty-one, maybe twenty-two, and Lark is early forties, tops."

I grabbed a rag from under the bar and wiped down an area to the left of Rafferty. After a beat, I locked eyes with my sister. "Nope, Lark will be forty-nine next week. That puts twenty-eight years between them."

Mickayla stepped closer to the bar. "Okay, but why do you sound angrier?"

I dipped my chin. "What he does in his free time is his business, but he loves attention from younger women. She said the reason she wanted to see him was 'private'. What else am I supposed to make of that?"

Rafferty shook his head. "That seems like a stretch, Ry."

Mickayla spoke before I could respond. "He doesn't act on most of the attention he gets from younger women, Ryan. But you said it yourself, it's 'his business,' so maybe you shouldn't jump to conclusions here."

I took a deep breath, then leaned toward Mickayla. "I'll do that. But like you said to her, if she comes back, she's still gotta tell one of us what she wants before she'll get to Lark."

"Why are you three his keeper?" Alexandra asked.

Mickayla hurried down the length of the bar, came around to my side of the bar, and sidled up beside me. "It's part of proving ourselves to him."

I shot Rafferty a dry look. "I thought it was bullshit until now."

"Maybe she was a plant," Alexandra suggested.

Mickayla laughed. "Honey, Lark doesn't have the time to plan something like that."

I stared into space for a beat. "No, but I could see another brother doing that to fuck with us."

Mickayla shrugged. "Whatever. Time will tell. If she even comes back."

Alexandra's head bobbed in a couple of short nods, then she looked at me. "Yeah, and maybe you won't be here when she does."

"Fat chance. We get no days off here if we want part-ownership," I said.

"Really?" Alexandra asked.

"As Lark pointed out, small business owners don't get vacations in their first year," Mickayla said.

Alexandra tilted her head. "But not even *one* day off?"

"His terms," I said, looking between the two of them. "I'll see you when you leave. Have a good time."

Technically, the bar was in the midst of a soft launch, and this was our first Saturday night crowd. As much as I wanted to say the crowd was a mix that mirrored the surrounding neighborhoods, I couldn't deny what Alexandra had said. One glance through the patrons, and most people would say this was a biker bar.

Last night, a local band had played from nine until midnight. Killian and I had to run interference between a couple bikers and a group of three extremely loud and rowdy men. They weren't exactly rednecks, but they were similar. Those same men came in tonight. Fortunately for them, the bikers they riled up last night hadn't come back.

At least, not *yet*.

Tonight, Lark had a different band scheduled. The Muzzle Kings had shown up over an hour ago and were planning to play until one in the morning. Based on their first set, they featured a decent mix of rock covers and original songs. They were on a break, and a few of the older patrons left for the night.

Rafferty and Alexandra wandered out, and we said our goodbyes.

Through the glass doors, I watched them swing onto Rafferty's Harley. A stab of jealousy ripped through me. Not that I had a thing for Alexandra, but I wanted something like what they had. They'd been best friends growing up, until they weren't, and recently they got their heads out of their asses and were giving it a shot.

But I'd never find something like that. My parents loved each other so much and were so vocal and visible about it that I knew I'd never find that kind of love for myself. To be honest, I wouldn't want it if it came with the amount of pain and suffering they'd gone through.

The door opened and Blood, Volt, and Tundra trudged into the room.

Fifteen minutes later, the two bikers from last night followed them inside, giving me chin lifts as they passed me.

Killian was wandering the room collecting empties during the band's break. He snuck over to me while carrying a stack of pint glasses almost as long as his arm. "That ain't good. You should have told them—"

I shook my head. "No fuckin' way I'm gonna deny two bikers entry for those assholes. Hell, it might force Lark to take a stand."

"If you believe that, you and I should swap places."

I dipped my chin. "Lark doesn't want us doin' that."

Kill arched a brow. "How would he even know? Especially since we don't have road name patches on our cuts." He grinned. "Won't be long before we won't be able to do this sort of thing because we'd have to swap cuts, and I know we'd hate doing that."

As usual, my brother had a way of tempting me to do...not exactly a bad thing, but most likely the wrong thing.

Risk should have been his middle name. Many months ago, I made the mistake of telling some of the brothers that should be Kill's road name, but they laughed at me because we'd only just started prospecting.

More often than not, I wound up taking the risk with him, but that's what brothers did for each other.

"Come on," Killian drawled into the ensuing silence.

With a sigh, I turned my hands up. "Fine, but don't mess up the till. We're charging a cover starting at ten."

Killian's head moved in two short nods. "Yeah, we gotta tell Lark to promote the cover charge more. I'm certain that's why it filled up so much earlier."

I nodded, moved out from behind the counter, and took the stack of glasses from him. "I agree. We make more than the ten dollar cover in the amount of alcohol those people order."

He grinned. "Yeah, I wonder if they'd come in if we charged the cover even earlier. An extra ten bucks a head is always an extra ten bucks."

I shrugged a shoulder. "Why mess with something that isn't broken?"

I hit the kitchen to offload the glasses, then wandered behind the bar to help Lark and Mickayla deal with the crush of people getting their drinks before the music started again.

Mickayla sidled up to me, putting three cocktails on a tray. "Take those to table two, and please stop switching with Kill. Lark might confuse you two occasionally, but that's happening less and less these days. He's no dummy, and neither are you."

She was right, but she was also jealous of our ability to swap places. Rather than respond to her comment, my eyes slid to table two. The three rednecks sat at that table, and their eyes were pinned on my sister.

"We need to hire some servers."

Mick chuckled. "Too soon, and seriously, get out of here before Lark hears you and figures out the switch y'all pulled."

I put the drinks on the table as fast as I could without spilling them. Two of the men had expressions that said they wanted to chat with me, which meant my goal was to avoid all conversation.

Before I could leave the table one grabbed my wrist, earning a death glare.

"Sorry, man, but she's your sister, right?" the man wearing a black baseball cap asked me, and let go of me.

This was why Killian should have been on the floor. This jackass never would have touched him.

I managed to contain my sneer as I looked down at him. "She's our bartender tonight. That's all you need to know."

The band started up again, and I busted my ass for the duration of their set while people ate, drank, and were generally merry.

The man wearing the baseball cap had switched to ordering Blue Moon drafts, which came with an orange wedge as a garnish. I hadn't thought anything of it, until just before the band was done with their second set.

The asshole who'd grabbed my wrist wadded up the orange rind and launched it through the air at one of the bikers who'd been here last night.

Before I could attempt to talk anyone down, all hell broke loose.

The biker who hadn't been hit by the rind moved faster than I thought possible and had one of the laughing jackasses out of his chair. With a hand at the asshole's throat, he was shoving him toward a wall, and one of the other rednecks tried to pull him off their buddy.

The guy who'd been hit with the citrus had his eyes fixed on the only guy still at the table. The one who flicked the fruit.

The asshole stood and glared at the biker as he drew closer to me.

"Sir, let me get them out of here," I said in a low voice.

"Nobody pulls that shit on me without feeling my fists," the biker said.

I didn't disagree with him.

Without moving my lips, I muttered, "One throw. Be fast."

The biker's body gave a slight twitch. With one hand he grabbed the asshole by the collar of his t-shirt, then he used his free hand to land a vicious left jab to the man's nose.

From the corner of my eye, I saw Volt and Tundra were breaking things up with the other biker and the two rednecks. After a quick glance in the opposite direction, I noticed Lark and Blood were keeping things calm on that side of the room.

The brawl ended almost as fast as it started, thanks to the band's lead guitarist causing ear-splitting feedback on the sound system. Funny how that screeching sound made most everyone stop what they were doing.

I grabbed the fruit-flicking asshole and escorted him outside.

"This is the second problem you've caused in as many days. Another time and you're barred. Your buddies, too."

"Fuck you," he spat at me.

I fought off a lip curl but raised my eye brows. "If you want to play it that way, you can be barred right here and now."

A knowing gleam hit his eyes. "You aren't the owner, you're just his lackey."

I ignored the barb and stalked into the bar.

Back in the main room, the band had started a rock ballad from the late eighties. My guess, this was an attempt to ease the tension. It appeared as though most of the patrons had stuck around.

Killian sidled up to me. "Did you really let that guy take a swing?"

I didn't know where Lark was, and a fib came easily to me. "No, man. He told me he was cool—"

"I'm not Lark."

I twisted my head so I could lock eyes with him. "Would you let that shit go if you were in his boots?"

Killian chuckled. "Fuck, no. I also wouldn't have let you get there first, though."

I shook my head. "Whatever. You want to stay out front or what?"

"No fuckin' way. I forgot how damn boring it is up here."

Chapter 3

Stay Calm

Ivy

Four months later...

"I've been thinking," Chad said, popping a tray of chopped potatoes into my oven.

Every Sunday, I got together with him and we made dinner together. Our close friend Kristen joined us when she had the time, but tonight she had a family dinner.

Except for around the holidays, we kept it very casual. Since we were at my place, I was wearing one of my favorite Jane Austen inspired t-shirts and a pair of silky-soft lounge pants. Chad was dressed as casually as could be expected in a colorful pair of madras shorts and a mushroom-colored polo shirt.

"You've been thinking... I'm not sure if that's good or bad."

He leaned against the counter and grabbed his glass of white wine. "I think you messed up going to that bar by yourself back in May."

I nodded. "Because you wanted to come with me, but Chad—"

"No, because you were too direct. That makes you hell on wheels at your job, but this needs a softer touch."

I nodded once. "Go on."

"See, if Kristen and I had been with you, we wouldn't have just asked to see Lark. We'd have found a spot at the bar, ordered something, and been more discreet."

My lips quirked with skepticism. "You mean we'd have hung out and waited for Lark to show himself."

"No, I mean we'd have been *discreet*. Asking them why the bar's called what it is...it's a new business. They've got to get the word out, and most people love talking about themselves."

I shook my head. "They'd have seen right through that."

Chad swirled the wine in his glass then put it on the counter. "Maybe so. Under the circumstances, I think fate has sent you a sign, Ivy."

I turned my gaze toward my kitchen window, trying not to roll my eyes. "You've told me that before."

"No, I haven't."

I shifted my gaze back to Chad. "Not in so many words, but—"

He crossed his arms on his broad chest. "Why are you so determined to talk to this man?"

"I just want to meet him. That isn't wrong," I said in a small voice, mainly because I'd told Chad this numerous times in the past.

"No, it isn't wrong, but you also want him to meet Debra."

"Yeah, because maybe she's curious about the man whose genes I share."

"Or maybe she isn't," Chad argued.

For some reason, I couldn't entertain that idea – no matter how logical it might be. "It's also up to him, Chad. The fact he has three people gatekeeping for him makes me wonder what he's hiding."

Chad grabbed his wine glass. "Could be hazing."

"No way," I scoffed.

"Ivy, you didn't do Greek life—"

"This isn't college."

"No, but a club is a club and a lot of them have rituals, rites of passage... you know, *hazing*."

I narrowed my eyes at him, but the effort was feeble seeing as my best friend was looking out for me, or trying to anyway. "Something tells me you're wrong. I just wanna meet Lark and I'm going back there after work tomorrow."

Chad pressed his lips together while his cheeks puffed out like he was holding in his anger. "You've always been too independent for your own good."

I shrugged. "Nothing wrong with being independent."

"Sure, except you'd do *everything* yourself if you could."

"That's not true. I do group-like things." I paused and nodded. "I definitely can't do my job all on my own, there's plenty of people I depend on to close deals, and I'm part of professional groups."

Chad smiled. "Yeah, because your boss forced you to join them." He tipped his wine glass toward me, his eyes darting to my t-shirt. "I gave you that shirt not because you love Jane Austen, but because you're the most obstinate and headstrong woman I've ever met. At this point though, even the society of headstrong and obstinate girls wouldn't take you."

I smirked. "Of course not. They're obstinate and headstrong."

His posture slumped. "Oh, my Ivy. You got answers for everything."

"Except this Lark guy, which is why I'm going tomorrow night."

"It's been months since you were there. I thought you'd let it go."

I wandered to the freezer, pulled out a bag of edamame, and popped it in the microwave. "Nope. I've been watching the bar in the afternoons and early evenings for the past few weeks."

Chad's body tensed. "Jesus! Why are you keeping things from me?"

I set the microwave to run and faced him. "Because I'm obstinate and headstrong? Anyway, their sister leaves at five for a break that's been taking roughly two hours. She comes back a little after seven. Killian leaves at six and Ryan leaves at six-thirty during the week, so I'm going in at six-forty-five. Fifteen minutes should be plenty of time."

Chad sipped his wine. "The way you described those two men...I thought you couldn't tell the difference between them. I suppose that doesn't matter as long as you see both men leave. But, are you sure you're right about their schedules?"

"Sure, I'm sure."

Chad shook his head. "I should meet you there. I'll—"

He couldn't be there, that I knew for certain even if I didn't know exactly why.

"No! Chad, I'm good. It's just a conversation."

"Yes, it's a life-changing conversation. Which could leave you in emotional tatters."

That sounded dramatic, but Chad knew me well. Part of what fueled my headstrong obstinance was to make sure nobody could hurt me...and that was ultimately why I didn't want Chad there. If I got rejected, it would hurt, but it would also be incredibly embarrassing (which was a different kind of pain), and I didn't want anyone I knew witnessing that.

I shot my friend a gentle look. "I'll call if I need you."

Chad matched my gentle look but paired it with a gleam of sternness in his eyes. "No, sweets. You'll call me before you leave there, so I know you're good."

As usual, Chad was right: I should have brought him with me – not that I would *tell* him that.

Traffic on the Buckman Bridge put me over an hour behind my usual schedule for scoping out On a Lark Bar and Grill. I pulled up to my normal spot at six-fifteen. Five minutes later, Ryan came outside. There was a remote chance it was really Killian, but as bad as traffic was all over town – Ryan had to be leaving early.

He threw a leg over his motorcycle, and I glanced away at the sight. Something about watching him climb on his bike made my belly flip and my breath catch.

What was that?

I might be attracted to him, but I wouldn't let that attraction grow.

The roar of the bike's engine got my attention. The moment I lost sight of the bike's tail light after he got on US 90, I hopped out of my car and beelined toward the bar and grill.

As I strode along the sidewalk leading to the front door, a tall man wearing a baseball cap backwards blocked my path.

"About time you came out to play," he said in a low voice.

Vaguely, I suspected he was the man who'd beaten on my car hood the first time I'd been here.

"I'm sorry, I don't know you."

He grinned, exposing yellowed teeth. Then he turned his head to spit, and I noticed the bulge of chewing tobacco in his cheek. "Don't matter. I remember you. Scared you so bad, you jumped like a rabbit. Made my fuckin' day."

I didn't like his vibe, but something told me being bitchy wouldn't help me here, so I softened my tone. "Listen, I'm not interested. It's not you, I'm in a crazy place at work right now and—"

I cut myself off when he chuckled. I read books, and I always found 'dark' to be the worst word to describe a chuckle. But now I'd actually heard one and I fought off a shiver.

"Don't care if you're 'interested' or not. I get what I want. Bonus, I saw how that prick bouncer drooled after you."

I stepped back two paces. "He doesn't even know me."

"Bullshit. You followed him home four nights last week."

Well, crud.

To an ignorant observer it probably looked that way, but there were only two ways back to the Interstate from here. Of course I probably went the same way as Ryan – or Killian did. My guess was this guy didn't know the difference between them any better than I did.

I shook my head. "I'm just here to talk to the owner. Now, if you'll let me pass—"

From his hip, he brought up a handgun. "Bitch, you're comin' with me."

Fear raced through my veins and my mind froze. The strap of my purse slid down my arm and I vaguely heard something hit the ground. I wanted to run, but he'd probably shoot me. For a second, I considered grabbing his arm and pushing it away, but he'd probably shoot me. As things stood, he'd take me somewhere else, and probably shoot me.

A few feet separated us. The man's eyes darted to the side as someone hopped over the low metal fence delineating the smoker's patio.

Next thing I knew, one of the triplets stood in between me and the other man. I didn't know which one because he had his back to me. His vest looked different up close compared to the last few nights. The backside featured a large, embroidered patch of a skull perched on an upturned fist with wings jutting out to the sides. An arched patch above the skull read "Riot MC," and a curved patch at the bottom read, "Jacksonville, FL." From what little I knew about the biker culture, having this patch now had to be a big deal.

I was pulled from my thoughts when he said, "Let her go."

The tobacco chewing man scoffed. "Look at that, you got a nickname now. 'Nickel.' Must be because that's all your life's gonna be worth."

Nickel's voice dropped an octave. "You got an issue with me, be a man and take it up with me."

Movement from my other side diverted my attention. Another man had wandered up to us, and he had a gun aimed at me.

Nickle's head shifted just enough to see the movement.

"We'll take it up with both of you. Come with us or I'll shoot her."

From over Nickel's shoulder, I saw the tobacco-chewer smirk. "Hand over your gun, asshole."

I heard him sigh before giving up his weapon.

The man took it and waved us toward the other side of the lot.

Before I could move, the second man grabbed my bicep and dragged me to a beat-up, dark green Nissan Frontier. He shoved me into the back of the cab. "Slide over, bitch."

I did as ordered, expecting him to follow me, but then I smelled leather and saw Nickel had climbed in beside me.

"You got cuffs?" the man at the door asked.

"Rusty didn't tell me to bring cuffs," the tobacco chewer said.

"Dammit, Campbell, do you think these two won't try to run us off the road?"

"I got zip-ties, Boyd."

"Well, move your ass and get 'em," Boyd said from the door.

I opened my mouth thinking someone would hear me scream, but Nickel grabbed my thigh. "Don't. It'll make it worse," he whispered.

I whispered back, "Are you Killian or—"

"Ryan. Stay calm," he whispered.

I almost choked with my urge to laugh. "Impossible," I muttered.

"Shut up back there," Boyd said, brandishing his gun.

The door to my left opened. Campbell stood there holding his gun in one hand and a zip-tie in the other. At some point he must have chucked his tobacco because the bulge in his cheek was gone.

From the other side of the cab, Boyd leaned toward us. "Put your fuckin' gun away, Campbell, and get her wrists bound. She does anything, I shoot the biker and then I shoot her."

My eyes slid to the side and saw Boyd had the gun held inches from Ryan's head.

Ryan's head moved in an imperceptible nod for me to cooperate.

I held my wrists out and Campbell wrapped the zip-tie around.

"Don't cut off her circulation," Boyd said, not a moment too soon.

Campbell gave a low pitched chuckle. "Oh, right."

I couldn't fathom why we weren't fighting these two assholes, but I had to trust that Ryan had good reason for me not to fight back. Maybe he was biding his time and letting them think we were coming willingly. Then again, a loaded gun made resistance a bad idea.

The moment my wrists were bound, Campbell shut my door. I heard the sound of flesh hitting flesh and suddenly Ryan slumped against me.

I let out a scream.

The cab dipped as Boyd put a foot on the running board and leaned inside. "Shut up, Ivy, or I'll shoot him for good measure."

"What'd you do?" Campbell asked from behind Boyd.

Boyd angled out of the truck and jerked his head toward Ryan. "No way he was going to let us zip-tie him, so I pistol-whipped him to knock him out. Get his wrists and let's go."

Campbell grabbed Ryan's wrists while I sat there fuming and struggling to think of a good way to get out of this. I could shove Ryan's body at Campbell, but Boyd would shoot me – hell, he'd probably shoot us both.

Once Campbell shut the door on us, I kept my gaze on Ryan's chest. I needed to know he was breathing because I'd never been around someone who'd been knocked out. After a moment, I saw a slight rise and felt a rush of relief.

Suddenly, my door was wrenched open again. I twisted my head and saw Boyd standing there. Too late, I realized his fist was zooming toward me. Pain exploded behind my temple and my vision went dark.

Chapter 4

Something That Big

Ryan

"Jeez, Pop once told me moving a limp body is the hardest lifting you'll ever do; he wasn't kidding. For a such a little thing, she sure is heavy."

Even though I'd woken up earlier when the truck bounced along a dirt road, I'd dozed off again. Those words immediately brought me out of my heavy stupor. I didn't want either of these assholes touching her. I didn't want *anybody* touching her.

"Looks like he's coming to, leave her for now," Boyd said.

"Maybe he can carry her. I don't want to throw my back out, man," Campbell said.

These assholes didn't know their heads from holes in the ground, and definitely had no business abducting anyone.

My door was thrown open and Boyd held his gun pointed at me and jerked his head to the side. "Outta the truck, nice and slow."

I couldn't stand that I'd let this go so far. Seeing Campbell talking to Ivy outside the bar made my blood boil, then I'd seen him holding a gun and that boiling blood rushed to my ears. Maybe if I'd taken a moment to think, I'd have been able to handle this whole situation better, but it was like my instincts were on a trigger-wire that wasn't under my control.

Whoever drove us, must have left the ignition switch in the run position because the digital clock was still lit and the radio was still on. As I slowly swung my feet toward the exit, I made note of the time, five minutes after seven.

Standing in front of Boyd, he eyed me up and down. "For once, Camp, I think you got a great idea. We'll let this jackass carry her dead weight."

He grabbed my bicep and marched me to the other side of the truck. It wasn't lost on me that I'd marched him out of On a Lark the same way. Both men looked at me with blank expressions as we stood staring at Ivy.

I cut my gaze to Boyd, who seemed to be smarter than Campbell, though that wasn't saying much. "I'm strong, but I can't carry her with my wrists tied."

The two of them exchanged a look. I'd wanted to tell them her wrists needed to be untied as well, but that would be pressing my luck.

Finally, Boyd nodded. "Yeah, I can see that. Camp, cut his tie." He leveled a look at me. "I'll be right next to you and if you pull anything, I shoot her in the head."

Campbell started to grab my wrists, but his eyes darted to my hip. "Boyd, get his phone. We need to get her phone, too."

"Good catch," Boyd said and snatched my cell off my belt.

They fumbled around Ivy's pockets, and I realized I was grinding my teeth.

Why did I react this way?

"Can't find anything, she must have dropped her purse or some shit when you pulled the gun," Boyd said.

Campbell came back to me and cut the zip-tie, narrowly missing the inside of my wrist.

Asshole.

With my hands free, I quickly slid an arm under Ivy's knees and my other arm along her shoulders. I slid her out of the cab and started walking toward the front of the truck.

We stood before a run-down farm house. The siding was painted a drab shade of olive green, most of which had chipped off. Many of the windows were boarded up, and the stairs to the front porch were on their last legs. The first step had fallen down on one side.

I raised my leg higher and used the second step to get onto the porch.

"Slow down, motherfucker," Boyd said.

If I'd had more of my bearings, I'd have set Ivy down and taken on Boyd and Campbell. Unfortunately, the pain in my head was so intense, I felt dizzy every so often from it.

Campbell pushed past me and opened the door. Boyd tipped his head for me to go in the house. The inside was worse than the outside. No light fixtures, just bare bulbs. Wallpaper hung off the walls like the room was molting. The entire place reeked of must and stale weed. We moved through a kitchen and I noticed there were no doors on any of the cabinets.

Boyd passed by me, unlocked a door, and pushed it open. "Put her in there."

I trudged into the room and felt ill. It was barren except a thin mattress on the floor. I put Ivy down as gently as I could.

When I straightened, I heard the door close and a lock clicked.

At least they hadn't separated us.

I dug my pocket knife out and sliced the zip-tie binding Ivy's wrists.

Her hands felt cold, so I took them both in mine and massaged them. I ignored how much I liked holding her hands.

On a sigh, I crossed to the other side of the room and sat down, fuming that they knocked out a woman who was probably pregnant.

Sleep beckoned to me, but I had to stay awake. Not just because I might have a mild concussion, but also because I needed to stay on my toes for these assholes. They never should have gotten the advantage on the two of us, but beating myself up about it wasn't productive.

Times like these made me wish I had twin telepathy with Killian. Or even Mick. She'd freak and then she'd jump for joy that I was stuck with this woman who got under my skin. However, we didn't have true telepathy. Best case scenario, one or both of them knew I had a massive headache, but wouldn't know I'd been knocked out.

Back in high school, Mickayla had played basketball and during a practice she fell and landed on her arm, breaking it. Killian and I both knew something was up because we'd both had a sharp, fleeting pain in our left arm, too. That was the extent of it for us. It wasn't like I could hyperfocus on the word taken or kidnapped and make them realize what was going on.

I forced myself to concentrate on the sounds coming from the kitchen – not that there were very many. Boyd and Campbell weren't the brightest crayons in the box, but there had to be a reason they brought us out here to a run-down house in the middle of nowhere – or so it seemed. I had to remind myself not to make assumptions.

On a Lark was in a small shopping strip on a rural stretch of US 90. The building seemed so out of place, it was like it popped up out of nowhere, but it had been there for over twenty years. One of the first things Lark had insisted Killian, Mickayla, and I do was to drive around the area in a five-mile radius. Then he expanded it to ten. As I recalled that research, it struck me that this place could be close to the bar, and yet, it could be over half an hour from the bar. If the time I'd noted in the truck was right, then we'd been on the road for over half-an-hour. The problem was I had no idea how fast they'd driven. With an open stretch, plenty of people got the lead out on US 90.

Yet, even as I considered all that, my gut said we were as far west as they could take us. If I'd been out for just over thirty minutes, we could be as far as Sanderson or even Olustee, depending on whether they'd gotten onto I-10 or stuck to US 90. Either way, we were well over twenty-five miles from the bar and I didn't think we could walk back – assuming I was right about where we were. It was highly unlikely we were still in Duval county, I was pretty certain about that.

Dammit! I really should have grappled with Campbell – gun or no gun.

I shook my head because that wasn't true. I couldn't put Ivy in danger.

It made no sense to me though, because I didn't even know this woman. Except for the fact she wanted to talk to Lark about something that was *private*. Which I believed could only mean one thing, but my sister was right: I couldn't make assumptions about something that big...but hell if I could stop myself.

Out of habit, I reached for my phone holster and shook my head. It sucked not knowing what time it was, and the only window in the room had been boarded up so I couldn't even rely on waning sunlight to gage the time.

Shit.

It had to be closing in on seven-thirty, and if they knocked Ivy out soon after hitting me, then she was past the half-hour point. She had to wake up soon.

Otherwise, I was going to raise holy hell to get her an ambulance because she definitely had a concussion.

Pots clanged in the kitchen – or it sounded like pots, then I heard male voices and the sound of a door slamming.

I heard Boyd's muffled voice from outside. "Yeah, we got two of his kids."

"One of his kids, that bitch isn't his sister," Campbell said.

"Shut it, Camp," Boyd hissed.

Just when I thought they couldn't be more ignorant, they proved me wrong. To be fair, though, I could see it. But only because I was young enough to be Lark's kid.

Still, assumptions led to trouble.

When I heard him again, Boyd had raised his voice. "What the hell do you mean we weren't supposed to take anyone yet? You don't have any way of—" He paused abruptly, then said, "Contact the club, man."

After a much shorter pause, he said, "Then call the bar."

"What's the problem?" Campbell asked.

From Boyd's response, I guessed he ignored Campbell. "Too bad, we've got them at the old house. We can't let them go now. You said we'd get paid no matter who we took. Make those bikers pay. We've got one of the sons and his girlfriend."

That was so fucked up.

I couldn't think of another group of bikers who would pay these men to take me, Mickayla, or Killian. They would just do it themselves.

"What do you mean they want the fuckin' old man?" Boyd yelled loud enough it made me jolt.

Another short pause.

"We could still ransom these two back to Lark," Boyd said in a normal voice.

There was a much longer pause after that.

Then I heard Boyd speak again. "Come on, Campbell. Rusty wants us back in town."

"We're just gonna leave them here? He isn't tied up," Campbell said.

"So what? We locked them in that room. Even if they get out, they don't know where they are, it's gonna be dark in under an hour, and we have his cell phone. If they leave, they'll have to walk, and they won't get far before we come back."

My head twisted toward Ivy when she made a moaning sound and shifted on the mattress. Her eyes weren't open yet.

I heard the truck start and then the engine noise quickly faded away.

We were alone, which ought to be good, but Ivy needed to wake up if we had a shot at getting out of here.

CHAPTER 5

BOUNCER SCHOOL

IVY

I BLINKED, THEN WINCED in pain. I had one helluva headache. Chad got migraines any time the weather changed. Everything I felt made me think of him, though I wasn't nauseous.

I took a deep breath and opened my eyes. The room was dim with only a sliver of yellowish-orange light coming in under the door. Then I remembered I'd been taken. My entire frame tensed and I heard someone shush me. I looked in that direction and saw Ryan sitting on the floor with his back against the wall.

"Where are we?" I whispered, sitting up on a thin, bare mattress.

"No fucking clue. I came to in the truck and we were rambling down a long-ass dirt road in the middle of the woods to this house. We could be anywhere within a forty-five minute radius of the bar."

"Why do you say that?"

"Because I caught sight of the clock on the truck's dash before the dipshit cut the engine."

I rubbed the side of my head. "Is it normal for someone to be knocked out for so long? And how did they get me in here?"

Ryan stared at me for a moment. "They made me carry you inside."

My head tilted. "With your hands zip-tied?"

He chuckled. "No. I told them I needed my hands free and they agreed."

I bit my lip. "Sorry I wasn't conscious. Maybe we could have—"

He shook his head. "No, they still had a gun trained on me. We have to bide our time."

I started to nod, but stopped since it made my head throb. "Not to be self-centered here, but do you think I have a concussion after being out for forty-five minutes."

He shrugged a shoulder. "You might have a mild one, but it's not unusual for someone to be out for half-an-hour or so."

"Do they teach that at bouncer school?"

He chuckled, then hissed. "Don't make me laugh, and no. I learned that when my uncles taught me and Killian how to fight."

"Oh."

I couldn't let myself dwell on the visual of him and his triplet learning how to fight.

The shaft of light under the door faded. I wrapped a hand around my neck, then shook my head. "Did you convince them to cut my zip-tie too?"

"No, they have my gun, and they remembered to take my phone at the last minute, but they didn't take my pocket knife. I cut you loose after they locked us in this room."

"They reversed the knobs?" I asked.

"Surprised you know they'd have to do that, but it seems so."

"I'm in real estate. I've seen all kinds of trippy things people do to houses."

I glanced around the room. It was bare bones, with a window that appeared to be boarded up, and a small doorless closet. The mattress had seen better days, and I had to wonder if the hardwood floor wasn't more comfortable – though it was probably dirtier. Maybe. There wasn't enough light for me to see how clean the mattress was.

"Chad's gonna kill me," I muttered.

"Is that your boyfriend?"

I laughed and let out an immediate short sigh. "Yeah, let's agree not to make each other laugh. Chad is definitely my friend, but not my boyfriend. He likes men as much as I do, let's put it that way. Actually, he'd say he loves them more."

"Got it. Why is he going to kill you?"

"He told me not to go back to the bar without him, but I went anyway, and it seems he was right. It's going to burn him up that he was right and he won't be able to lord it over me because he'll be worried sick when he finds out I'm missing."

"We haven't been gone that long. If we're lucky, he won't have to find out."

My lips quirked to the side. "I'm thinking we have to make our own luck here."

"That's fair."

"Anyway, he knew when I was supposed to get there, and I was going to call him when I was done. He's going to be crazy with worry, if he isn't already."

I heard him take a deep breath. "You can't do anything about that, so my advice, is to not think about it. Doesn't do you any good."

"Sure," I muttered, not meaning it at all. Telling me not to think about something was like erecting a huge billboard with the word 'Worry' in big, bold, neon letters.

We lapsed into silence and at first it was oddly comfortable. Probably because we both had headaches. Then my curiosity went into overdrive and I knew I was in trouble.

Silence *and* curiosity made a poisonous combo. The silence was killing me, and my curiosity was eating at me from the inside out.

Still.

A big part of me wanted to know why he put himself between me and a gun, and a smaller part of me figured that was dangerous information. I supposed I needed to thank him. But, he could have been shot and I had no idea why that made me so angry.

"Stop thinking so hard. You're making my headache worse," he said.

My head snapped up and I sliced my gaze to him. "I'm making *your* headache worse? You've got yourself to blame, buster."

He stared at me. Those blue eyes unreadable and unnerving.

My ears rang with the punishing quiet and I couldn't stop myself.

"Why did you do that?"

"Do what?"

"Get between me and that asshole?"

He looked away from me. "It doesn't matter."

"Putting yourself in that kind of danger always matters, Ryan. I just don't know why you'd do it."

That earned me his full attention. "You're pregnant. Someone has to protect you and your baby."

Much of my body dropped: my stomach pitched, my heart sank, and my mouth fell open while my eyes widened.

Then a deep-rooted, soul-lightening laughter bubbled up from my belly. I threw my head back and let it rip, even though it made my head throb.

Who'd have thought I'd laugh my head off during my first (and hopefully last) kidnapping?

That thought brought on another wave of hysteria and I clutched my stomach – which instantly reminded me of his words and I sobered.

"What the hell is so funny?" he demanded.

"You think I'm pregnant."

He *almost* hid his lip curl. "Why else would you be looking for Lark about a *private* matter. You're exactly the type he goes for."

Ulk. More than I needed to know.

"You are...you couldn't be more wrong," I said, then held up a hand. "Come to think of it, no, you're maybe twenty-five percent right."

His eyes narrowed. "That's nonsense. I'm either right or I'm wrong. There's no percentages to it."

I crossed my arms. "Is that why you have a problem with me? You think I'm pregnant."

He hissed out a humorless chuckle. "No. It's that a woman should know better and keep herself protected. After today, I see staying safe is a challenge for you."

I pursed my lips then powered through my anger. "We'll get to that last part in a moment, but do you really believe it's the woman's responsibility to prevent a pregnancy?"

He sighed. "No, it's on Lark, too – hell, as often as he taps twenty-some-thing-year-old ass, I'm shocked he didn't take better care."

So much to unpack here.

"I sense you have an issue with age gaps," I said.

He shook his head. "No, it's not for me. I could give a shit who a brother fu—sleeps with."

I chuckled. "If you say so."

"Are you gonna clear up your nonsense? I'm one-hundred percent right, not twenty-five percent."

I tilted my head. "It's not your business since it's a private matter, but I'm not pregnant."

"Whatever," he interjected.

"Lark has a baby, yes, but I *am* that baby. That's why I'm looking for him. He's my biological dad."

He put a finger to his temple and rubbed. "There's no way. Lark just moved to Jacksonville two years ago, and you don't sound like you're—"

"Stop. You're making all kinds of assumptions. My mom went to a sperm bank, chose to use his deposit based on the information he provided. I'm not wrong, and...should we get out of this alive, I'd appreciate it if you didn't tell him. It's my news to share."

He stared at me like he was trying to figure me out then gave a slight nod. "Are you from Memphis?"

"No. We lived outside Atlanta until I was nine, and my stepdad got a great job offer in Jacksonville."

His head reared back a touch. "Wait...you said your mom chose Lark – but you have a step dad. Did he get no say in—"

I waved a hand toward him. "No. Mom hadn't found the right man, and had saved her money, so she decided to go for it."

His expression shifted, and I couldn't tell if he was shocked or impressed. "All alone?"

I shrugged. "Yeah. After she had me, she remained single. Her parents were around and helped her out a ton, though I don't remember much of that since I was so little. There was another man she was serious about until...it fell apart. That forced her to explain things to me about my father situation much sooner than she'd have liked."

Luckily she hadn't married Ed, but I didn't want to share that.

I mean, Ryan's attitude seemed a bit kinder now that he knew I wasn't pregnant, but he obviously didn't like me. To be fair, I wasn't too enamored by a man who jumped to conclusions like he was at a trampoline park, and he apparently judged women who were attracted to older men. He might have claimed he didn't care who Lark slept with…but that didn't ring true from the way he said it.

"You're doing it again," he muttered.

He sat on the floor with this back against the wall and his legs bent, resting his wrists on his knees.

"Doing what?"

"Thinking too hard. Whatever it is, let it go. We're gonna need our energy."

I arched a brow. "That's easier said than done. I can't understand why someone wanted to abduct us. I'm not even part of your world. Why not leave me behind?"

He flicked a hand up in a dismissive gesture. "Two possibilities. First is because you saw them, and they didn't want you to report me going missing. Second, and I think this is more likely from a conversation I overheard earlier, Boyd thought you were my sister Mick."

A nervous chuckle escaped me. "If he actually mistook me for your sister, he'd be especially dumb then, because she's the definition of gorgeous."

He stared at me for a long moment.

"What?" I asked.

"You're ten times prettier than my sister."

"Whatever. I wasn't fishing for compliments, but thanks."

CHAPTER 6

SHE HAD A KNACK

RYAN

SHE COULDN'T BE ONE of those women who didn't know she was stunning.

Jesus, this woman. What was I gonna do with her?

Nothing, that's what.

That wasn't true. I would keep her safe because even if she wasn't pregnant, she had a knack for finding trouble.

Yeah, that overshadowed her beauty. She'd be a handful for any man. It's one thing to go looking for Lark, but the moment she walked into the bar should have told her it was a fool's errand.

Maybe that was too harsh.

I couldn't imagine life without my dad. His brothers – now my brothers – would step in if something had happened to him, but it would never be the same.

"Are you sleeping?" she asked.

"Not sleeping," I murmured, but kept my eyes closed.

"Shouldn't we try to break out of here?"

I opened my eyes. She stood across the room leaning against the wall.

My lips twisted with skepticism. "That could work, but then what? Somebody out there will shoot us."

Her eyes widened. "That's the thing. It's too quiet. I don't think anyone is here," she said in a low voice.

I paused to listen as hard as I could before I met her gaze. "If we're alone, why did you lower your voice?"

She gave me a dirty look, and hell if I didn't feel it in my balls. "I don't want to jinx anything."

I rose from the floor, went to the wall, and listened hard.

I didn't want to be in here any more than she did, but I didn't want them to cuff me again either. Especially if they were going to cuff me to *her*. More than that though, I didn't want them to separate us – even if she drove me crazy.

My troublesome girl hadn't thought about that.

My? What was that shit?

She wasn't my girl.

She was trouble though.

Between Killian and Mick, I'd been in the middle of all kinds of trouble my whole life. And I loved it.

Fuck.

No. This wasn't the time or place for thoughts like that. I had at least a year before I'd be ready for a woman like her. I was here to start fresh (because finding what Mom and Dad had would never happen).

Ivy wasn't my type.

Besides, we needed to get out of here.

We both jolted when a door slammed somewhere in the house.

"Not alone any more," I whispered and returned to my spot on the floor.

"There is a bed. I'm sure it's more comfortable."

I dipped my chin. "Which is why I'm leaving it for you."

I heard kitchen noises through the walls. The beep of what I assumed was a microwave, even though I hadn't seen one earlier. The muffled sound of pots or pans clanging were heard, then it fell quiet.

A few minutes later, Ivy said, "Oh, no."

"What?" I asked.

"It smells like bacon. That's cruel and unusual punishment," she muttered.

At her words, the scent registered and my empty stomach rumbled.

She was right – it was cruel. Until then, I'd been able to ignore my empty stomach. Filling this shithole with the smell of food made my hunger impossible to deny.

"Do you think they're going to feed us?"

I sighed. "I'm trying *not* to think about food at all."

She nodded. "But that might be our chance. Two of us to one of them."

"You don't know there's only one, and since there were two of them earlier, we shouldn't assume there's only one now."

She pouted her plump lips as she thought about it. "Sounds that way."

I quirked my lips skeptically. "We thought we were alone five minutes ago also."

She threw her hands up. "Okay, I get it, but we should be ready even if we have to play this by ear."

I nodded. "You're right."

Before I could say more, the sound of heavy footsteps approached the door.

"Food's comin'. No plates, just a pan and two forks."

Ivy nodded at the door. "Okay. Thank you."

My mouth dropped open with my disbelieving look and I heard the footsteps move away. "What the hell are you thanking him for?" I hissed.

A devious grin made her green eyes sparkle. "He doesn't *have* to feed us and he gave us info."

I closed my eyes and fought for patience. "We have to be a team, so this is no time for you to be enigmatic. What are you getting at?"

Her expression shifted to solemness or even disappointment. "As much as I hate to sacrifice what smells like good bacon – he shows up with a pan – I can take it and hit him in the head with it."

"I don't have a good feeling about that."

She lowered her chin toward her shoulder. "He won't expect me to attack, Ry."

I liked hearing her shorten my name, but I couldn't let that distract me. "I know that but how many times have you hit someone with a skillet? And a hot one at that?"

She looked abashed. "Do you have a better idea?"

Reluctantly I said, "Unfortunately, no."

"Well, say a prayer because I think he's headed our way."

A key scraped in the lock and I hurried to the door.

Ivy gestured for me to stand against the wall near the door. I paused long enough to widen my eyes at her while mouthing 'be smart,' before I pressed myself against the wall.

A lazy smile slid across her face, there and gone before the door opened. More light poured into the room and I saw she held her hands down at her lower abdomen, both wrists close together as though still bound. That was a great touch since I didn't want Boyd or Campbell to know I had a knife.

Not yet, anyway.

Her eyes lit up and she grinned. "Tell me I smell bacon cheeseburgers. If it's just bacon, that's fine, but—"

"It's hot dogs, bitch. Move so I can put this down. The cast iron is about to burn me through the potholder," Campbell said.

That was all I needed to hear. I nodded at Ivy, she stepped back. Campbell stepped forward, the skillet in his right hand.

I grabbed his elbow and forced it toward his face.

Campbell overcame his surprise quicker than I expected and fought back. I stomped on his foot, and he howled so loud, I saw Ivy wince. He tried to throw the pan at me, but he missed. Four hot dogs skittered across the floor as the iron skillet landed two feet from my boot.

Ivy scrambled to the pan.

"Don't touch it, you'll burn yourself," I said.

Her side-eye rivaled an eyeroll from my sister. Like Mickayla, she didn't listen to me, and grabbed it anyway.

In the meantime, Campbell whirled on me, wrapping both hands around my throat. With my left hand, I brought my knife up and plunged it into his neck.

He let out a shocked cry and squeezed harder.

Suddenly, he lurched toward me at the same time I heard a dull thunk from behind him. Then like a cartoon character his eyes rolled back in his head and he collapsed. I moved out of the way right before he could fall on me.

I leaned over to pull my knife out of his neck. Blood seeped onto the floor.

Ivy gasped. "What'd you do that for?"

I almost chuckled. "It's my only weapon. Boyd could be out there or someone else. Let's go."

We hurried out of the room. It quickly became clear that nobody else was in the house. As we crossed through the kitchen I saw there was a plate of bacon and scrambled eggs.

Ivy stopped, tilted her head back, looked up at the ceiling, and said, "Please let this be safe to eat."

She grabbed a rasher of bacon and popped it in her mouth.

"Are you nuts?" I asked.

She swallowed. "No. Anyone who leaves bacon behind is nuts. Besides, I have no idea what time it is, or when I might get to eat again, and I'm starving."

I recalled Boyd's words about us having to walk and I grabbed one of the two remaining rashers.

"Screw it," Ivy said, picking up a fork and shoveling eggs into her mouth.

She held the utensil out to me. My gut said we didn't have time for this, but I needed my energy. I took the fork from her, loaded it up with eggs, and chowed down.

———

One step onto the wrap-around porch, and I saw the beat-up Nissan.

"You think the keys are in his pocket?" Ivy asked.

I did, and yet, I couldn't imagine Boyd underestimating Campbell's stupidity and sending him back here alone.

"Maybe. We need to stick together, so let's go check his pockets."

"I'm not arguing with you, but why do you say that?"

"If Boyd's here, he's twice as smart as Campbell, and that means he's even more dangerous. I don't want either of us to be blindsided."

"Fair. I've had enough of that for a lifetime," she muttered.

I wanted to dig in on that comment about being blindsided, but we needed to haul ass out of this dilapidated mess as soon as possible.

Mid-way through the kitchen, Ivy put a hand on my chest to stop my progress. I enjoyed feeling her touch there, but willed it out of my mind.

"Let me check his pockets, you stay here in case Boyd comes inside."

I shook my head. "We both go because I doubt you're cool with dead bodies."

Her eyes slid to the side and her internal debate was almost visible. Finally, she said, "You're right. We'll go together."

At the door to the bedroom, I had her stand back and I quickly went inside, found the keys to the Frontier and got out of the room. In the hall, I grabbed her hand, and tugged her toward the front door.

She resisted as we left the kitchen. "What are you doing? He had the keys?"

I faced her. "Got the keys. If Boyd's on his way back here, this is our only chance. We need to take his truck, and I'll get us back to Lark's."

She pressed her lips together and visibly warred with herself. "As much as I love that idea, we're just going to leave him here? I mean, if we move him outside the house somewhere, that might buy us more time since it'll reaffirm that Campbell left. The floors are dark enough, they might not notice the blood stain."

She had a point.

I tipped my head to the bedroom. "Let's hurry. Gonna need your help to move him though."

Chapter 7

Skillet Attack Plan

Ivy

"I'M GONNA HAUL HIM up to his feet, get his arm over my shoulder, and you need to get in a similar position on his other side so we can move him like a three-legged-race," Ryan said.

My stomach lurched since I really didn't want Campbell's head anywhere near mine.

I took a deep breath and gave a nod. "Fine. I guess you know more about moving dead weight than I do."

After what felt like five hours but was probably only fifteen minutes, we left Campbell in a small copse of trees and palmetto bushes.

Ryan and I walked at a rapid clip back to the house.

My nerves got the best of me and I blurted, "I can't believe we got kidnapped."

"This is no time for blame," he said.

"I didn't blame you."

He grunted. "The way you said it made it sound like you blamed me."

"I didn't."

"Then what's with the tone?" he asked.

"It wasn't tone, but I thought one of us would have fought back."

"You'll have to forgive me for protecting a woman who I thought was pregnant."

He wasn't being snippy…and yet, there was something off. But I decided to let it go.

"Very noble, but you should know a woman's pregnant before you assume. It always leads to trouble."

"All right, Mick," he muttered.

I grinned. "I knew I liked her."

We hurried to the truck. Ryan aimed the key fob at the vehicle and pressed a button. The headlights flashed and I heard the locks go.

"Thank goodness we're getting out of here," I said.

Ryan nodded. "Yeah, but if I don't find my cell in the truck, we're gonna search the house."

"Really?" I asked.

"Yes, really, Ivy. We need to let people know we're headed back. Hell, my cell will be able to tell us where we are."

"I'm sorry. I'm just antsy and scared Boyd will return."

"Right. You help me look and this will go faster."

His cell wasn't in the truck. We ransacked the kitchen, but it wasn't there either.

"Shit!" Ryan yelled, making me jump.

I took a deep breath. "I'm sorry we didn't find your phone, but people got by without cell phones for years. We can get back and—"

"What if there's no gas in that truck? Or just enough to get to a corner store?"

I shrugged. "Then we get to the corner store and ask them to call the cops."

His eyes widened. "Yeah…and what about the body we left behind?"

I hadn't wanted to dwell on that. Reflexively, I shrugged. "It was self-defense. Either way, we need to go."

Lights flashed through the kitchen as I heard another vehicle approach.

"Fuck," Ryan hissed.

I scrambled back to the small room where we'd been held, and I grabbed the skillet.

Ryan charged in behind me. "What are you doing?" he whispered.

My lips tipped up. "Skillet Attack Plan. It worked once. Might work again."

Clomping footsteps coming through the house could be heard.

Then, a man yelled, "Campbell! Quit fucking around. We gotta go."

The walls were paper thin since I heard the man sigh. Then the steps came closer. "If you're messing with that woman—"

Ryan's eyes widened and I saw him grip his knife tighter alongside his thigh.

A key scraped in the lock, then the man said, "You motherfucker. Always gotta stick your dick in anything that moves."

Boyd pulled the door open and came into the room. Ryan lunged forward, plunging his blade into Boyd's gut.

Boyd gasped, but reached for a gun on his hip.

I hustled up beside them, raised the iron skillet, and whacked Boyd in the face.

Over his grunt, it sounded like his nose broke, and blood gushed down his face.

With better reflexes than I expected, he grabbed my wrist.

Ryan yanked his knife free and went for Boyd's neck.

Boyd's grip on my wrist weakened and I pulled my hand free. I swung my arm back to hit him again.

"Don't," Ryan said.

Was he kidding?

"Why?" I asked.

"A second blow could be seen as premeditation."

I wasn't a lawyer – and I didn't think he was either – but he had so much certainty in his tone, I dropped my arm.

Boyd sunk to his knees, then he fell awkwardly to his side.

Ryan looked at me. "Pretty sure he's heavier than Campbell. You up for moving him, too? Or do you wanna leave him?"

I fought off a sigh. "Dealer's choice."

"Check his pockets. We'll leave him, but we're taking his vehicle and his phone."

We couldn't unlock Boyd's phone, but the GMC Canyon he drove was decked out with navigation and more than enough gas to get us back to On a Lark. Ryan's phone wasn't in the glove box, but he seemed resigned to it being a lost cause.

Out of habit, I lifted on the center console for a tissue since that was where I stashed mine, then I shook my head. "Sorry."

"What for? I don't think I checked there for my phone."

I nodded. "Ah. I was on auto-pilot and going to grab a tissue." I lifted the lid again and reached inside. "I think you're in luck," I said, pulling out a cell phone in a black hard-shell case.

"Yes," Ryan hissed.

He took the phone from me, and used his finger print to unlock it. Then, to my surprise, he handed it back to me. "Pull up my contacts and call the bar."

I shot him a look, but his eyes were trained on the road. "If you say so. I thought for sure you'd want to call your brother."

He shook his head. "No. We're closer to the bar, and I never told Lark I was leaving. Put it on speaker."

I did as he asked, and once the other line rang, I held the cell toward him.

"Where the hell have you been?" a gruff voice demanded.

The level of irritation in the man's voice sounded eerily familiar. If I wasn't mistaken, I sounded the same way when I was overly worried about someone.

"Lark, I'm sorry. Those assholes we tossed out months ago took me and a woman hostage. From what I overheard, they wanted me because they thought I'm your son."

"Are you shitting me, Nickel?"

"No," Ryan said with heavy emphasis.

"Well, where are you now? It sounds like you're driving."

"Two of the assholes are out of the picture, and I'm driving his truck back to town. We should be—"

"*Don't* bring that vehicle here. This is the first place they're gonna hit looking for you," Lark said.

"Shit, you're right," Ryan muttered.

"There's a side road on the right off US 90 about a mile after you cross into Duval county. Take that and park the truck in the brush. I'm sending Adam to pick you up."

———

We walked into the bar and Chad launched himself off his stool and hurried to me. He wrapped me up in a bearhug.

"Thank God, you're okay," he whispered in my ear.

"Yeah, I'm sorry I had you worried."

He leaned back, but didn't let me go. "Girlie, *you* didn't abduct yourself. Come on, Lark has your purse."

The food in my stomach morphed into a lead weight.

Before dragging me to a stool, Chad shifted his gaze to Ryan then to me, a smile spreading on his face. "Now I know what you were talking about months ago. God felt generous giving us more than one of him."

My eyes widened, but a thrill shot through me hearing Ryan's deep chuckle.

"Need you to tell my mom that. She jokes that God was testing her with the three of us."

Chad let me go and held a hand out to Ryan. "I'm Chad. Happy you and Ivy are back safe."

Adam wandered to us. "Nickel, Lark wants to see you in his office."

Chad led me to a barstool.

"Why didn't Lark give you my purse?" I asked, settling next to him.

"Because he doesn't know me."

"Did you tell him—"

Chad aimed a pointed look at me. "No. I wouldn't do that to you, but I did insist on calling the cops, but he wouldn't hear of it."

Considering the conversation Ryan and I had back in the house, that was probably a good move.

"Hello? You *are* going to report this, aren't you?" Chad demanded.

I breathed in deep through my nose. "Not tonight."

"Ivy Felicia," he started, his voice rising.

I rested my hand on his arm. "Listen. A lot happened, I'll tell you all about it, but tomorrow. Okay?"

Chad's face set with a blank look. "Fine. But I don't like this. I want something done to these bastards."

A door near the bar opened, and Ryan came back into the room. He sauntered toward me and Chad with my purse in his hand.

"I fully understand the sandwich craving you had by the way. He is fucking hot," Chad muttered.

"Stop," I whispered before Ryan drew even with us.

"Here's your purse. Lark's on the phone with our club president. He'll be out soon."

Knowing I didn't have to face Lark yet filled me with so much relief, it surprised me.

Hell, maybe it was a sign.

I gave a single stiff nod. "Thanks."

Ryan returned my nod and sauntered away.

I had to leave. My head was pounding and all I wanted was to go home. I rummaged through my purse to make sure my keys were there, then I slid off the stool.

Chad stood. "What are you doing?"

I hated lying to Chad, but I had no choice. "I'm going to the bathroom. I'll be right back."

He gave me a long look. "All right."

I went down the hall toward the bathroom, noticed the door to the smoker's patio, and went out that way.

In no time, I was at my car.

I jumped when I saw movement at my side.

"I knew you'd do this. Why are you running away *now*, Ivy?" Chad didn't let me answer. "We spent four days in Memphis. He's in your backyard. You've come too far to just leave."

I sighed. "Chad, I don't know what my problem is. No, that's not true. Losing Jeff sucked. It still sucks because Mom's so... empty. I want to help her and I got it in my head and my heart that this could help. Now, I see I'm wrong."

"You don't know that."

I felt my eyebrows shoot up and I lowered my chin. "I do know, because whether that man is good or bad or something in-between, nobody can replace Jeff."

Chad stepped closer. "Of course not, sugar. But it doesn't mean your heart didn't lead you to someone who might give you a new kind of love – even if only for you. No shade, but I don't see Debra being drawn to Lark." Chad widened his eyes. "He's got *edges*."

I wasn't sure if Chad emphasized the word 'edges,' to be dramatic, or if he and Lark had chatted while I was missing. I reached out and gave his hand a squeeze. "Today has been *a lot*. Can you see why I just want to go home?"

He nodded. "Yeah. Are you sure you're good to drive? I can—"

I went up on tiptoe and kissed his cheek. "No, honey. I'll be fine. But thank you. I'll call you tomorrow."

CHAPTER 8

MANY FORMS

RYAN

THE MOMENT I NOTICED Chad and Ivy were gone, I rushed outside. The two of them were chatting next to her car. I thought they would come back to talk to Lark, but then she climbed into her car.

"Shit," I whispered.

As she drove away, I hurried over to Chad, ignoring my pounding headache.

He heard me approach and turned to me. "Is there a—"

"She was knocked out by those bastards. She isn't good to drive, man. Give me her address, I'm following her home."

He aimed an unhappy look at me. "In that case, I'll follow—"

I shook my head. "Let me. Two of the men are out of commission for now, but that doesn't put her in the clear. One of them made a phone call, and at least one other person is involved from what I heard. Time's wasting. Help me out here, I need her address so I can catch up to her."

He hesitated.

"I'm not going to hurt her."

His lips quirked and he cocked a brow at me. "Hurt comes in many forms, so make sure you don't. She lives in Ortega."

He gave me the name of her townhouse complex and I ran to my bike.

Railroad tracks ran parallel to US 90, and I heard a train whistle in the distance. It sounded like it was coming from the east. I didn't want the train to hold me up and I sped toward the crossroad that would get me to I-10. As I approached Chaffee Road I almost thought I'd lost her. Luckily, she'd been held up by the train.

Once we were on the Interstate, I let her gain some distance, so she wouldn't get suspicious. Chad's words tumbled through my mind. *Hurt comes in many forms.*

That was true, but he made it sound like *she'd* been hurt. That irritated me more than it should.

We were almost downtown when she exited onto McDuff Avenue. A car cut me off at the last minute, but I made the light and kept following Ivy. Ten minutes later, we both drove into a small complex of townhouses not far from Highway Seventeen.

She pulled into a narrow drive for the first unit, and I parked my motorcycle behind her car. She threw open her car door and twisted out. "Why did you follow me? We're free."

"You need someone around. You probably have a concussion."

One of her sculpted brows rose. "Not sure if you're the best candidate since you have one too. I heard how hard they hit you. It had me so worried, I stared at you for a good minute to make sure you were still breathing."

I resisted the urge to flirt with her, but the fact she stared at me definitely stroked my ego.

"Can you take that magnet off your car before we go inside?"

She nodded. "I normally take them off so they don't get stuck. Chad has an ex who ran marathons and one of his magnets wouldn't come off. But seriously, Ryan, we're free. I can have Chad come over instead."

I crossed my arms. "We're free, but I killed two men to do that. They're gonna find out and they're gonna come after you."

She lowered her chin. "But you killed them."

I didn't point out that she helped. "They don't know that, but they *do* know you were with me. I'm not leaving."

What went unsaid was that I got her into this. I was going to make sure I got her out of it.

She peeled the magnets off her car and stowed them under the passenger seat. I walked her to the door of her unit, keeping an eye out for anything suspicious.

She led me inside her townhouse. The foyer was wider and longer than I expected with two closets to the left, and a staircase to the right. I followed her deeper inside. The U-shaped kitchen appeared to be fairly new, and a living room-dining room combo sat just beyond it. At the far end of the living room, an open doorway provided a glimpse of what appeared to be a master bedroom.

She started toward the kitchen, then stopped, and slowly shook her head. "Well, I'm starving, but it's been almost a week since I bought groceries. Your choices are a Boston Market frozen dinner or a chicken pot pie."

"I'm not hungry."

She gave me a pointed look. "After the day we had, you can't come to my house and refuse to let me feed you."

My eyes narrowed. "Why are you so insistent?"

Her eyes widened. "I'm starving, and I'll feel incredibly rude if I eat and you don't. It's almost nine o'clock, you have to be hungry."

The way my head hurt, I wasn't sure eating was a good idea. Then again, a full meal might alleviate the persistent ache.

"I don't want to eat your last frozen meal."

Her head jerked and those green eyes lit up. "I almost forgot. There's some left over jambalaya we can have instead."

That gave me pause. Dad made jambalaya when I was growing up. His was top-notch, and my favorite dish. "Did you make it yourself or is it from a restaurant?"

Her head tilted. "I made it. I'm not a half-bad cook, even if I'm saying so myself," she said with more sass than I expected.

This was even better than riling up my sister. Not only was it fun, but I found it made Ivy more adorable.

I threw my hands out in surrender. "Jambalaya it is, but you should know, you got big shoes to fill. My dad makes some of the best jambalaya."

"Great."

Ivy forked up a bite of andouille sausage, but didn't put it in her mouth. "I think this is overkill. They aren't going to come here for me."

We were seated at her oval dining table, me across from her. I'd finished eating before her. If there'd been more jambalaya, I'd have had seconds. It wasn't quite as spicy as Dad's, but it was damned good. I leaned back in my chair. "You're the first unit at the front of the neighborhood. You aren't exactly in the safest position."

She smiled. "Which is why I have a gun."

Given her profession, that didn't surprise me. "Is it in your purse?"

"No, it's in a lockbox in—"

"You should get it now, Ivy."

She chewed her food and swallowed. "I'll do that before you leave. Surely, you have better places to be. That reminds me, where do you live?"

I swallowed down a chuckle. "Why? Gonna send them my way?"

Her brows drew together and she almost frowned. "No, you followed me home. Fair's fair in my world."

"I live at the clubhouse."

Her eyes widened. "You have that as your address on your license?"

I fought off a grin because that was what my sister said when we moved into the clubhouse – the brothers would never let us give that address. "No, my license still lists an old address."

She tilted her head. "That's not too smart."

I chuckled. "Makes it harder for them to track me."

"They know where you work."

"Yeah, but that's a problem for me and Killian."

She stood and grabbed my empty plate. "Well, you should be on your way. I'll be fine."

A loud buzzer went off near her door. She gasped and fear shrouded her face.

I pressed my lips together, tamping down my anger. The next thing I knew she was at the door, talking into an intercom. "Who is it?"

I hurried up behind her as a garbled male voice said, "Amazon delivery."

A zing of awareness shot through me when I grabbed her hand before she pressed any more buttons. I lowered my lips toward her ear and whispered, "You got a camera out there?"

She nodded and pulled her phone from her pocket. On the screen a man in a uniform walked away.

"Were you expecting a delivery?"

Her eyes slid to the side. "Probably. I have subscriptions for certain things."

I didn't trust this. Something about an Amazon delivery this late bugged me. "Humor me. Go get your gun."

"It's a package."

I stared into her jade-green eyes. "It could be a trap."

She kept staring at me and twisted her pursed lips. "Okay, I'll humor you."

She hurried through her dining-living room combo and into her bedroom, then came back with a small handgun.

"I'm going out the side door." I held out my hand. "Give me your keys. I'll come in with the package if it's all clear."

She went to her purse, plucked out her keys, and handed them to me. "Why do I need my gun if you're going out there?"

I tucked the keys into my pocket. "In case I'm ambushed and they come in here."

Her chest rose and she exhaled slowly. "Be careful, Ryan."

I shrugged off my cut, hung it on a chair, and went out a side door to a small yard. I crept out through a gate and up the sidewalk. At my bike, I pulled my gun out of the saddlebag. Across from her unit, a sports car was parked in a space perpendicular to the street, the engine ticking. A sedan had been backed into a space next to it and someone was in the driver's seat – watching Ivy's building.

As I stared at the windshield, I noticed a light coming from below, then the person looked up and I realized they held a cell phone most likely.

At a regular pace, I walked along the sidewalk and then up the two steps to her door.

I glanced back at the car as casually as I could. The driver had tipped their head down, focused on the phone. I grabbed the box and unlocked the door and I let myself into Ivy's unit.

She stood in the foyer when I entered. "Just a package, right?"

I quirked my lips. "Is it normal for someone to sit out in their car on their phone at this time of night?'

Her eyes lit and she smiled. "Oh, that's Mr. Billings. He smokes in his car and scrolls his phone."

"I don't care. You need to come with me."

"I thought you didn't have a place."

I grinned. "It isn't a place someone in your line of work could sell, but I'm taking you to the clubhouse."

Her head reared back. "Taking me? I can follow you, seeing as I have to work tomorrow."

A wry laugh escaped me. "That's funny since most bosses don't like their employees to be on the job if they have a concussion."

She narrowed her eyes at me.

I twisted a hand toward what I assumed was her bedroom. "Put your gun in your duffle and let's go."

She crossed her arms under her breasts, and my fucking cock took notice. I took a deep breath and willed myself not to get hard.

"Chad doesn't live that far away. How about you drop me off with him?"

That made sense. Hell, it would probably work out better that way, but her obstinance —no, *resistance* – drew out something inside me. A strange need to wear her down...and having her in my room wouldn't hurt either.

I shook my head. "You'd put him in danger like that? Does he have a gun?"

Her silence brought something else to mind.

"You got a problem with bikers?" I asked, grabbing my club cut and putting it on.

Her lips pushed into a pout and she dropped her hands to her hips. "No, I just don't want to be around Lark. I know I was looking for him, and that none of this makes sense, but I'm guessing he stays at the clubhouse, too. Or he'll be there."

I nodded once. "That's understandable. But no, he has a place closer to the bar, and is only at the clubhouse when we have meetings or cookouts."

I didn't tell her it was highly likely we'd have a meeting in the morning, but I didn't know that for certain.

"I still think this is overkill."

"Would your mother see it that way? I'm guessing you're her only kid."

Her eyes darted to the side. "Yeah, I'm her only child." She looked at me with attitude. "You're way too observant."

"Get your bag, Ivy."

She stared at me a beat, then turned around, and went to her bedroom. I liked watching her walk away even more than I did the first time she came to the bar.

Again, I got the feeling she was trouble, and I was screwed.

CHAPTER 9

TROUBLE

IVY

I CARRIED MY DUFFEL bag out of my bedroom, and Ryan took it from me. He stood close while I locked my door, but he was scanning the area outside my townhouse.

He led me to the end of my driveway. I realized we'd be riding on his motorcycle and I nearly tripped.

"Are you okay?" he asked, looking down at me.

"I'm fine, but are you sure you're alright to get both of us to your clubhouse?"

His lips quirked up. "Feeling better now that I've got food in my belly, and it isn't that far from here. Probably five miles, maybe six."

"Oh," I said.

"Why'd you stutter-step?"

I shrugged. "Nothing big. I've just never ridden on a motorcycle before, and I forgot that you followed me on your...is this a Harley?"

He opened a leather saddlebag and to my surprise, my duffel fit with no problem. After he closed the bag, he faced me. "No, it's a Triumph. Once I'm on the bike, you climb on behind me. Under the circumstances, I'd like you to hang on to me."

"What circumstances?" I asked reflexively.

"The fact that I don't trust you aren't at one-hundred percent and there could be someone looking for both of us."

It was on the tip of my tongue to remind him that was enough reason to take me to Chad's, but I didn't want him to be in danger either.

I nodded. "Got it... Nickel. That's what I'm supposed to call you, right?"

"Yeah, at the clubhouse that'd be good, though I don't care if you call me Ryan in private."

I didn't expect I'd spend much time with him in private after tonight.

He swung a leg over his motorcycle and I found I'd been wrong last week. I didn't stop myself from watching him mount his bike because it was an intrusion, I'd done it because it turned me on so much.

"Grab my shoulder, use the foot peg, and hop on, Trouble. "

I did what he said and managed to settle behind him more easily than I expected.

His head turned toward his shoulder. "Hang on to me."

I suddenly felt awkward. I wanted to put my hands on his waist near his hips, but that felt entirely too intimate. I'd look like a fool if I held onto his shoulders. I decided to put my hands on his lower ribcage. "I hope you're not ticklish," I muttered at the same time he started the engine.

He shook his head. "I'm not," he said loud enough to be heard over the bike.

Then we were off. He started slow, but once we were on 103rd Street he took off. We had to be going ten miles over the speed limit. I had a bad habit of speeding, but speeding down the road on a motorcycle was so much better.

From the circuitous route he took to get to Blanding Boulevard, I got the impression he knew as many back roads as I did, and I wondered why that was. For me, it was an occupational necessity. The average person – and especially someone who was new to town – didn't normally go out of their way to take side streets.

I took in the large patch for the Riot MC on the back of his leather cut. Perhaps he knew the same shortcuts for reasons I didn't want to know.

He slowed to turn off of Blanding Boulevard and after a half-a-mile, he turned left into a property surrounded by a black iron fence. A two-story building took up a chunk of the property. There was plenty of room for bikes to park, and a grassy section where there were cars and a couple other motorcycles parked.

He eased his bike into a space next to a beat-up Kia Rio, lowered the kickstand, and shut down the engine. "Do you need help getting off?"

That sounded like fun.

I hung my head at my wayward thought, grateful he couldn't see me smirking and biting back my laughter.

"What are you smiling about?" he asked.

My head shot up. "I didn't think you could see me."

"I can see you in the side mirrors, Ivy. Do need help?" he asked again.

I moved my head in a circular nod. "I imagine I might."

He grabbed my right hand and guided it up to his shoulder, then he took hold of my left hand. "Put your left foot on the peg, stand, and if you need to, use your hand on my shoulder to help you while you swing your right leg off."

I followed his instructions, and managed to dismount without making a complete fool of myself. While he swung off the bike quickly, I still noticed how well he filled out his faded jeans. He turned around and I swallowed. I hadn't realized I stood so close to him, and I stepped back. My heel caught on something and I started to fall. Ryan lunged toward me, wrapped his warm hands around my biceps, and caught me.

That was good and bad. It was good for all the obvious reasons, but it was bad because now we stood even closer to one another and I smelled his leather vest and faint traces of his cologne or deodorant. Worse, I didn't like that combination, I *loved* it.

He stared down at me like he was weighing his words. His hands slid up to my shoulders and back down in a soothing manner. "You actually trip or are you not feeling well?"

I pressed my lips together. "I tripped. There must be a root or something in the ground."

"Are you prone to being clumsy?"

When I was feeling awkward, absolutely.

Still, we hardly knew each other and I was embarrassed. "Not really, I'm just a little... nervous, I guess."

"How's your headache?" he asked, a thread of skepticism in his tone.

"It's getting better."

"Think you're lying, but let me grab your bag," he said, dropping his hands and side-stepping around me.

I took a deep breath and rubbed my arms. Next thing I knew, he grabbed my hand and he led me to a large concrete patio with six wooden picnic benches. We went in through a back door and I heard the clack of pool balls and alternative rock music played, but it wasn't blaring.

He led me to a narrow staircase and dropped my hand. I followed him to the second floor, and down a long corridor with four doors on each side of the hall. This building was much larger than it seemed from the outside. My real estate brain wanted to calculate the square footage, but my head was starting to pound again now that I didn't have anything to distract me from the pain.

He stopped at the second door, unlocked it, and led me inside. There were rectangular windows set high in the wall, which allowed some moonlight to filter inside. He hit a lamp on a nightstand and set my duffel on the floor next to the bed.

"So this is my room for the night?" I asked.

He dragged his fingers along his jaw, the expression in his eyes calculating. "Yes, but it's my room, so really, it's our room for the night."

A sinking sensation went through my belly, but it was tinged with excitement.

He must have read the look on my face. "If Killian isn't staying here tonight, I can sleep in his room if it makes you more comfortable. But fair warning, he's probably using his room tonight."

I shook my head and waved a hand in front of me. "I don't want to be more of an imposition." I shrugged and looked him in the eye. "It's just sleeping after all, right?"

He stared at me for a beat. "That's right."

The way he said that, my stupid nerves fired up and I filled the silence. "It's not like you're attracted to me or anything."

With a head shake he turned away from me while shrugging out of his leather vest. He hung it on a wall hook next to a dresser. He opened a drawer and pulled out a neatly folded black t-shirt, then bent to a different drawer and pulled out a scrap of white fabric. I watched him put them on the bed, then he reached behind his neck and yanked his t-shirt off right in front of me.

What in the world?

He pitched the t-shirt toward a hamper in the corner of the room, then locked eyes with me. "I wouldn't put words in my mouth, woman. I'm gonna shower because I'm guessing I'm quicker than you, and I know I got sweatier than you moving that fuckin' body."

"Okay," I whispered, doing my level best not to take in the tattoos on his chest, or his very well-defined muscles, or the smattering of chest hair that I found so appealing.

Picking up the white fabric that I realized was a tank-top undershirt, he trudged closer. "You're sexy as hell, but you're also trouble. And I'm not in a place in my life where I can afford more trouble."

My eyes widened, but with that parting note, he went into the en-suite bathroom and closed the door before I could retort.

Little did he know, I wasn't trouble. Not even a little bit. Hell, if he had let me talk to Lark months ago, we wouldn't even be in this darn mess.

I heard the shower start, and I struggled against my vivid imagination thinking about him being naked... and wet. A remote control sat on the nightstand next to the lamp. I snatched it up, aimed it at the flat screen on the wall, and the announcer commentary from *Monday Night Football* filled the room.

I didn't follow football much until the playoffs, but I needed a distraction from Ryan.

Desperately.

No sooner had I perched a hip on Ryan's made bed than someone pounded on his door.

"What the hell, Nickel? You're late for the pool tourney!" a male voice yelled.

The man pounded again, and I hurried to the door, opening it a smidge and felt confused for a second. Ryan and his brother looked so much alike, it took me a beat to realize Killian was standing in the hall glowering at me.

"Hi, um, he's taking a shower. I'm not sure if he's going to be—" I cut myself short when I felt the heat of someone who could only be Ryan standing behind me.

"What the fuck, Kill? You've never pounded on my door."

Killian's eyes darted from me to Ryan. "You've never been three hours late before either. I'd ask why she's here, but I'd rather know why the fuck she's got a shiner."

My hand darted up to my face. I didn't have a black eye...but then I recalled how red and puffy the area around my face was when I used the bathroom before leaving my townhouse.

"We got ambushed outside the bar. Thought Lark or Volt would have shared that shit. We both got walloped in the head, and I'm thinking she might have a slight concussion."

"No such thing as a 'slight concussion', and you know it. The two of you should go to the emergency room."

"Which would force someone at the hospital to call in the cops and shit. No. That isn't happening. I'm keeping an eye on her, and we'll get up every forty-five minutes or whatever the fuck we're supposed to do."

Killian scoffed. "You cannot rely on WebMD or some shit—"

"Called Abby, and you know she's not gonna steer us wrong."

Even though I didn't know Killian very well, I swore a devious expression filled his eyes. "Well, unless you're going to sleep soon, you should come downstairs...and bring her with you."

"Whatever," Ryan muttered from behind me and slammed the door shut in Killian's face.

I turned around. "I'd say that was rude, but I'm guessing you've done that to him plenty of times before, being siblings and all."

"Yeah," Ryan clipped out.

My eyes watched a droplet of water slide down his neck, to his bare chest, and further down, which was the moment I saw he was only wearing a towel wrapped around his trim waist. My mouth went dry at the sight.

Oh my God.

The things I wanted to do to him...no.

No, that wasn't a good idea.

He huffed out a breath through his nose. "Fuck. Don't look at me like that, Ivy."

I tilted my head. "How about not standing so close to me like that, hmm?"

"Don't get cute," he ordered.

"I'm not being cute."

He dipped his chin and one of his eyebrows ticked up and down. "You are, even though you don't know it. And your facial expressions are out of control."

I opened my mouth to argue, but he was right. Even Chad had told me my facial expressions put me on par with Dorothy from *The Golden Girls.*

My gaze moved past him and I swatted my hand out toward the bathroom. "You go get dressed or whatever, and we won't have to talk about this."

He nodded. "I'll do that." His finger came up and traced along the edge of my temple. "Then, I'm taking you downstairs so you can ice this."

"I can just go downstairs while you—"

His index finger went under my chin and tipped my face up. The insistent look in his eyes sent a thrill through me. "No. You don't go down there without *me.*"

My brows furrowed. His statement didn't sound like a warning, it almost sounded proprietary.

"It's just a bag of ice," I whispered.

His expression turned serious. "But that isn't just some room down there. It's our common room. If you're not with me... not sure Killian will be able to stop whatever might happen to you down there."

"Something would happen to me?"

"Since nobody down there knows who you are... something could. Bottom line, you wait five minutes for me. Got it?"

"I got it."

Slowly, he dragged his finger out from under my chin. "Don't be scared. Once they know you're... with me, it'll be fine."

I didn't know why he hesitated before saying 'with me,' but I sensed it went back to his proprietary tone.

He turned around and my mouth dropped open. Colorful ink depicting the Riot MC patch covered his back. It was impressive and gorgeous, but made even more so by his rippling muscles. My eyes wandered down his legs. I admired his thick calves and the intricate scorpion tattoo wrapping around the bottom of his left calf. The bathroom door snicked shut, and I shook my head.

If anyone was trouble around here, it was definitely *him.*

CHAPTER 10

ONE MORE THING IN COMMON

RYAN

THIS NIGHT COULDN'T END fast enough. I thought being stuck in a room in the middle of nowhere was torture, but no, *this* was real torture. Having her on the back of my bike, in the clubhouse, in my room, and soon in my bed... but not being able to do a damn thing with her because I'd told her she'd be safe here. Yeah, I had a masochistic streak all right.

Then I'd almost told her she was mine.

Good God.

I couldn't have a woman right now. I may have earned my patch, but working for Lark felt like I'd signed on to be a never-ending prospect for him.

That wasn't totally true.

He ran the three of us ragged in an effort make us *feel* just how grueling and harsh the restaurant and bar industry really was.

I didn't want to add a woman into the mix right now. Definitely not one like Ivy, who not only wasn't from my world, but also deserved a stable man who lived in her world.

Watching her interacting with Killian though, practically barring him at the door, some instinct in me said she could hack it around here. Not just hack it, but even fit in with brothers and their ol' ladies.

Shit.

I quickly put on my tank and pulled on my jeans. I'd forgotten to grab a clean pair, but I'd take care of that while Ivy showered. The way she looked at me earlier had me fighting off kissing her. And for her to think I wasn't attracted to her. That was ridiculous... then again, she thought she wasn't as gorgeous as my sister. I was exactly the man who could show her reality.

I stepped out of the bathroom to find her watching *Monday Night Football* with a hip propped on my bed.

"You could take your shoes off and get comfortable, Ivy," I murmured as I wandered to dresser.

"I didn't want to mess up your bed, especially since I need to shower," she said.

With a pair of socks in hand, I sat on the edge of the bed opposite her, and tugged them on. "Let's go get you some ice, or I can run down and get it while you shower."

She stood. "No, I'm curious about this building. It's deceptively large."

"That's the damn truth," I muttered, shoving my feet into my boots.

"Why do you say it like that?"

I chuckled. "As a prospect, we had to scrub every inch of flooring and all kinds of other chores to maintain the clubhouse. Trust me, you figure out how big this place is real fast that way."

Once we were downstairs, I grabbed her hand and led her into the common room. Not many brothers hung out here on Monday nights, so I didn't expect for there to be anything too wild and crazy happening.

Killian, Tundra, Rafferty, and I normally played a pool every Monday night. Now that Rafferty and Alexandra were serious, he'd been hit and miss around here. As we rounded the corner of the bar, I saw Rafferty lining up the cue ball to break a fresh rack and Tundra stood to the side holding a cue stick.

Tundra was older than us by about twenty years, and his eyes narrowed on Ivy. "What the hell happened to her?"

"Who is she?" Tic asked.

Tic also stood holding a cue stick. They must have asked him to fill in for me. He earned his patch around the same time as me, Killian, and Rafferty, but he'd started prospecting before us. I didn't trust him. It took him longer to patch into the club. He loved the club lifestyle, but he rarely listened to the rest of us –

about anything. It was one thing to march to the beat of his own drum, but it was a whole other thing to ignore his brothers. It rubbed me the wrong way, and I despised that he'd taken an interest in Ivy. I had to shut that down.

I stopped and twisted my head toward him. "She's Ivy, and she's off-limits to you."

His brows shot up. "Is she now?"

"Yeah. It's not a challenge. Forget you even saw her."

Tic opened his mouth, but Tundra cut him off. "Leave it, man."

Tundra wandered to the bar while I loaded ice into a plastic bag. "This have something to do with you being late?"

I nodded. "Those assholes who caused two fights at the bar when we first opened came back around. They saw her making an approach, and one of them cornered her and pulled a gun. I got in between them, but never pulled my piece. I should have just shot the asshole—"

Tundra shook his head. "No. That would've gone bad fast."

I sighed. "Then one of the others came out and had a gun trained on her. They took us to a run-down dump way out near Sanderson."

Tundra's jaw ticked and he looked away. "Where are they now?"

"Out of the picture," I muttered and tied off the bag of ice.

Tundra locked eyes with me. "You're in the clubhouse, Nickel. I'm your brother, say it straight."

I handed the bag to Ivy, but kept my gaze on Tundra. "Two of them are dead, but at least one other person knows or soon will know they're gone because someone named Rusty was calling the shots."

"Why'd they take you two?" Rafferty asked, sidling up to Tundra.

"They think I'm one of Lark's kids," I said. I glanced at Ivy holding the bag of ice. "Put that to your face, woman."

She raised the bag to her temple, but shook her head while doing it. "Pretty sure this is a lost cause, Nickel."

I shot her some side-eye because deep down I preferred her calling me Ryan.

"Why did you bring her here?" Rafferty asked. "Pretty sure she can ice that bruise at home."

"I'm a realtor, and there's a magnet on my car that lists my name and phone number. They shouldn't be able to find my address that way, but Ryan, I mean Nickel, didn't want to take that chance."

Tundra's lips quirked into a small smile. "Always better to be safe than sorry."

I went behind the bar and put down a pint glass. "You want anything to drink, Ivy? There's a half a bottle of red wine back here, but who knows how long it's been sitting around. Or there's some white wine—"

"Or tequila helps with bruises," Tundra said.

Ivy laughed. "It does not."

Tundra leaned forward. "How would you know? I'm guessing you've never had a shiner before."

Was he flirting with my woman?

Dammit. She wasn't mine.

Ivy pulled the ice away for a moment. "No, I haven't, but I've had tequila before and those headaches almost rival the one I've got right now."

I narrowed an eye at her. "You said it was getting better."

She shot me a small smile. "Yes, but being on your motorcycle had everything to do with that."

I had a sudden urge to throw her over my shoulder and ride as far as my Triumph would take us. Rather than give into the urge, I forced myself to ask, "Do you want something to drink? Otherwise, I'll grab you a water."

She shrugged a shoulder, which drew my attention to the line of her collarbones which were on full display in her wide-necked blouse.

"This is a bad idea, but after this day, I don't give a damn. I could go for vodka and cranberry or I'm good with vodka and a twist of lemon or a lime if you've got that," she said.

We were more than good with that. My favorite liquor was vodka. I went to the side-by-side fridge and pulled a bottle of vodka from the freezer. A lemon and a lime sat on the counter close by, I grabbed both. When I turned around, I saw Ivy watching me.

I nodded at her.

"You forgot glasses," Tundra said.

My eyes slid toward him. "Got some in my room."

"No ice?" he asked.

"This has been in the freezer."

"Not gonna socialize?" Tundra kept at me.

I fought off a frown. "So you can flirt with her some more? We'll pass."

Tundra roared with laughter. My anger flared because nothing about this was funny.

Tundra clapped a large burly hand on my shoulder. "Nickel, when I'm flirtin' with your woman, you'll fuckin' know it."

"Whatever. If you're around, you'll see us in the morning," I muttered.

Ivy reached out and took the fruit from me. I jerked my head toward the other side of the room and she walked in front of me. The way Tic eyed her up and down didn't escape me, but I kept my reaction in check.

I shifted the vodka bottle so I could hold her hand before she got out of the common room. From the corner of my eye I saw her head turn and I looked down the dim hallway. Another biker and one of the club groupies were halfway down the corridor making out. She'd pushed forward and had him up against the wall, and he had both hands wrapped around the globes of her ass. She pulled away and kissed his neck. In the dim light, I recognized Killian.

"Goddammit," I hissed.

"What?" Ivy whispered, twisting her head around to me.

"Don't worry about it. Let's go," I whispered, and hurried us up the stairs.

Inside my room, I put the vodka on my dresser and took the lime and lemon from her.

She put a hand on her hip. "What was that all about?"

I moved to my closet to grab a towel, then went to my bed and picked up the black t-shirt I'd left there. I held them out to her. "Like I said, don't worry about it. You need to shower before you have a cocktail. Here's a towel for you, there's a washcloth in the bathroom."

Her head reared back. "That seems over the top, too."

I chuckled silently. "It's not over the top if I'd rather you shower with all your wits about you. That's being safe."

She tipped her head to concede the point. "What was the problem downstairs? Two people were making out, which isn't something I haven't seen before."

"It was about to become much more, Ives."

She shrugged. "I'll take your word for it. I mean, I'm not a voyeur, but your reaction was... over the top."

I tipped my head back for a moment. "Not if you consider that was Killian down there, and I'd rather not see him gettin' some."

"Oh. Well, that makes more sense. At least you don't think I'm a prude or so delicate I need to be protected from seeing people making out."

I closed my eyes, turned my head a tick, then held up my hands before I looked her in the eye. "Please, go take your shower. It's getting late."

While she showered, I checked my phone. I had a string of texts from Mickayla.

> **What the hell! How did you get taken from in front of the bar?**

> **Hello?**

> **This is no time to ignore your triplet, Ry.**

The last message came in an hour ago. I wondered how she knew about it so fast when Killian hadn't known.

I sent her a text to set her mind at ease.

She responded instantly.

> **The only good thing is that I hear you followed a certain woman home.**

I rolled my eyes and sent her back a GIF that said 'goodnight.'

> **I bet it will be.**

> It isn't like that. Now I need to get some sleep.

I put my phone away and went to my desk in the corner of the room. In a large drawer, I had two highball glasses and I pulled them out. I should have had a prospect bring me a bucket of ice, but I hadn't wanted to give Tundra another reason to give me shit.

It had surprised me when Ivy suggested vodka over tequila since that was my go-to liquor, too. I poured two fingers into each glass when I heard the bathroom door open.

I looked over my shoulder and swallowed. She wore my t-shirt and it hit at her mid-thigh. Her legs were long and curvy, making my hands itch to touch them.

She put her duffel bag next to the bed. "Please tell me you didn't do anything else to that vodka. I saw that it's Tito's and really it just needs a squirt of lime for me."

I grinned. "Nope, haven't done anything to your glass yet. Get over here, and you can doctor it yourself... or I'll do it."

She chuckled and sidled up to the dresser. "We forgot to grab a knife downstairs, so I'm not sure how we're going to manage this."

I pulled my pocket knife out of my pocket and put it on the dresser in front of her. "You can cut it if you want. I cleaned the blade earlier in the bathroom when I got dressed. I'm more of a gimlet man, but there's no lime juice down there because we used it all last night."

Her eyes widened and she looked up at me. "Wow. We have one more thing in common then, I guess."

My brows arched. "One more?"

"I'm not exactly counting, but so far we have three things in common. Being abducted, apparently a mutual attraction, and our drink preference."

Every time I thought she couldn't stir up trouble, she went and did it again.

I left her comment alone and twisted a hand at the lime. "You gonna take care of that, or should I?"

She held her hands up. "Have at it. I don't want to get juice all over your dresser."

My dirty mind served up visions of her getting a different kind of juice all over my dresser. I took a deep breath and exhaled before I grabbed the lime and cut it in half.

I handed her one half. "Have at it, Ivy."

While she fiddled with the lime, I squeezed as much out of the other half as I could, careful not to get seeds in the glass.

"Geez, you must have strong hand muscles," she said, carefully putting the other half on the dresser.

I grabbed that half and squeezed the rest into my glass. "Yeah. It's important to have strong hands when you're dealing with drunks."

She raised her glass to mine. "Here's to escaping that creepy house."

I tapped my glass against hers and took a sip.

She slammed hers back. "All right. Hit me again, Nickel."

"You aren't getting drunk, woman."

Her head tilted. "Not trying to get drunk. But, I'd say today calls for two cocktails, not one."

I poured a single finger of vodka into her glass. "There you go. That's it, Ivy."

"Cool," she said, and sipped at it, then wandered to my bed.

Chapter 11

We're Even

Ivy

Between the vodka and discovering new things about Ryan at every turn, I found myself letting my guard down more and more with him. I needed to protect my heart here.

I'd had two long-term relationships, and both had wrenched my heart in different ways. William left me on the hook for an apartment lease, which was why I hadn't bought any property. My credit seriously needed to improve. The other ex-boyfriend, Austin, had been more controlling than I liked, but the worst thing was when he brought another woman home with him – out of the clear-ass blue – and wanted to experiment. I liked to think I was open-minded, but that sort of thing should have been discussed before hand. The two of us.

Ryan didn't give me those kinds of vibes, but he also wasn't willing to go to the law about the crimes committed against us... which basically made us criminals, too.

That should have put the ultimate damper on my attraction to him, but he'd made a good point. It wouldn't look like self-defense – especially since we'd moved one of the bodies.

He downed the last of his cocktail and poured himself another.

My snark couldn't be denied. "That's it for you, too, right, Nickel? Or is it a one-way street here?"

He glanced over his shoulder at me with a cynical smirk. "This is it. Thanks for the reminder, smarty."

I set my glass on the nightstand while shaking my head. "I'm just saying...double standards suck."

"That they do," he muttered, moving to the other side of the bed.

The clinking sound of his belt buckle stole my attention and I glanced his way in time to see him drop his jeans to the floor. He wore shiny royal-blue boxer briefs that appeared to be made of nylon.

I fought all of my reactions to seeing him in his skivvies.

"You all right?" he asked, pulling the comforter out from under the pillow on his side.

"Yeah," I said, my voice higher than normal. I cleared my throat. "I'm going to brush my teeth."

I stood, bent to my bag to dig out my toothbrush and heard Ryan groan. My eyes darted to him. "What's wrong? You sound like you're in pain or something."

"You could say that. It's not every day there's a gorgeous woman in my room wearing my shirt and bent over like that and I can't do something about the pain she's putting me in."

With my toothbrush and toothpaste in hand, I quickly straightened. "To be fair, seeing you in your boxer briefs leaves a woman in a certain state, too. So I'd say we're even."

His eyes widened. "We're far from even, Ives."

I shook my head and went to the bathroom. To get my mind off Ryan and how insanely attracted I was to him, I brushed my teeth with vigor.

Earlier, I'd noticed the bathroom had been remodeled and I'd meant to ask him what company they'd used because even at a glance I could tell it was excellent workmanship. I kept a small database of general contractors, plumbers, electricians, and other companies that could help my clients spruce up their homes to get the most bang for their buck when their property was listed. Nothing about the tile work or the flooring appeared to be done half-way.

Thoughts of my database made me think about my schedule for tomorrow and my back straightened. If I wasn't mistaken, I had a closing tomorrow... and I didn't have my car.

Shit! Why had I let him talk me into riding on his bike?

I set my toothbrush in a counter-top holder, rinsed and spit, took care of other business in the bathroom and went back into the bedroom.

Ryan sat with his back against the headboard and a paperback in his lap. I didn't know why that took me aback, but it did.

"Whatcha reading?" I asked.

"Now you're back to being cute."

I pulled the comforter and sheets down on my side, and climbed into the bed. "No, I'm not. I'm curious to a fault, especially about books."

"Re-reading a police procedural."

I shoved my legs under the covers and my foot grazed the side of his leg. The unexpected thrill that gave me couldn't be ignored.

He set the paperback aside, tossed the covers off, and left the bed.

The torture continued as I watched him saunter to the bathroom. Something about him in the white tank was more mesmerizing than him being shirtless and in a towel. Like the clingy material better defined his muscles.

This was going to be a long night.

I heard the water running in the sink. I settled further into the bed and turned out the lamp.

The best way to avoid the temptation of watching Ryan move around the room was for me to rest my eyes. As soon as I closed them, my exhaustion washed over me. Seemed being kidnapped took it out of a girl.

I pulled the covers up and turned onto my side.

Ryan climbed into bed a couple minutes later and killed his light. Then I noticed a faint light behind my eyelids, and I figured he was checking his phone.

"You sleeping?" he asked.

"Not yet," I said, cracking an eye open. This man was hot even in the dim light of a freaking cell phone.

"I set an alarm for an hour. Figure it'll take us both ten minutes to get to sleep. Either way, we're gonna have to wake up every so often for a few hours."

"Great," I muttered. "In the morning, my boss isn't going to like hearing I didn't get a full eight hours."

"You aren't going to work tomorrow."

I pushed up to an elbow and stared at him. "I've got a closing tomorrow, Ryan. I have to be there. You have no idea how hard it is to get all the parties at the same place at the same time to get a deal done. It's non-negotiable."

Suddenly, Ryan pushed into me, and I was on my back with his forearms framing my head. "Woman, your health and your safety are more important than a closing no matter how difficult it is to coordinate. Pretty sure your boss will feel the same way, and if he doesn't, fuck 'im, he isn't worth working for."

"She," I said on autopilot.

"Whatever. She ought to be understanding in this fucked up sitch, and what I said still stands. If she doesn't get it, it's not worth working for a bitch like that."

The phone cast a dim light into the room allowing me to see the intensity in his blue eyes. I loved how fierce he was about my health and safety, but feeling his body heat and having him hovering over me like this turned me on in a big way.

I kept staring at him willing myself to keep a stoic facial expression because otherwise, I'd give away how much I wanted him to kiss me.

His face came closer. "Do you get me?"

"Yeah," I whispered, pressing my lips together at the end.

"What time's your closing?"

"Eleven," I murmured.

"I'm thinkin' we can get you eight hours between then and now. Just won't be uninterrupted."

The light from the phone went out, and in the darkness I felt bolder. I reached up and stroked the side of his bicep. "Thanks. I appreciate it."

He sighed and I felt his nose graze along side mine. "You don't need to appreciate that. Let's get some sleep, though at this point it's gonna be hard as hell to sleep next to you."

"As if," I whispered.

He rolled away on a chuckle. "Woman, you griped about seeing me in my underwear, but you're over there in my shirt without a bra, and I'm doin' my damnedest to keep my hands off you."

"What if I said you didn't have to?"

"You deserve better than that."

"That makes no sense. We're both drawn to each other. We could scratch the itch and make out before sleeping."

"That will make shit worse, woman. I won't be able to stop, and if I did, I'd have blue balls instead of fighting a painful hard-on."

He was probably right. Rather than argue with him, I twisted away from him and murmured, "Good night... for now."

I heard him exhale hard, and I knew he found a sliver of humor in my words. Crazy as it made me, I felt better for that.

The most bizarre trilling sound woke me from a dead sleep. It kept going and I shifted. I made out the sound of Ryan not exactly snoring, but definitely making the same sounds as Darth Vader, if the Sith Lord ever slept. More forcefully than necessary I rolled toward him. He still didn't wake, and I began to worry that he'd suffered more of a concussion than I had.

I reached out and nudged his arm. "Nickel. Ryan, wake up."

He snorted in a breath and his body jolted. "Whas goin' on?" he asked in an almost boyish voice that made me bite back a smile.

"Your alarm's going off, big guy. We both need to be awakened every so often, remember?"

The way he took in a deep breath couldn't be missed, and then he sat up, twisted to the nightstand and grabbed his phone. He disabled the alarm, put the phone down with a clatter, and flopped back to the bed on his back.

I couldn't help but laugh, and even though it was silent, my body shook with it.

"Are you fucking laughing at me, Ives?"

My smile widened, my lips parted and I laughed out loud. "Yeah. You're the one who insisted on waking up on a schedule and yet, you're the one who can't stick to the plan. Add to that, you sound almost – don't take this the wrong way – boyish when you first wake up, and it's funny to me."

He sighed and groaned at the same time. "Glad I'm entertaining to you. How are you feeling? Still got a massive headache?"

"No, but more importantly, do you?"

"No. Not unless I count you giving me shit for how I sound when I first wake up."

"That wasn't shit. I thought it was cute," I said, then wished I hadn't. Seeing as I couldn't take it back, I tossed the covers off me. "I'm hitting the bathroom, while you reset our ridiculous alarm."

"Not ridiculous, woman," he muttered.

I wandered into the bathroom shaking my head, but didn't respond.

When I returned to the bedroom, Ryan rolled out of bed.

"Aren't there other side-effects associated with a concussion?" I asked just before he hit the doorway to the bathroom.

He paused, but didn't look at me. "Yeah, but neither one of us had those. Don't know about you, but I'd rather wake up every so often, than find myself in the hospital because my brain swelled in my sleep."

Mental note: someone didn't like having their sleep interrupted. Then again, neither did I.

I rolled to my side, and realized I was facing Ryan's side of the bed. It wasn't ideal, but I figured I'd switch when he came back to bed.

The next time I woke up, it wasn't because of an alarm. It was because I was burning up and a heavy arm rested along my waist. I opened my eyes and in the dim moonlight coming into the room, I saw the outline of Ryan's white tank top against his skin.

How was I pressed up against him like this? No, why was I held tight to him like this?

As gentle and slow as I could, I tried to pull free of his hold without waking him. That was no easy task, let me tell you.

I had eased his arm off me, and managed to pull away from him by an inch when his breathing shifted.

"Ivy," he said, his voice almost questioning.

"Yeah," I whispered, trying not to wake him up fully.

"What are you doing?" he asked.

"I'm... giving you space."

"Alarm go off?" he asked in a husky voice.

"No."

Light from his cell phone filled the room, then I saw him fiddling with the screen for a bit before he put it back on the night stand.

"Everything all right?" I asked.

"Will be once you get back over here."

I did a long blink, not that he could see it in the darkness. "Pardon me?"

"You were out cold earlier, and the only way for me to get some sheets was to pull you closer to me. I'm not fighting for sheets with you, so get your ass over here and let's go back to sleep, Ives."

Nobody called me that. Scratch that, Ed had called me 'Ives' when I was little. He was long gone once Mom learned what a jackass he was to me. As much as I wanted to tell Ryan to stop calling me that, there was something downright therapeutic about the way he did it. In fact, I almost *liked* it – but my jury was still out.

How weird was that?

I curled up on my side of the bed. "Um, I'll just be right over here, on my side of the bed. I mean, it's a queen so everything is nice and cozy."

Ryan slid his arm under my neck, along my shoulders, and pulled me toward him. "Don't fuck with me, tonight, woman. We're both too tired for that. See you in another hour."

"Thought it was every forty-five minutes?" I asked like an idiot.

He chuckled. "I've been stretching it out. My guess is we don't have real concussions. Those pussies didn't have what it takes to give either of us concussions."

I rested my arm along his abdomen telling myself *not* to enjoy this. But that was like trying not to enjoy ice cream. One of my favorite things about being with a man was this – snuggling up to him and falling asleep made me feel safe and like I belonged with him.

It had been nearly a year since my last serious relationship, and I'd forgotten how much I missed this. Which was the very reason I couldn't relish this. Later tomorrow, we would go our separate ways when the threat had passed. I had to remember that.

CHAPTER 12

IRON-CLAD

RYAN

I WOKE UP AGAIN to my fucking alarm at five o'clock. My back felt stiff. I stretched an arm out and encountered cold sheets.

I bolted upright and saw a strip of light at the bottom of the bathroom door. My eyes closed as I sighed.

What was Ivy doing to me?

I didn't get worked up over a woman this way. We hardly knew each other, but there was a bond between us that seemed iron-clad. Part of me never wanted to let her go, but I would have to soon. We couldn't get closer.

She didn't need to get involved with me.

I lived for bar fights, and even before prospecting, I loved causing trouble with Killian.

She didn't need a man with my temper. Hell, I'd jumped to all the wrong conclusions about her – I didn't deserve someone like her.

The bathroom door opened and she padded back to the bed. "Is that the last alarm, Nickel?"

I sighed. "Yeah."

The bed jostled while she got situated. "Good. Can I ask you something?"

"Sure."

"Yesterday, how did you know a second blow could be seen as premeditation? You were so certain. Did you go to law school or something?"

I chuckled. "Or something. Mom's a lawyer. She started as a public defender, which is how she met Dad."

"Was she his lawyer?" she asked, her tone full of interest.

"No. Not at all. It's a long story, but now she practices family law."

"I see. What's your dad do?"

"He paints custom art on bikes and the occasional car."

"Really?"

"Don't get excited, the business is owned by the Biloxi chapter."

"Oh, so... why aren't you with the Biloxi chapter?"

I had to shut this conversation down – for her sake and mine. "Do you really want to chat or are we goin' back to sleep?"

She gave a dejected sigh and I felt like an ass. "Sorry. I'm just curious."

"No, Ives, I'm being' an asshole. Mick came out here for school and me and Kill didn't like the idea of her being so far away."

"I only met her once, but she seems like she can take care of herself."

I laughed. "Yeah. It's the men she attracts who never know how dangerous she is."

"Dangerous?" she scoffed.

That made me smile. "She stirs up trouble better than you do."

"I don't stir up trouble! Whatever. I'm still surprised you didn't start with the Biloxi chapter."

I shook my head. "My family is incredibly close, but I knew we needed to break away from that. Us moving gave our parents time to focus on our sister."

"But she's here."

"No, our younger sister."

I heard and felt her shift in the bed. "Your parents didn't have their hands full with you three?"

My body shook with my silent laugh. "Fuck if I know. Things happen. We love Mabel to pieces... and sometimes I think that's why she's so spoiled."

"But it isn't," she murmured.

It threw me how well Ivy could read me.

"No, it isn't. I don't know what happened, but she's been a handful for the last five years. Now... she's gonna be twenty-one soon and I'm not sure she'll ever get her act together."

"That's sad. Why not stay in Biloxi to be there for her?"

I scoffed. "Dad would have liked that. He accused me and Killian of taking the easy way out."

"Why would he say that?"

It struck me that I hadn't even talked to Killian about this shit. After a beat, I said, "We saw how the VP's son was treated when he prospected. Dad thinks we were trying to avoid that."

Her brows drew together. "Were you?"

My head wobbled. "Not many people seek that shit out, and no question that Block, Tiny, Brute, and Cynic would love giving us shit. Even more than we take here. Bottom line, we came here because of Mickayla – and that's the worst part of it. Dad doesn't see that it's harder being out here."

"What about your mom, though?" she asked.

"Mom thought having us a day's ride away from home would be good for everyone. Mabel was fourteen then, and I guess we all had hope. Since then, Mabel's shoved the three of us away."

She slunk further under the covers. "I didn't mean to bring up something that was a downer."

"Don't sweat it," I murmured.

"Sleep well."

I let it go at that for a beat. She wiggled around next to me, the sheets moving with her, and I had to speak up.

"Ivy. Are you for real right now?"

"What?" she whispered.

"Get your sweet tush over here. I'm not fightin' you for sheets... and you don't want me to, believe me."

She sighed. "Take your sheets. I don't think we should snuggle sleep because there's plenty of mixed signals between us already. Sleeping like that makes it worse."

Dammit. Her logic couldn't be argued, but hell if I didn't want to argue anyway. Not to mention I wanted to clear up those mixed signals by kissing her breathless, but that flew in the face of my earlier decision.

But was it really a decision?

The next time I woke up, I heard Ivy speaking in a low voice and it sounded like she was in the bathroom. I opened my eyes and saw the door was open just a crack.

My head didn't hurt half as bad as it did yesterday, which I took as a good sign. This pain could be knocked out with a couple Advil. I tossed the covers off, and pulled on a pair of gym shorts. I wandered toward the bathroom and overheard snippets of Ivy's conversation.

"Yes, ma'am, I'll be at the closing. That's definite, Belinda."

She went quiet, then said, "No, a doctor didn't tell me I had a concussion, but my gut tells me I should take it easy today."

That almost sounded convincing, but the pitch of her voice shifted enough that I wondered if her boss was calling bullshit on her excuse. Then again, I knew she was lying.

"Right. I'll be back at it tomorrow, and I'm sorry for the inconvenience."

She said her goodbyes after that and I backed up and sat on her side of the bed.

Her eyes widened a touch when she came out and saw me. "Oh, sorry. I didn't know you were up."

"No need to apologize. What did you tell your boss? Sounds like your lie didn't go over so well."

She shrugged and my eyes darted to the hem of the t-shirt rising up on her thighs. "I said I had an accident and bonked my head on a cabinet when I fell."

My lips quirked to the side. "Rookie mistake. Never give more detail than necessary."

Her head tilted. "You're a skilled liar, huh?"

I dipped my chin. "Wouldn't say that. I know how to get out of things when necessary."

Slowly, she nodded once. "I see. Well, the bathroom's all yours."

I stared at her, and if she were any other woman, I'd have told her to climb on my lap right then and there, but as she'd already pointed out, there were plenty of mixed signals between us.

"Um, are you okay? Or just not awake? I can't tell if you're staring at me for a reason or just in a zombie trace."

I almost smiled. "Not a trance."

Her brows arched. "Is there a problem?"

Aside from my growing hard-on, no, but I either had to shower again to give myself some relief... or I had to figure out a way to flirt with her.

She stepped closer. "Would you mind checking under that pillow? I think I left my hair tie somewhere in the bed."

And... there was my opportunity.

"I'm not stopping you from checking."

She blinked. "You're kind of in the way, Nickel."

"Ryan."

She gave a slight frown. "I thought I was supposed to call you by your road name."

I shrugged a shoulder. "I like it when you use my real name."

Her eyes slid to the side and back to me. "Okay. Are you going to scootch over, Ryan?"

"Nope."

She narrowed her eyes for a beat, shook her head, and moved so she could step between my leg and the nightstand. I widened my legs to stop her and she put a hand on my shoulder.

"What are you doing? It's almost like you're flirting with me or something."

I wrapped my hands around each of her thighs. "Would it be a problem if I were?"

"Last night you said it would be."

"It's funny what happens when you sleep on a decision." I slid my hands up an inch. "Is this okay?"

Her eyes held a sultry heat. "I'd tell you if it were a problem."

I slid one of my hands higher while tugging her toward me. She bit her lip and climbed onto my lap. My hands glided up her soft thighs and I felt the edges of her panties...no, thong if I wasn't mistaken. To verify, I let one hand drift around the globe of her ass – her bare ass.

"Thong," I whispered.

She inhaled pressing her tits against my chest. When she exhaled she settled into me more.

"You gonna kiss me?" I asked.

"Was going to ask you the same thing."

I pulled my hand that wasn't at her ass out from under her shirt and drove my fingers into the hair at the back of her head. She tipped her face down while she rounded my neck with an arm and cupped the back of my head with her hand.

My fingers clenched in her hair and I gently tilted her head before I pulled her lips to mine. It made no sense to me, but I swore I felt a charge run through my body. I opened my mouth to touch my tongue to her lips. She opened and I traced my tongue along her lips and further into her mouth. Her other hand slid along my chest and around to my back while she pushed her weight forward.

Before she could push me to my back, I semi-stood, twisted, and planted her on her back on the bed. Neither one of us broke the kiss. I kneaded the globe of her ass, making her moan. That sound went straight to my rock-hard cock.

Her tongue surged forward into my mouth. I let her have her way with that. Then she heaved up and rolled me to my back, breaking our kiss.

She had a triumphant smile on her face, her cheeks were slightly pink, and I wanted to take her picture – she looked so fucking hot.

"That was some kiss, Ryan."

"Yeah, so why'd you stop?"

She brought her face closer, her lips a millimeter away from mine while reaching back to my hand. "I'm thinking you can put this hand to better use... elsewhere."

She kissed me, and guided my hand around her hip and inside her thong. I groaned because feeling her wet heat set my cock to throbbing. If she wanted me to put my fingers to good use, I wouldn't deny her. I started with my index finger and played with her while she plundered my mouth.

Fuck.

I could get used to this.

I felt her get wetter and I added my middle finger to the mix.

She broke the kiss with a satisfied sigh. "Yeah."

"Sit up and ride that, Ivy."

Her eyes were heated and almost glittered at me. She sat up and began to ride my fingers, but then I watched her hands move down toward her thighs and she whipped my shirt off.

"Oh, fuck," I muttered at the sight of her firm, round tits. On autopilot, my free hand reached up and fondled one of her breasts.

She put her hand over mine and bucked her hips. "Yes, honey."

If she was going to come, it wouldn't be on top of me. Not like this. I wanted to watch her do that with my cock deep inside her. I rolled and had her pinned under me in no time, my fingers still inside her sweet pussy. I pulled them out and she mewled.

"Ryan, I was so close."

I yanked my tank off. "I know." I leaned down and kissed her. I'd meant for it to be short, but she hiked a leg around the back of my thighs, and I kissed her long and hard.

She pulled back, while grinding her hips into mine. "Then why'd you stop?"

Her hip action made me buck once and I loved feeling her tits against my bare chest. "Because the first time I make you come, it's gonna be on my tongue, woman. I want to watch and taste you."

"Oh my God," she muttered.

I pulled her thong off and spread her legs. At the sight of her glistening pussy, I licked my lips. Then I sprawled on the bed, slid my hands under her legs to her ass, and flicked her clit with my tongue.

She gasped. "Oh, God. Do that again."

I chuckled, then gave her what she wanted. She squirmed. I lapped at her pussy, loving the salty-sweet taste of her.

It didn't take long before she was practically riding my face. I liked that she was completely uninhibited. That I'd made her lose control.

"Ryan," she moaned.

I hummed against her.

"Yes," she hissed.

A knock sounded at my door, and her whole body went stiff. I lifted my head and looked toward the door, willing whoever was on the other side to go away.

Another knock came, this one even louder.

"Go away!" I hollered.

"Wake up call! Officers want everyone up and at 'em."

"Fuck," I whispered, and knifed off the bed.

I opened the door an inch, using it to keep most of my body out of view. A prospect stood on the other side. "Got your fuckin' message. Now, leave."

The disappointment and fury rolling through my body couldn't be denied, and I slammed the door shut.

Blowing out a breath, I turned to face Ivy. She looked so damned good in my bed. Her green eyes were warm on me, her teeth were sunk into the corner of her lower lip, and she'd closed her thighs.

I wandered back to the bed. "You all right?" I asked.

"Yeah, that was just... unexpected." She looked at me like she was trying to hide her disappointment. "I'm guessing we have to cut this short."

I pressed my lips together. "You guessed right. I'm gonna hit the bathroom."

I dressed and went back to the bedroom.

"Do you regret it?" I asked.

"No," she chirped then she added, "I mean, I hate that we were interrupted. That was so freaking hot, it's not funny. Nobody has made me so—"

"I was there," I said with a smile, trying to ease her rambling.

She sighed. "Right. But we're going our separate ways after this morning."

I wasn't so sure about that. I wanted to be certain the threat had passed. She kept talking before I could refute her.

"And, I'm sure you'd rather have a woman who's more accustomed to your world."

"I didn't say any of that, Ives."

She made a fine point, though. It would be easier if I found a woman who understood the club dynamics, but the bigger issue was my work. The bar would always be my mistress, and Ivy struck me as a woman who would be all about family. I wouldn't be ready to build a family for a good long time.

She nodded. "Yeah, but we probably shouldn't have done that after all."

"You're the one who suggested it."

"Last night."

I thought that was splitting hairs, but at the same time, I got it. Something about kicking the day off with a bang was different from ending the day like that. It felt raw and couldn't be blamed on lowered inhibitions because of alcohol or some shit.

"If you're hungry, we probably have some eggs downstairs. Or I can get a prospect to run out and get something for you."

She shrugged. "I'm good with eggs if it's not a problem."

CHAPTER 13

GOT BUSY

IVY

DOWNSTAIRS, THERE WEREN'T ANY eggs in the fridge. Instead, Ryan had found a package of frozen cinnamon-raisin bagels and a container of cream cheese. We were sitting at a small two-person Formica table when a tall woman with dark brown hair and hazel eyes walked into the kitchen.

She wore khaki pants and a green polo shirt with a logo for Jacksonville University School of Dentistry. Her head tipped a bit to the side when she locked eyes with me.

Her gaze moved to Ryan and she grinned. "Hey, Nickel. What's shakin'?"

He looked over his shoulder at her. "Not much. Are you working today?"

"Sort of. I have one class and half a day in the Orthodontics clinic."

"Cool," he said, then tipped his head toward me. "This is Ivy. Ives, this is Alexandra, Bluff's woman."

I smiled at her. "Nice to meet you."

She returned my smile. "Likewise." She cocked a brow at Nickel. "It is so weird hearing you use Rafferty's road name."

"You know that's who he is around here."

"Yeah," she said on a sigh and turned to the fridge. "But it doesn't make it any less strange."

The back door opened and three older men wandered into the kitchen, all of them wearing leather vests. One had eyes strikingly similar to Alexandra's, and his name patch read 'Cal.'

The second man had dark hair worn long and loose with a well-trimmed goatee. His name patch indicated he was 'Volt'.

The last man's name patch read 'Blood.' He too had long hair and a goatee, but his hair was pulled back in a ponytail. He locked eyes with me and smiled. "Do you still have a headache?"

My eyes widened, but I managed to shake my head.

"Good. Nickel called my wife after you two got back. That's why I asked."

Nickel shifted to look at the men. "Are we—"

"Church. Half an hour," Volt said.

I glanced at the time on the stove. I needed to leave by ten-fifteen to get my car and make it to the law firm.

"Um, Ry— I mean, Nickel, I need to leave in twenty minutes to get my car and—"

He sighed. "Can you try to push it by an hour?"

My eyes closed and I took a deep breath. It was difficult enough being a realtor. Add into the mix me being under thirty, and both customers and colleagues had preconceived notions about me being flaky or unprofessional. So I always did my best to keep my appointments — *especially* closings. It was the best part of the whole process after all.

I opened my eyes. "I'll check, but it's just up Blanding from here."

Alexandra crossed the kitchen to the toaster. "Not to interrupt, but I can take her. I have to go that way for class. I'm leaving in fifteen minutes."

Ryan dragged a hand down his face. "If she takes you, leave your magnets off the car. Where are you going when you're done?"

"I was supposed to meet Chad for lunch. He knows I have a closing today. Then, I'll go home."

Ryan didn't say anything.

"I'm grateful you went out of your way to keep me safe last night," I said in a lower voice.

That got me a heated stare – or at least it felt that way – I could have been imagining it.

"I'm gonna be at your place when you're done with all that."

"You don't have a key."

"I'm gonna be at your place."

"That really isn't necessary," I whispered.

"You really don't know that."

I tried not to roll my eyes when I glanced away from him. "I guess you'll just be hanging on my doorstep or something."

"Don't worry about it. Let's hit my room so you can grab your bag."

"I know that area. Your place isn't far from Rafferty's house," Alexandra said, starting her car after I told her my address.

"Really? Being that close, why did you two stay at the clubhouse last night? If you don't mind my asking."

She stopped to pull out of the compound and looked at me. "He had drinks and decided we'd stay there."

"How long before you become a dentist?" I asked.

She turned onto the side street leading to Blanding Boulevard. "Another two years at least. Did Nickel ever let you talk to Lark?"

I shot her a sidelong glance. "How did you know about that?"

She chuckled. "I saw you approach him at the bar months ago. Even from a distance, anyone could see you two had sparks."

Well.

I ignored the 'sparks' comment. "I haven't spoken to Lark yet. But let's say, Ryan won't stop me when I'm ready."

"It's not my business, but don't be frightened of Lark. Even if they're one-per-centers, they're all good men at heart."

That confused me. "I'm sorry, what?"

She glanced at me and back to the road. "The club used to be outlaws, but they've gone legit."

Okay, maybe some of those shows were right.

Alexandra read into my silence. "You didn't know. Geez, Nickel is gonna kill me."

"No, no. Don't worry about it. I mean, I helped him with our kidnappers. Crap. I shouldn't have told you that."

She laughed. "Don't sweat it. Club business stays in the club."

My brows drew together. "Are you sure?"

"Yes. You probably didn't notice but Cal's my dad. I hugged him while you were talking to Nickel. The club is a big family, and tight like one, too. People assume it's a gang, but it isn't."

I nodded, since her relationship to Cal explained his eyes being so similar to hers, or vice versa. "I see. That must be why Lark wouldn't call the cops like Chad wanted him to before we came back."

She let out a wry chuckle. "Yeah."

I didn't have anything to say to that.

"You're too quiet. I don't know you, but you seem freaked out."

"Not really," I said.

She laughed. "Lie to me all you want, but don't lie to yourself. That's just wrong."

"I'm not," I fibbed. *I was the off-spring of an outlaw!*

"You are, so to keep you from really losing your mind today – Nickel said he'd be at your place, right?"

I nodded. "Yeah, waiting on me."

She pulled into my neighborhood and parked, then she turned to me. "He'll be waiting, but he'll also be inside, Ivy."

"He doesn't have a key."

Her head tilted. "He won't need one because he'll pick the lock."

"He's gonna break inside," I muttered.

"Only to keep you safe."

It struck me that there was more than one kind of safety involved here. Nickel breaking into my home wasn't dangerous for me. But spending more time with him might lead to him breaking inside my heart – and that didn't feel very safe at all.

I shook off my thoughts and unbuckled my seatbelt. "Thank you so much for doing this. You're a lifesaver."

"Not a problem. Have a good closing. Hopefully, I'll see you around the clubhouse soon."

I grinned. "That would be awesome, but I don't think things are like that with me and Nickel. We got away. They aren't going to find me."

———

At a quarter to one, I met Chad at the Metro Diner. He sat at a table sipping a cup of coffee, and I noticed he'd ordered a glass of strawberry lemonade for me.

As I approached, his lips pulled together and he gave me a stern look. "Ivy. You naughty girl."

I sat down and returned his stern stare with my own. "I don't know what you're talking about."

"This is *me* you're talking to, girlie. You and that man got busy with a capital B."

I closed my eyes and sighed. "*If* we did, it doesn't matter, *and* it doesn't make me naughty."

"You know I don't mean it like that."

My head tilted. "Half the restaurant heard you call me naughty."

He shrugged a shoulder. "Maybe a quarter, and I should have kept my voice down. Sorry." He leaned forward. "But tell me, was it good?"

"We were interrupted and now I'm thinking that was for the best."

His eyes narrowed. "You didn't get busy?"

I sipped my lemonade. "We— this is *so* not your business."

"We're best friends. Tell me."

"Third base," I muttered, putting my glass down.

"For you or him?"

"Me. And he is talented."

His eyes widened. "Stop right there. You're making me blush."

I giggled. "You asked. And it takes more than that to make you blush."

"You're right. Getting interrupted always sucks – no pun intended – why do you say that's for the best?"

"He and I shouldn't get physical."

He dipped his chin to give me a wry look. "Girlfriend – I'm not saying this to stroke your ego, but the way he looks at you... I'd give up a lot for a man to look at me that way."

I took a deep breath. "You almost sound like Alexandra."

He twisted a hand up. "Then you should believe us. What's holding you back? After you answer that, we need to discuss Lark because between both these men, I've never known you to chicken out so much."

I sighed. "I didn't chicken out. I was overwhelmed."

"With Lark, sure. Ryan, I don't believe you. It's been a long time since Austin did you dirty. Give that hot biker a chance."

I leaned toward him and lowered my voice and asked, "Even if he commits crimes?"

Chad sat back. "That's too vague. What are we talking about here?"

Our server came to take our orders. Chad never deviated from the fried chicken and waffles because he so loved their strawberry spread. I always tried to order something new and went with the Shepherd's Pie.

"How's your day going?" I asked.

Chad laughed. "You aren't changing the subject. Spill."

I told him about the crimes Nickel and I committed in order to escape.

"I don't see a problem," he said.

I widened my eyes. "Chad, we *moved* one of them, and took the truck," I said, being careful of my words in case someone was eavesdropping.

"It's a moot point now."

I sipped my lemonade. "Stashing the truck bugs me most."

"Yeah, but finding that at the bar would be worse – so I understand Ryan's thinking."

"Lark's. It was his idea," I corrected.

"Okay... so when are you going to call Lark?"

I shrugged. "I'm not sure. Even if you can justify what Ryan and I did – Alexandra mentioned the club hasn't always been legit. My guess is that Lark has done far worse. Do I really want to know more?"

"Yes, you do."

"That was rhetorical."

"He isn't just an outlaw. He isn't just a bar owner." He paused and gave me a nod. "You're right that he didn't really make you who you are – Jeff and Debra had far more to do with that – but he's... I can't explain it. He reminded me of you before he found out you were missing."

"How so?" I asked, feeling intrigued.

"The way he greeted me for one thing. I've been at your open houses and it was the same bright smile and easy manner."

I wobbled my head. "The smile is probably genetics, but good business people know how to be personable to make a sale."

Chad shook his head. "It's more than that. You'd have to see it to know....W hich is why I'm giving you a hard time about it."

If there was anything Chad loved to do it was give me a hard time about stuff. Especially when I was procrastinating.

"Tomorrow evening."

He grinned. "Love it. We can take Kristen with us. She needs to see your man up close."

"He's not my man, Chad."

"That's what you think. When are you seeing him again?"

I arched a brow. "Supposedly when I'm done here. He's going to be waiting for me at my place. Alexandra thinks he's going to pick my lock. What do you have to say about that?"

Very slowly, Chad smiled. "I think he sounds better than Austin by a long shot already."

I closed my eyes and shook my head.

CHAPTER 14

SAFE

RYAN

ALL THE BROTHERS WERE gathered for church and the session had been called to order.

"Nickel, tell everyone what went down yesterday outside On a Lark," Volt said.

As quickly as I could, I rehashed how Ivy and I were taken and what we did to escape.

Volt glanced at me and then to Lark. "What do we know about those bastards?"

"Not as much as I'd like," Lark said. "We have names for two of them, but they're dead. And the first name of the ringleader."

Volt nodded. "Since you had Nickel drop the truck somewhere specific, did you check to see if it's still there?"

"It was when I drove to town earlier this morning. I'll check again before I open the bar this afternoon," Lark said.

"Any idea what MC they were referring to?" Volt asked, his eyes on Lark.

Lark turned his hands up. "Your guess is as good as mine, brother."

Blood locked eyes with me. "You said your girl used the skillet on those bastards – did you wipe it down?"

"The first time she had a pot holder." I thought hard and shook my head. "Second time she probably didn't use the pot holder, and neither of us thought to—"

"Don't worry about that now," Blood said.

"Easy for you to say," I muttered.

Volt sat back in his chair. "By now they know those two are missing and that the truck's gone."

I shook my head. "Boyd mentioned that another MC didn't care who they took. My question is why would another MC let someone else do their dirty work?"

Lark turned his gaze to me. "That's hard to say when we don't know *who* is willing to take one of us right off the street."

Blood shook his head. "We can't try to guess how these assholes think – it's a waste of time. Lark do you have cameras working?"

"Yeah, and Adam's putting in another to catch the adjacent parking lot, since that's where they parked yesterday."

"Do you need a couple brothers outside for the next few nights?" Volt asked.

"Wouldn't hurt, even if my gut says no."

Blood glanced around the room. "Who's in for tonight?"

"I am," Tundra said, his voice firmer than I'd ever heard it.

Volt frowned. "You sure? You're at Platinum's tonight."

Tundra gave a slight head shake. "Dayside. I'm off at five-thirty. Plus, I'm used to dealing with assholes like them."

"Your call," Volt muttered.

Cal, Beast, Razor, and Liar were all-in to patrol the parking lot. It felt like overkill, but I sure as hell didn't want my siblings, or anyone else, to go through that shit either.

Lark leaned forward to get Volt's attention. "I'm giving Nickel the night off."

I looked at Lark with questioning eyes.

"Don't argue," he muttered.

It flew in the face of what Lark had told us – no days off – but for once I wouldn't argue. The ache in my groin was killing me, and I knew just the woman to help me with that.

"Think that's the most sympathy I've ever seen from Lark," Blood said.

Lark glared at Blood. "He'll make it up at Thanksgiving."

Great. Though, that might work out in the long run because Mom wanted all three of us back in Biloxi for Christmas. It was too soon to talk to Lark about those plans.

Ricochet cleared his throat. "I have a question."

Volt nodded for him to speak.

"How about I let them take me?"

"They aren't going to come back that soon," Patch, our treasurer, said.

"They're dumb enough, they might," Lark said.

"No. I don't want you doing that," Volt said.

"Standing offer," my triplet said.

"Same," I added immediately after.

"They gave you a concussion," Lark said.

"Yeah, and I want the mastermind behind it shut down."

"You two earned your patches, but remember, we don't do shit solo," Volt said.

"Or duo," Blood added.

"Got it," Ricochet said.

There was a pause.

"We're gonna watch the lot. *But* will that tip off the cops if they come around?" Bluff asked.

Roll gave his son a dose of side eye. "You're a biker. Cops show, act like you were outside for a smoke or some shit."

Volt nodded. "If cops show, we know nothing."

"Right," I said.

"Sounds like as much of a plan as we're gonna get," Lark said.

"Agreed. We'll meet again on Saturday. Sooner if new shit develops," Volt said, and tapped the gavel to the table.

While the others filed out, Ricochet came to me. "What are you gonna do on your day off? Sleep off your headache?"

I fell in step beside him. "No. I'm going to Ivy's to make sure she's safe again tonight."

"When did making sure she's safe become a euphemism for sex?"

"Shut up."

He stopped in the middle of the hall. "Wait... you *didn't* tap that?"

I gave him a dry look. "She's not a 'that,' and strenuous activity is a no-go with a concussion."

He rolled his eyes at me. "Your head's so hard there's no way you had an injury."

"Safety first."

"Right. You meeting up with her or what?" he asked.

"I was at her place last night before coming here. I'm headed back there now," I said, ambling toward the stairs.

"Is she there?" he asked, following me.

"Don't know. I'll pick her lock if she isn't."

We'd made it to the second floor and stood near the laundry area.

My brother made a sound almost like a scoff. "Damn, you haven't even tasted her pussy and she's got you wrapped."

"Didn't say that," I muttered. With anyone else, I'd have kept that to myself, but Killian knew when I was lying.

His chest heaved with a silent chuckle. "Knew it. We're tougher than those bastards."

"They still knocked me out," I said, walking to my door.

"Whatever. Have fun...keeping her safe," he chided and sauntered past me toward his room.

"Fuck off," I muttered.

Ricochet roared with laughter.

I unlocked Ivy's door with ease, slipped inside, and twisted the deadbolt behind me.

Last night, I'd taken in her space, but here alone, I could admire how organized and well-decorated it was. The walls were a glossy egg-shell color which I liked because most people only used glossy in their bathrooms. A beige couch with small blue flowers took up a good part of the living room. It was feminine in an understated way.

I did a quick, cursory walk through of the upstairs and downstairs to make sure I was alone, then forced myself to mind my business. If I got to be in Ivy's bedroom, I wanted it to be her idea. Not because I'd decided to camp out there while waiting.

The TV remote sat on the coffee table. I snagged it and channel-surfed. Nothing caught my eye, and I turned it off. I pulled off my boots, stretched out on the sofa, and immediately understood why Ivy bought this furniture. It was so comfortable, I didn't want to get up. I wished I'd brought my paperback with me. Since I hadn't, I decided to rest my eyes.

My body jerked when I heard a key in the lock. I opened my eyes in time to see Ivy step inside, close the door, and lock it.

She stared at me for a moment. "Alexandra was right."

I sat up and ran a hand through my hair. "Right about what?"

She hung her purse on a hook by the door. "That you'd be waiting inside."

I sensed something bothered her, but I didn't think it was me being in her home. "What else did she tell you?"

She shrugged a shoulder and edged deeper into the living area. "The club used to be outlaws, and she hinted that in some ways it still is."

I shook my head. "Something else is bothering you. Did your closing go smooth?"

She nodded. "Yeah. All good."

"Then what's bugging you?"

Standing in the middle of the living room, she crossed her arms under her breasts. "I hardly know you, I don't think I should tell you what's bothering me. At the same time, the fact you picked up on something bothering me is crazy."

She hardly knew me?

Four hours ago, I had my tongue down her throat and my mouth on her pussy. Still, things were moving fast with us, and I could see where she was coming from.

I gave her my most skeptical look. "You know I'm a triplet. I'm from Biloxi. I'm in the Riot MC, and I work at a bar. What more do you need to know? My political background?"

One of her eyebrows lowered while the opposite one arched with her confusion. "You're political? I'd figure as an outlaw you wouldn't be."

I stared at her for a moment. "The people who say they don't *do* politics, don't realize politics are *always* doing them."

"Wow."

"Don't sound so surprised."

She looked abashed for a beat. "I'm guessing you're a Republican."

I took a breath. "You guess wrong. I'm a Libertarian, but registered to a different party specifically so I can vote in primary elections."

Her head reared back and she unfolded her arms. "Now, that surprises me."

"It shouldn't. The whole system is fucked because the things we need most are term limits on the Supreme Court and definitely Congress. It'll never happen though because the legislation has to be passed by Congress. They won't and not just because it doesn't serve them, but it doesn't serve their donors who got them the seat. The whole system is for the rich and by the rich."

She shot me a questioning glance. "With that attitude, why do you vote?"

My lips tipped up. "Because if you don't vote, you have no right to complain."

She lowered her head in a half nod. "Is that how your dad sees it?"

I gave a silent chuckle. "No. That's all my Uncle Mick. I also vote because it makes me feel like I've done something."

Her head tilted to the side a touch. "Even if it's spitting in the wind."

"Maybe. It's like Nina Simone says in one of her songs, 'too slow.'"

Her brows furrowed. "You listen to jazz?"

"Aunt Stella and Uncle Mick do. I'm from Mississippi. You can't grow up there without hearing 'Mississippi Goddamn' and really *listening* to it."

She looked at me with awe, which was totally misplaced. After a moment, she said, "You should run for office."

That took me by surprise so much, that I laughed straight from my gut. "You need to do something," I said when I had myself under control.

"What's that?"

I stretched my arms out on the top of the couch. "Kiss me."

She opened her mouth and closed it as reluctance shone from her eyes. "Nickel—"

"Ryan."

"We shouldn't."

"Why?"

Her gaze shifted away from me and she sighed.

"Just kiss me, Ives."

That earned me her eyes. They were narrowed, but I liked riling her up.

"Only one person has ever called me that."

"Should I stop?"

"I'm not sure. The way you do it is... almost nice."

There was way more to this story, but this wasn't the time to push for more. Or it would defeat my main objective.

"Come here," I said as gently as I could.

She came to me.

I grabbed her hand, tugging her onto the couch. "One kiss."

She shifted toward me, put a hand on my shoulder and pushed up. Our lips met and as if she felt the same zing of sensation that I did, her lips parted. My tongue swept into her mouth. She tasted like strawberries and lemons. I felt her other hand drive into the hair at the back of my head. It felt like her fingers were twisting some of my hair.

I wrapped my arm around her back and pulled her closer. The kiss kept going. She rose up on her knee and twisted her body. Then she settled her ass in my lap.

I groaned because that was exactly where I wanted her.

She broke the kiss and rested her forehead on my collar bone. The sound of her panting breaths filled the room. "Why did I give in to you? I knew that was going to happen." She raised her head. "One kiss, eh?"

I rubbed my hands up and down her back. "Are you really complaining?"

She still had a hand in my hair, playing with it, staring at me.

"What's bothering you, Ivy? You may not know me *that* well, but we're far from strangers. I might be able to give you a different perspective."

She didn't exactly roll her eyes at me, but they did go up and to the side for a beat. "That's what I'm afraid of."

I chuckled. "What is it?"

With her deep inhale, I felt her breasts press into my chest. Ignoring that was damned difficult, especially since that kiss had my cock at the ready.

She dropped her hand from the back of my head and sat back. "Chad is insistent that I go to the bar tomorrow night to talk to Lark. The problem is that I don't think that's such a good idea any more."

I didn't either, but that was for different reasons.

"Why not?"

She shook her head. "I can't talk to you like this." Her hands went to my shoulders so she could get up, but I tightened my grip on her body.

"You can totally talk to me like this."

Her eyes flared. "Ryan, this is serious."

I widened my eyes at her. "I know it is. Most men don't want to be surprised by anything, but they damn sure don't want a surprise kid to show up. The fact he donated sperm surprises me, and yet, given his road name, it makes sense. I don't have the full story on why they named him Lark. It's either that he's so damned methodical and a type-A planner that he'd *never* do shit on a lark, or it's the fact he does *everything* on a whim."

She shrugged. "My gut says he's a total planner because I am, but that's the thing. What difference does it make? What am I going to get out of telling him that mom chose him to make a baby and here I am? I'll probably fuck up his life... Hell, Chad was right. The universe was giving me a sign when you kept me from seeing him the first time."

I hated hearing the defeated tone in her voice.

Tightening my arms, I pushed up and gently laid her down on the couch and settled my weight on her. "It wasn't a sign. I made assumptions and it got us both in a fucking mess. Lark's cool."

"So you think I should tell him tomorrow night?"

I glanced away for a beat. "What I think doesn't matter. Going to the bar tomorrow night isn't happening though."

She dragged her fingers down my spine. "Why not?"

I pulled a hand out from behind her and cupped her cheek. "Tonight, there's going to be brothers patrolling the outside lot. Those bastards behind our abduction are going to come back. I don't want you around the bar until they've been dealt with, so you going to the bar isn't happening."

"Are you patrolling the lot tonight?"

Instantly her facial expression shifted to shock, like she hadn't wanted to ask me that.

"Are you concerned about my safety, Ives?"

She shook her head. "It's official. Please don't call me that."

I nodded. "Are you worried about me?"

Her expression became abashed. "Maybe. I hadn't meant to ask that out loud. I usually have more self-control around people."

My lips tipped up. "Tonight, I have the night off, and I'm spending it with you."

"Why?"

I swallowed back a chuckle. "Are you shitting me right now? We got interrupted back at the clubhouse, but our chemistry is off the fuckin' charts. I'm gonna taste more of you, you're gonna taste me, and we're gonna do that in a number of ways."

"Ryan," she whispered.

"What?"

"This isn't a good idea," she whispered.

I dragged my nose alongside hers. "I'm not gonna hurt you."

"Casual isn't an option for me."

I felt one of my eyebrows lift. "You're after a commitment."

She frowned slightly. "I didn't say that, but you..." She sighed. "You're different."

That was vague, and yet, I understood where she was coming from because deep down, I felt the same way about her. Something about her was different from other women I'd seen in the past.

I tucked a lock of hair behind her ear. "I'm not after anything, serious *or* casual. I'm practically married to the bar these days. Most women expect so much attention—"

She shot me a look. "I'm not most women."

With a grin, I nodded. "Believe me, I got that."

Her eyes danced over my face. "Do you think this is just a weird form of Stockholm Syndrome?"

I turned my head to the side and huffed out a disbelieving chuckle. When I faced her, I tried to keep my tone level. "No. I don't. If it were that, you'd be mourning the death of at least one of those assholes."

"Going through trauma connects people, though," she muttered.

I hesitated a moment. "Yeah, but the thing is, on the day you showed up, my astute sister pointed out that you tick all of my boxes. So...don't downplay what's going on here."

She gave a reluctant nod. "That's fair."

"Right. I don't want to pressure you into anything, so if you want me to stop, I'll get up and leave you alone, once I get someone else here to keep you safe."

CHAPTER 15

UPSTANDING WOMAN

IVY

I DON'T THINK I'D ever had any man be so direct with me. While I loved that he was willing to leave me be, I knew I didn't want anyone else here but him.

He began to shift his weight, and I reached up and traced a finger along his lower jaw. "No. I want to see what happens between us – even if it scares the hell out of me."

He tipped his head and his ocean-blue eyes filled with curiosity. "What is there to be scared of?"

I laughed. "Don't ask stupid questions."

"Fair. Are you sure I didn't pressure you?"

I smirked. "No, but telling me that I ticked all your boxes is a very smooth move."

He chuckled. "I'll keep that in mind. Even though my dick is hard as a fuckin' rock right now, I'm gonna give you a choice. Your buddy wants you to talk to Lark. Something tells me you don't want him to be there. Am I right?"

I widened my eyes. "Get out of my head!"

He grinned a boyish grin. I loved that look on him, it softened his features and drew me to him. "If you want, I'll call Lark and make sure he has time to talk to you this afternoon. That way, your buddy isn't there, and if it doesn't go the way you want, it's private."

My teeth sunk into my lower lip as I debated that.

"Ivy," he half-said, half-groaned.

I let my lip go and grimaced. "Sorry! That sounds good actually, but can we do that after we finish what we started?"

He shook his head. "No. Thing is, I know his schedule. You want this, it'll be better to go in the afternoon before any of the happy hour-slash-early-bird dinner people show up."

"Fine," I said, not hiding my petulant tone.

He smiled and sat up. "Don't worry. When we're done, no matter how it goes, I'll take you out for a nice dinner and *then* we'll really finish what we started."

I sat up. "Awesome. That sounds like a plan. Are we going on your bike?"

He stood, paused, and looked down at me. "It's almost twenty miles from here, are you sure you want that? You'll have to do something with that beautiful hair of yours if you do."

My hair wasn't exactly my armor, but like most women, I felt better when I knew I looked my best.

With a short nod, I said, "Okay, we can take my car."

"Let me call him first."

I nodded and hit the bathroom.

Nickel left the office and I settled into a chair across the desk from Lark.

While I drove us here, I'd thought about what I'd say ...and of course, now all of those thoughts went by the wayside.

"Don't have all day, lady," Lark said with a smile.

I wrung my hands in my lap. "Yeah, I know. This isn't like me."

He leaned forward and I took in how handsome he was for an older man. He had curly, dark hair – which would explain why my hair was so curly when Mom's was stick-straight. One thick lock of it was a silvery gray and it was so expertly done, I almost wondered if he had it colored, but his weathered skin and calloused fingers told me otherwise.

"I'll have to take your word for it, darlin'."

Mom called me 'darlin'' all the time, and for some reason hearing Lark use that term kicked me into gear.

"Okay, this is bizarre, but here goes nothin'. You donated your sperm in Atlanta twenty-seven years ago."

Lark's face froze and he sat back in his chair. "Yeah," he drawled.

I twisted my hands up in front of me. "You may not recall, but you didn't check the box for no-contact. Mom gave me the information she had. And... I've been looking for you in Atlanta, and Memphis over the past seven months."

"Moved here a year ago," he muttered.

"Yeah. I figured that out four months ago, but Ryan wouldn't, I'm sorry, Nickel, kept me from you."

He nodded.

"My mom chose your donation for her IVF treatment."

"How old are you?" he asked.

"Twenty-five."

He grunted and I couldn't tell if it was a grunt of that checks out, or something else.

"That's why I was here Monday, but... Things went awry."

He laughed. "'Awry'. Yeah. Getting taken at gunpoint is exactly what awry means."

I stared at him.

"Sorry. What do you want from me?" he asked.

"Nothing, I suppose."

His brows drew together. "Nothing? I doubt that."

I shook my head. "I'm not here for back child support or anything."

He shook his head. "You couldn't demand that even if you wanted to, that's spelled out in the contract."

I did a slow nod. "Right. Mom knew what she was getting into, and still she would mention how much she wished she knew the man who made me who I was."

"I didn't make you into anything."

My head tilted. "No, and I said the same thing. But, looking at you, I can see where I get my hair because it's never been from Mom."

He kept quiet, and I began to feel awkward. My gut had been right. This was a bad idea.

I stood. "You're busy. I don't want to take up more of your time."

He stood, but leaned a hand on the desk. "Did something go wrong in the past year?"

"Wrong, how?" I asked.

His beard moved with his lip twitch. "Don't know if your Mom married or whatnot, but when I signed the forms, they gave me some pamphlets about what to expect if I got contacted. Most of the time it'd be because home life was crap, but I can see that isn't the case for you. So, I'm guessing something changed."

I pressed my lips together. "Yeah, I suppose you might say that. My step dad who essentially helped Mom raise me, he died a year and a half ago. No matter how curious I was about you in my teens, I'd never make Jeff feel like he wasn't my dad."

Lark dipped his chin. "There you go. Sorry you lost your dad. Guessing he wasn't much older than me, which means he died young."

"Yeah. Fifty-five."

He shoved a hand in the pocket of his faded jeans. "Look, I'm not tryin' to be standoffish, but I'm not anyone's father figure."

Yep. Bad idea. And, I was even more grateful that Chad wasn't here.

I nodded, kept quiet, and took a sideways step toward the door.

"But it's good to know my donation amounted to an upstanding young woman."

My eyebrows arched. "You don't know me well enough to say that – especially after what happened in that dilapidated farm house."

He shook his head. "Did you get out alive? Did you keep Nickel from getting hurt any further? Yes, and yes. Where I'm from, that's the measure of an upstanding woman."

I nodded again, moved closer to the door, but paused when he spoke.

"That friend of yours – he knows about me, right?"

"Yeah," I whispered.

Lark's eyes hardened. "Do not let him tell people about me. My gut says the trouble you and Nickel got into has something to do with me. Those dumb fucks thought the *triplets* are my kids and abducting one would devastate me. They get word you're my kid – even if I don't know your mom – you're in even more danger."

"Why would they have a problem with you?"

He arched a brow. "You work in real estate, surely you've heard of 'not in my backyard.' There's plenty of folk 'round here who don't want a bar in the area. Even if it's a restaurant and bar. Narrow-minded assholes don't need reasons to start trouble if it gets them what they want, which is me out of the picture."

"I see."

"That's another reason I can't have you hangin' 'round here trying to get to know me. Those bastards have been raisin' hell here since our soft open. They get dealt with, maybe we can get to know each other."

I gave him a wan smile and opened the door. "That sounds like a plan. Take care, Lark."

The office door opened to the main barroom, and Nickel sat on a barstool so he faced the doorway.

His full lips formed a slight pout as he stood and came to me. "Did he hurt you?"

I shook my head. "Not like you mean."

His gaze shifted to a point over my shoulder. "What did you say to her?"

"Don't like your tone, Nickel," Lark muttered.

"Don't care. I'm not your employee right now."

"No. Even my brothers don't take that tone."

I put a hand on Ryan's chest, and felt his heartbeat hammering against my finger tips. "Ryan, please."

He tipped his head down and stared at me. "Are you sure you aren't hurt?"

I gave him a small smile. "I'm sure. Let's go."

He slung his arm around my shoulders, turning me toward the exit, but also bringing Lark into view.

Lark cocked a brow at me. "Looks like searching for me wasn't such a waste after all."

Oh boy.

We went out to my car and Ryan stood at the driver's side door. "I'm driving us back."

"I don't—"

He stepped closer to me. "Nope. You're covering, but I know that did a number on you. Give me the keys."

"It's not that bad."

"Which also says it's not that good. Let me drive, you don't know where we're going."

"We're going to my place."

He shook his head. "I'm taking you out. Let me drive."

I handed him my keys. "Fine. But this seems early for dinner."

He pressed the button to unlock the car. "It's four-thirty, and with traffic, it'll be five-fifteen by the time we get to where I wanna take you."

I wandered around to the passenger side and got in the car. I buckled up as he started the engine and adjusted the mirrors.

"Did he argue with you?"

"No."

"Did he tell you to jump in a lake?"

I chuckled. "No, but he made it clear he wasn't sure what he could do for me at this point."

Ryan sighed. "Was he a dick about it?"

"No, and that's why I didn't want to follow through. Something told me it would be anticlimactic."

He reached out and squeezed my thigh, then left his hand there. "It is a lot for a man to wrap his head around.

I shook my head. "I'm not so sure about that. If it'd been a one-night stand, sure. But he signed a form that allowed for contact *and* they gave him a brochure on what to expect when an adult child makes contact."

Ryan looked at me and back to the road as he guided the car onto the Interstate. "That shit doesn't make sense."

"What do you mean?"

His hand rubbed up and down on my thigh. "Why allow a kid to contact you if you don't want a relationship?"

I shrugged a shoulder. "I don't know, but it was roughly twenty-seven years ago that he...donated."

"You're twenty-seven?"

I glanced at his profile. He hadn't shaved today, and I loved how his sandy-blond stubble made his jawline more pronounced. "Twenty-five. You sound surprised."

"Didn't realize you're almost two years older than me."

I laughed. "That explains so much."

"Whatever, Trouble."

"Trouble?"

"Yeah, you've been causing trouble since I met you."

I scoffed. "Puh-lease. I could say the same thing about you. Trouble like this never found me until I met you."

He squeezed my thigh. "Nope. I know how to spot a troublemaker and you're just like Mickayla."

His hand on my leg did things to me. To be fair, his hands on me *anywhere* did things to me. "We could go back to my place and I'll cook. I don't need you to take me out."

His gaze cut to me and back to the Interstate. "You *need* me to take you out. When we get back to your place, it'll be the opposite of anticlimactic."

"So, you're promising me the climax I missed this morning."

He moved his hand on my thigh higher toward the juncture of my hip. "I'm promising you multiple climaxes, baby."

I struggled against putting his hand where I really wanted it, but it wouldn't be safe for him to touch me like that while driving.

He chuckled. "There you go earning your nickname. Can see the thoughts on your face. You're pure trouble, Ivy."

I picked up his hand and moved it to his thigh. "Pretty sure you're the troublemaker here, Nickel."

I slid into my side of the booth at Poe's Tavern across from Ryan, and set my bag of books next to me on the bench seat. "You are going out of your way to earn brownie points with a woman who has explicitly told you it isn't necessary."

His lips spread with a sly grin. "Not all those books are for you, Ivy."

"Possession is nine-tenths of the law, Nickel. I'll be reading them even if I've never heard of this Eighty-Seventh Precinct series."

"Good thing I know where you live then. I'll be able to get my books when you're finished with them."

"Breaking into my home to wait for me is one thing, but breaking in to steal books is a bridge too far, mister."

"Don't be cute when I'm too far away to kiss you," he ordered.

A man with his hair in man-bun sauntered up to our table and put down two cardboard coasters. "What can I get you to drink?"

"You trust me?" Nickel asked.

I nodded.

He turned to our server. "Two gimlets with Grey Goose, make mine a double. And two waters."

"You got it," he said, and left.

"Why isn't mine a double?" I asked.

"Safety first, Trouble. Besides, you can have more than one. That's the only drink I'll have until we get back to your place."

"Have you been here before?" I asked.

"Yeah. Their burgers can't be beat, and Mickayala says their tacos are great, too."

I nodded and took in the extensive menu, every item gave a nod to an Edgar Allen Poe work.

"You got a few things you need to handle tonight," he murmured and I glanced up at him.

"Like what?"

"I'm going out on a limb here, but does your mom know you found Lark? And you need to tell your buddy that tomorrow night is off."

This man was entirely too smart. It wasn't going to be easy telling Mom I'd found my biological dad. She'd been rather ambivalent about me seeking him out. In fact, that led to me trying to hide my trip to Memphis from her, but Chad goofed and let our side trip slip. When Mom asked why we'd go to Memphis, he'd fibbed about us wanting to see that place too.

"Yeah. Mom doesn't know that I found him here in town, so you're right. I need to let her know, but I'm not doing it tonight. That feels like something I should do in person. And that's not me procrastinating," I added when I saw the look on his face. "She's probably going to be miffed that I didn't tell her he was actually in the Jacksonville area."

He nodded. "I can see that, but your man, Chad, needs to be reined in."

I threw my head back and laughed. "Don't ever let him hear you say that."

Ryan's eyes were bright and steady on me. "Fuck," he whispered.

"What?" I whispered back.

"You're a fucking stunner when you laugh, Ivy."

I felt my cheeks heat. "Thanks," I muttered.

"Can you text Chad, so he isn't planning to bring other friends of yours to the bar."

"Oh, my friend Kristen was going to come with him, but yeah. I can text him now." I wagged a finger in the air. "It's funny, Lark told me to make sure Chad doesn't tell anyone about why I've been looking for him. He seems to think that would make me a target. Like the reason they took you had everything to do with him, but he can't really know that yet, can he?"

He hesitated a moment. "We don't really know what the motivation was for those assholes, but that's the first I've heard of Lark saying he thinks they were really targeting him. Wish he'd have said something about that earlier."

"You mean at your meeting?" I asked.

"Church, yeah."

"Why is it called 'church'?"

Our server came to the table and put down our drinks. "Two Gray Goose Gimlets. Are y'all ready to order?"

Ryan shot me a questioning look and I nodded. "You first, though."

He ordered a crab cake sandwich, and I wound up ordering a Chicken Amontillado.

"Excellent choices," our server said, taking our menus and scurrying away.

I pulled out my phone and asked, "Are you sure you don't mind me texting right now?"

He nodded. "Yeah. Sooner is better than later, and this way if he's going to call you, he can interrupt dinner, and not what's happening afterward."

I pressed my lips together to hold back my smirk. "Got it."

Once I sent Chad a text, I set my phone on the table, face down. It vibrated seconds later.

Ryan held up a hand. "Check it. I may not know him well, but he damn sure cares about you. It's been my experience that people like that can be hard to come by, and I'd rather you put him at ease."

I didn't expect *that*, and I really wanted to dive into that statement from him because between his siblings and all the MC brothers he had, there were plenty of people who cared about him.

No sooner had I picked up my cell again, than it rang in my hand, Chad's name on the screen. "Hi, there. I can't talk for very long."

"You cannot send me that text and then cut this convo short," Chad said, his tone indignant.

"I'm sitting with Ryan at Poe's Tavern and this is after he just took me to the indie bookstore at the beach and bought me like five books. My friend, I can't talk for very long."

He inhaled sharply. "That's a strong move. Did he know you love books?"

My head tilted as I considered it. "He sat in my townhouse today waiting for me, so I'm guessing he saw my bookshelves and put it together. Are you gonna keep quiet about Lark and why I was hanging outside there so much?"

"Yes, but sweetie, you need to talk to Lark."

I pressed my lips together. "I did, and I'll tell you all about it later."

"Later, when? Because I'm guessing it *won't* be later tonight."

No, I didn't expect that either.

"If you can swing it, we'll do lunch again tomorrow."

"Fine, but we're going to Okinawa."

I shook my head. "We can't go there. It's community tables and no privacy."

"You are not helping here, Brummis. It's more of a hike for you, but we'll do Kickbacks."

It wasn't really more of a hike for me, but I'd let him think so. "Deal. I'll text you when I know my schedule."

"Have fun, and do that man every way you can."

"Chad!" I cried.

"Girlie. He is fine, and you know you want to. Live it up. You deserve it."

CHAPTER 16

SECOND LOCATION

IVY

I ENDED THE CALL, grabbed my purse, and ducked my face while I put my phone away.

"I'd ask you what he said to make you blush so hard, but I'm pretty sure I can guess."

I turned to Ryan and tried not to glare. "You shouldn't gloat."

His smirk looked almost boyish. "I'm not gloating now, but I damn sure will later."

"Ryan!"

A food runner put our plates on the table and I'd never been so happy to be interrupted before.

I heard his quiet, rumbly laugh before he said, "You're fucking adorable."

I stirred my drink. "Did you call me adorable?"

"Yep."

I sighed. "The last person to call me that was Jeff."

One of his eyes narrowed on me. "Is he the person who ruined 'Ives' for you?"

"No, not at all."

He nodded once. "Didn't you say your step-dad's name was Jeff? He passed away."

I took a deep breath. "Right. It's been hard for Mom. Much more than either of us expected."

"Was his death expected?"

I nodded. "Cancer. We thought the treatments were working, but it somehow spread."

He reached out and grabbed my hand. "Say no more, Ivy. Cancer fucking sucks."

"That's the understatement of the century," I muttered.

"Yeah. Why did Jeff call you adorable?" he asked in an exceedingly gentle tone.

I shrugged. "Mostly how I am with Mom."

As much as I loved thinking about Mom and Jeff, it had a somber feel I didn't want to mar my time with Ryan.

I picked up a french fry and dipped it in ketchup. "If you and your brother live at the clubhouse, where does your sister live?"

He swallowed a bite of his sandwich and sipped his drink. "She just finished her degree this past spring. Her campus apartment lease ended. She's recently moved into a double-wide near the bar."

"Is she renting?" I asked, paused, and held up a hand. "Sorry, don't answer that. I slipped into work mode."

He grinned. "It's okay. Yeah, she is renting because she wants to wait until we know where the second location is going to be."

"Second location?" I asked.

He nodded. "The goal is to build enough business at the bar that allows us to invest in another spot and have three to four bars in town. If they all do well, then Mick wants to get into franchising."

I forked up a bite of my grilled chicken. "That's ambitious."

As I chewed my food, he shot me a look. "What were really you going to say?"

"That *is* what I meant to say, though I left off the part that it's also very risky. The restaurant business is in general."

"That's for sure," he muttered.

"Is there a time line for this? And where do you and your brother fit in?"

He stared down at his drink for a beat, then met my gaze. "If we get the number of locations we need to make franchising possible, I'd be going to different markets and scouting locations and verifying applicants. But that's five to eight years down the road at least."

I nodded. That was most likely the real reason he didn't want a woman. He'd be out of town – if he even made Florida his home.

I sipped my gimlet. "That's exciting."

He shook his head and smiled. "That's funny because you sound anything but excited, Trouble."

With a sheepish grin, I conceded the point with a head tilt. "No, really. I would imagine between the three of you—"

"Four of us, Lark's got a heavy hand in this plan."

I did a slow nod. "Ah, well, I'm sure you'll be very successful."

He polished off his drink and chased it with some water. "Time will tell. Lark's made it clear not only does the market change, but our goals will change too, with time."

"Wise words," I murmured, and put the last bite of my chicken in my mouth.

Mom and Jeff had given me similar advice after I passed the real estate exam.

I swallowed my food and glanced around the tavern. "How did you find this place?"

"One of the brothers lives within walking distance."

My brows furrowed. "But your clubhouse is on the Westside. He has to cross the ditch and the river."

Most of the people who lived at the beach referred to the Intercoastal waterway as the ditch. The way Ryan grinned at my words, I knew I didn't need to explain to him.

"Yeah, but his woman loves her place and he loves her... So he's willing to make the drive – or ride, depending on the weather."

I nodded. "That was another occupational hazard coming out again. I'm all the time thinking about where people work and the commute time around here."

"I bet, but Vamp knows how much Killian and I love crab cakes and it's not every day you find a place with good crab cakes and a variety of craft beers on draft."

I leaned toward him. "But you didn't order a beer."

He matched my lean. "No, because I wanted to share the same drink as you."

That was rather sweet.

"You're blushing."

I pressed my lips together, willing my blood to stop rushing to my face. "I'm just surprised how sweet you can be."

A contemplative expression filled his eyes. "If it weren't for last night, and learning you're a vodka girl, I wouldn't have even known that about you. So ...I don't know. I guess you can call it sweet, but I just like that we have that in common."

"So do I," I said in a quiet voice.

"Are you done? If you are, I'll get our check because we have to go get dessert after this."

"Dessert? Is that code for—"

"No. When I'm out this way, I always hit Whit's. It's fan-fuckin'-tastic, as Mickayla says."

I popped another french fry in my mouth and washed it down with some water. "Ready when you are, big guy."

<hr>

No matter how quiet I tried to be, my exhale could be heard in the car.

"Are you in pain over there?" Ryan asked. Observant to a fault.

I felt stuffed to the point of borderline misery, but I would be all right with enough time to recuperate.

"We should have split the ice cream."

"Custard. And no way. I'll split plenty of things with a woman, but my custard is all mine."

I aimed some severe side-eye at him. "Really? That's the line in the sand for you? No woman gets to share custard with you?"

He rested his hand on my thigh. "Not on a first date. Sets the wrong example."

I chuckled. "What example is that?"

"That I'm down with that kind of game playing. You don't strike me as a woman who plays games. With three siblings, I know how to share and I decided a long time ago, I don't share my ice cream. It's better when a woman says she wants a full waffle cone as opposed to having to split it with her."

I shot him a look as he drove us across the Fuller Warren bridge. "So it *is* ice cream."

"You know what I'm saying. Are you gonna survive? Or should I stop at Walgreen's?"

"I'm good," I said.

"What time do you have to be at work in the morning?"

"That's right, I forgot to tell you. My boss was at my closing, so she saw my black eye. She's giving me tomorrow off."

"Sweet," he said in a low voice.

"Having a shiner is not sweet," I muttered. "I should have put on more make up before we left earlier."

He nodded at the road. "That's not what I meant. Hate seeing your face like that, but I'm glad you have tomorrow off because it means I have all night to do whatever I want with you."

Butterflies swarmed in my belly. I felt my cheeks heat and I looked out the window.

He lifted his hand from my thigh. Next thing I knew, he grabbed my hand and threaded his fingers between mine then he moved our hands to his thigh. "You're too fuckin' cute, Trouble."

In no time, he turned into my neighborhood and parked in front of my townhouse.

I tried to pull my hand away, but he kept hold and faced me. "Are you nervous?"

My head tilted just a touch. "A little, but that's normal."

He shook his head. "Nope. You have nothing to be nervous about with me."

I stared at a point over his shoulder as I contemplated that. Lots of things made me nervous about him, but I had to keep that to myself.

"Ivy, look at me."

I met his gaze, and lied through my teeth. "You're right. I'm being silly."

His lips pulled together and he gave me a hard stare. "No. I didn't say that. Let's go inside."

He had my keys and unlocked my door for us.

Inside, I hung up my purse and kicked off my shoes. From the corner of my eye, I saw Ryan tuck my keys inside my purse before he shrugged off his leather.

I turned and found Ryan *right* there. He grabbed my hands and pulled them up over my head, while simultaneously he backed me up against the wall. His head lowered and he kissed me hard, hot, and heavy.

At once it annihilated my nerves, it was so delicious and intense.

He let go of one of my hands, skimming his fingers down the side of my ribs and tugging my blouse free of my dress pants.

I shoved my free hand around his back and yanked his t-shirt free of his jeans. This morning, I hadn't had much time to explore his back. No way I'd let this opportunity pass me by. I slipped my hand under his t-shirt, enjoying the feeling of his warm, sleek skin and imagined the ink beneath my fingers.

He angled his head and took the kiss deeper.

I pressed toward him making him groan. He squeezed my hand that he held above my head. Then his other hand slid up under my bra and he palmed my breast.

Our kiss broke when I gasped, "Yeah."

He rested his forehead on mine. "Not nervous any more are you?"

I hiked a leg up alongside his thigh. "No, I'm not. Your shirt needs to go."

That earned me a deep, dark chuckle. He let go of my hand, reached behind his neck, yanked off his T-shirt, and tossed it toward the couch. "You don't have to ask me twice, baby."

With his chest right in front of me, I licked my lips and kissed his collar bone. Then I kissed a trail to his pectoral and took his nipple between my teeth and let it go.

"Fucking hell, Ivy. That went straight to my cock."

I smiled and peeked up at him. "That's the idea, Nickel."

"Didn't think you had that in you," he murmured.

"I'm glad you like it," I said, dragging my lips to the other side of his chest.

His hand left my breast so he could cup my cheeks and tip my face up toward his. "I'll like it better when I have you naked again. Bedroom or couch?"

"What about the wall?"

Heat flared in his eyes. "First time isn't happening against the wall, Ivy."

I unbuttoned my blouse. "Bedroom."

He pulled my lips to his. Another delicious kiss began, but this time, he wrapped a hand around my waist and walked us backward to my bedroom.

His other hand darted out and hit the light switch.

I broke the kiss and gazed up at him. "It's like you've been here before."

He arched a brow as he slid his hands under the lapels of my blouse. "Had to be sure I was alone earlier."

I loved having his big, warm hands on me. His eyes watched as he gently guided the satin off my shoulders.

My fingers hit his belt buckle, and I undid it.

He shook his head. "That's it, Trouble."

"Why?" I asked.

"How am I gonna get you undressed if I can't even get your shirt off?" he asked, guiding my hands away from him and easing my blouse off fully.

I had a hard time keeping my hands off of him, so I let my fingers trace the line of his sternum and the ridges of muscle lining his entire torso.

He found my bra clasp, undid it, and I had to stop my exploration long enough for him to pull my bra free.

"God, you've got great fuckin' tits," he said, his hands palming my breasts.

He sounded almost reverent. Then again, I'd never heard a heterosexual man complain at the sight of boobs.

I shoved my dress pants and my panties down, then went to work on the button of his jeans.

"Are you in a hurry?" he chuckled.

"You saw me naked already. Fair is fair in my world, and I'm determined to get you naked, too, mister."

He helped me out by unzipping his jeans and shucking them along with his boxer briefs.

Seeing him in all his glory was a sight to behold... it seemed he ticked all of my boxes, too.

"Get on the bed, woman. I'm not letting anything keep me from seeing you come on my tongue."

I sauntered past him. "You better not, my man."

A distinct pain scored through my tush a moment before I heard the sound of Ryan spanking me. I looked over my shoulder at him, my eyes wide with incredulity, but I caught sight of his round ass since he was bent over to pull his boots free and step out of his jeans.

"Couldn't help it, Ivy. Your ass might be as outstanding as your tits, but that's a damn close call."

I giggled and climbed up onto my four-poster bed. "Stop complimenting me. You're going to give me a complex."

He stalked to the bed. "Don't get humble on me now."

I felt my eyebrow arch. "Nobody tells me my ass is as great as my boobs."

He put a knee on the bed and hovered over me. With a hand planted on the bed near my hip, he leaned forward and I reflexively leaned back. "That's good because I don't like the idea of anyone else checking out your ass."

Using my index finger, I traced along his chest and followed the trail of hair leading to his groin. "Really?"

His blue eyes glittered at me. "Yes, really. Are you done teasing me with that finger so I can take care of you?"

I smirked. "Only if you promise I can take care of you later."

"That's a promise I can make, but it'll be much later because we're gonna take care of each other."

"Yeah?" I asked, kissing his cheek.

"Yeah," he whispered. "After I eat you out."

My teeth sunk into my lower lip.

He chuckled and kissed me.

Then he ate me out until I came on his tongue.

It was everything this morning had promised to be and *then* some.

My orgasm had just started to recede when the bed jostled violently. I watched Ryan hurry to his discarded jeans, dig out his wallet and get a condom.

He was lost in concentration as he focused on rolling the condom onto his thick, heavy cock. If we were going all night like he'd hinted earlier, I knew what I wanted to do next: join him in my shower and wrap my lips around him.

"Don't look at me like that, Ivy."

I let my eyes travel up the length of his body. "Or what? You aren't the only one with plans for tonight, sir."

"Spread those legs wider and move up the bed."

I obeyed him, for now, because I could see the determination in his eyes.

"Does your wall butt up against your neighbor's?"

My brows drew together and I hesitated.

He climbed onto the bed and lowered himself into a plank position over me. "Is anyone going to hear us? I'm not just going to fuck you, I'm probably going to pound you into this mattress because my cock is so hard it's already weeping."

I bit back a chuckle. "No. We're all good on that. Let the pounding begin."

He reached down and dragged his cock through my wetness. "It's going to begin, babe. Just not sure if I'll be able to stop."

I lifted my hips to help line him up. "Don't threaten me with a good time."

He laughed and drove his cock inside me by about half. I inhaled at the sensation.

"You good?" he asked, leaning into one arm.

The concern etched on his beautiful face hit me harder than I expected.

"Yeah," I whispered, feeling something warm bubbling inside my chest.

He pushed in more and I widened my legs.

"You feel so damn good," he murmured.

"Same, Ryan. Give me more."

His hand left his cock, traveled up my body to my breast. He rubbed his thumb over my nipple repeatedly. My hips jerked at the mounting pleasure that gave me.

He kissed my neck, then murmured against it, "You are so damned responsive."

"Are you teasing me?"

He lifted his head. "Not a fuckin' chance."

His body shifted, his cock drove forward, and I knew I had all of him. He angled his head and kissed me. I wrapped my hand around the back of his neck and kissed him back.

As the kiss went on, his hips began to rock, but it was slow and way too gentle.

He ended the kiss and looked me in the eye. "Are you ready? I need to go harder."

I nodded. "Yeah. I'm not made of porcelain, honey. I can take it."

He thrust once and it was clear he was holding back. "That's good, baby."

Then he grabbed my legs, hitched them up as high as he could, then he maneuvered his arms and my legs were draped over his shoulders.

"So fuckin' gorgeous," he whispered.

After that, he did what he promised and pounded into me. It was so raw, it was almost punishing, but in the most delicious way.

With my legs off the bed, I couldn't easily match his thrusts, and I put my hands above my head to push back against him. He swiveled his hips on an inward thrust. Pleasure scored through me. I tipped my head back and moaned.

My release was ever so close, but I needed more. I moved one hand to my breast and rolled my nipple.

"Fuck, yeah, Trouble. Keep touching yourself," Ryan encouraged.

My eyes found his and I dragged my fingers down to my clit.

"Do it, Ivy," he said, when I hesitated. "Make yourself come."

It wasn't going to take much. I stroked myself, and watched Ryan's thick cock pistoning into me. It was so erotic, and so damned beautiful. Ryan must have liked what he saw too, since his speed increased even more.

My back and my neck arched as I came.

I heard Ryan groan as his body went still. I opened my eyes just in time to see his head fall back as he came inside me.

He was gorgeous.

The sound of our labored breathing filled my bedroom. He moved his arms and lowered my legs, then wrapped his arms around me and rolled to his back, our bodies still connected. I loved that he could do that – move us both after what had to be the hottest sex of my entire life.

Yeah, I'd been right earlier. I couldn't do casual. Not with him.

He wasn't just different. He had the potential to be the one.

And that scared me to death.

"What's with the look, Trouble?"

"I don't have a look," I lied.

He watched me close for another moment. "You're scared."

Why was he so good at reading me?

"What do I have to be scared of?"

He tucked a lock of hair behind my ear. "Us."

Okay, I'd always wanted a smart man – but I was starting to rethink that.

He chuckled. "That look says I'm right." He rolled to the side. "Hold that thought, I gotta deal with this condom."

The gentle way he pulled out of me made me itch to have him back.

Again, he stared at me and I feared my expression shared too much.

He leaned over me and kissed my cheek. "That was more than a hot fuck for both of us. There's a reason sex complicates shit. We had a bond surviving our abduction. Now we cemented that bond."

"I don't know what you're talking about," I fibbed.

His head tipped to the side. "Are you gonna tell me that was just sex for you?"

The word 'yep' should have been right there at the ready, but not only could I not say it, I couldn't even nod my head. That was anything but *just* sex.

"Didn't think so," he muttered.

I watched him saunter to my bathroom, admiring his back tattoo of the Riot MC patch.

I lifted the covers and pulled them over me, getting comfortable.

Ryan came out of the bathroom and stopped in the middle of my room. "You're cute, but we aren't goin' to bed yet, Ivy."

"I know. I need to shower first, and I'm planning on you being in there with me."

One of his eyebrows ticked up and down. "I'm definitely down for that."

"I figured. I'm looking forward to tasting you."

He pulled back the covers and laid down beside me. "Don't be afraid, Ivy. I mean it. I'm not looking for a woman."

"Right," I whispered.

He continued. "Life's funny though. Most people find each other when they aren't looking. Hell, Uncle Mick would say *especially* when people aren't looking."

I turned on my side to face him. "I hear you, but—"

He shifted to his side. "Ivy, I'm saying, I'm willing to give this a shot if you are."

"You say that now, but I can't handle being ghosted for no good reason or blindsided by threesome requests."

He slid an arm around my shoulders and pulled me closer. "I'd never do that. Has it struck you that *you* might want to ghost *me*?"

"Not a chance," I scoffed, and wished I hadn't.

His lips quirked to the side skeptically. "I work with Lark and he's my MC brother. You aren't going to want to spend as much time with me if shit goes south with him. You might resent being around me because he'll be there – a reminder of what could have been. And you damn sure won't want to spend time at the clubhouse with me."

I turned my head away for a beat. "We've avoided him so far."

"Ivy. I'm serious."

I nodded. "So am I. Those are two separate issues."

"Yeah, but Lark will be around to some degree. We both have to take the risk here."

I nodded. "You're right."

"Yeah, but are we on the same page?"

I thought about it for a moment. I wanted to give this a shot. I knew it down to my bones. If things went haywire between me and Lark, that was between me and Lark. I'd figure out how to deal with him being part of Ryan's world.

I grinned at Ryan. "Yeah. We are."

"Good. I got one last condom and I need to be back inside you."

"Really? That soon?"

He pulled me on top of his warm body. "Woman, you hated losing that connection to me. Nobody's ever looked at me like that. I want that from you again. Only this time we're going slower."

I straddled him and felt his erection. "Okay, but I like it hard, Nickel."

"That's doable."

CHAPTER 17

AVOCADO

RYAN

Ivy failed to stifle her yawn from me. She was sitting on the counter, and I stood next to her holding a pint of Blue Bell Cookie Two Step ice cream. I glanced past her to the microwave which indicated the time was two-thirty-eight in the morning.

We'd polished off what little of the pint that was left in her freezer, and it was high time to call it a night. But I couldn't stop staring at her.

Then again, she'd tossed on a paper-thin white t-shirt she'd cut into a very loose muscle shirt. It was something she liked to sleep in, she'd told me. Seeing as it was indecent in at least three states, sleeping was about the only thing she could do in it. The edge of her areola peeked out the top with her breathing. Sheer torture for me, but I fucking loved it.

"No matter how hard you stare, it won't make my shirt disintegrate," she murmured.

I set the ice cream carton on the counter and stepped between her legs. "Wouldn't want it to, Trouble. This 'shirt' suits you so much it's not funny. Though, part of me wants to modify it."

She laughed. "Modify it how?"

I stepped closer and slid my hands under the shirt, up her stomach, and held her breasts in my hands. "Rip it, so your tits are out completely. But that would ruin the tease."

"Sure would," she said, her voice husky and her green eyes heated.

"Is there a drug store close? I need to fuck you on your couch."

She took a deep breath, pressing her tits into my hands. "I'm on the pill."

I closed my eyes at the gift she was giving me. When she spoke again, I realized she'd misread my reaction.

"I saw my doctor four months ago, I'm clean."

I opened my eyes. "Baby, that's good to know, but are you sure?"

Her expression turned guarded. "Yeah, I mean, as long as you're clean, it just—"

I slid my hands around to her back and pulled her closer. "Had my physical not long before you walked into the bar the first time. I'm clean too."

Her tongue peeked out to wet her bottom lip. "Then we're good, yeah?"

I lifted her off the counter and she wrapped her legs around me. "Yeah, babe, we're good. Real good."

She leaned down and kissed me. It was a straight shot from her kitchen to the couch, and I carried her there while her tongue tangled with mine. I broke the kiss, set her on her feet, and shoved my underwear off.

Her teeth sank into her plump lower lip, and I loved that she had that reaction to seeing me naked.

I sprawled out on my back on her couch. "Climb on, Trouble. I wanna watch you ride me. If you don't want that shirt ripped, you might want to take it off. Though it'll be more fun if you leave it on."

She blushed, then whipped the fabric off and dropped her panties before climbing on top of me. "Maybe the next time, honey."

I jacked my cock once, then Ivy took hold and lined me up. She sank down nice and slow. Her pussy gripped me in that slick heat and I exhaled slowly. It was unreal how much better she felt skin-to-skin. It felt right fucking her earlier, but this...this was better than anyone ever before.

The globes of her ass hit the tops of my thighs. She had me to the hilt.

Her hands rested on my pecs. "God, I love the feel of you inside me."

"That makes two of us, baby. But, it'd be good if you move."

A slow smile crept across her lips. "Yeah, but this time we're going slow."

I shot her a devilish smirk at her repeating my words. "Are you gonna do it hard?"

She returned my smirk and lifted up nice and slow. "Nope. You nearly wore me out earlier."

I took hold of her hips, but didn't try to control her rhythm, not yet. Instead, I enjoyed the sight of her moving on top of me. Between the way her tits bounced and the feel of her sleek pussy, I could get used to this.

She leaned forward, kissed me, but cut it short. Then she leaned back and rose up only to sink back down on me harder. Her tempo increased and I guided her hips down a little harder each time. She took her hands from my chest and ran them up her torso.

"Fuck," I hissed.

"Mmm," she hummed while playing with her tits.

"Ivy."

She ran one hand down to her clit and began to bounce faster. I couldn't hold back any more and pistoned my hips up with her downward thrusts.

"Oh God," she moaned.

As much as I loved watching her, I had to take control.

"It's my turn, baby," I said, while knifing up, twisting us both, and planting her with her back on the couch.

"Holy crap on a cracker," she muttered.

I chuckled. "Glad you liked that."

"Don't stop," she ordered.

My hips thrust into her and she raised her legs higher, giving me more access.

"Faster," she said.

I gave her what she demanded, and felt my balls draw up. "Fuck. I'm close, Ivy."

She put her hand between us and rubbed her clit. "Yeah."

I felt her pussy contract around me and I came long and hard, then I collapsed on top of her.

No doubt about it, losing the condoms made sex so much better.

It hit me that I'd given her too much of my weight and I lifted up a touch. "If I haven't told you, I really fucking like your couch."

She giggled. "Yeah, we definitely put it to good use. Not sure I can move right now."

I grinned. "We should get some sleep...in your bed. You want me to carry you to the bathroom so you can clean up?"

Her eyes darted to the side and back to me. "No, but that's thoughtful of you."

Slowly, I pulled out of her and that same look came over her face. I'd meant it earlier, no other woman had ever looked at me like that. Like that connection meant something to her. I grabbed her hand and helped her to her feet.

"I have a spare toothbrush if you want to brush your teeth," she said when she stepped inside the bathroom.

"That'd be good, Ivy. I'll wait until you're finished."

Fifteen minutes later, we were laying in bed.

Right before I nodded off, Ivy shifted to her side.

I turned so I was spooning her. "Woman, you better not steal the sheets like you did at the clubhouse."

She chuckled. "If I do, it isn't intentional."

"Goodnight, Trouble."

"Goodnight, Ryan."

Ivy shifted her mass of dark hair over her shoulder and peered up at me. "I would offer you breakfast, but I don't have any milk or eggs in the house."

My lips tipped up. "That's fine. I'll eat whatever you're having."

She sat up and held the sheet to her chest. "Normally, I make my own avocado toast, but the idea of giving you an avocado is outlandish."

I snatched the sheet out of her grip, then rolled into her, taking her to her back and pressing my chest to her tits. "Are you judging me because I'm a biker?" I asked in a teasing tone.

The skin around her eyes crinkled with her laughter. "No, I'm *guessing* based on your extremely well-honed muscles."

Her legs spread and my hips dipped lower.

I laughed and kissed her neck. "Avocados have a little bit of protein, so I'm down with your breakfast, Ivy."

She sighed. "Cool. Are we eating and then fucking or vice versa?"

I raised my head. "Fucking then eating."

Almost an hour later, I popped the last bite of toast in my mouth.

Ivy watched me over the rim of her glass of orange juice. "I can't believe that's your first piece of avocado toast."

"Yeah. I don't buy the things because they're never ripe when I need them. And if I'm at a place that serves it, I'd rather have something else on the menu. But Mickayla will be thrilled to know you popped my cherry."

She opened her mouth to speak, but her cell rang and she immediately frowned. "That's the office. I'm going to have to take it."

I finished my orange juice while she took the call.

"Are you sure they said their name is Boyd Huntington?" she asked.

The food in my stomach felt like a lead weight. She looked freaked but it didn't come across in her voice.

"Yeah. Did you tell him I wouldn't be in today?"

Pause.

"She did? She's the one who insisted—"

She stopped short, then sighed.

"Okay, all right. Text me his number and I'll get on it, Shayla."

She ended the call and put her cell on the counter.

I stepped into her personal space. "You aren't doing anything with this, Ives."

Her eyes widened. "What am I supposed to tell my boss? How would I know this person's misrepresenting themselves? I know Boyd's dead, but I can't very well tell my boss that. I mean, the cops haven't come around."

"Why would they? It happened in another town, and we didn't leave anything behind to put ourselves at the scene."

"Ryan," she started.

I shook my head. "Ivy, working in real estate is a dangerous job because you're in an empty house with a stranger. You and I know that guy's dead. Call your boss and punt this customer to a male colleague."

Her head tipped back and she pressed her lips together. She righted her head and looked me in the eye. "He demanded me specifically."

"Which is how you know it's a set-up."

She took a deep breath. "It's just a phone call."

"And I'll be listening in, Trouble. But first I have to text Lark and Volt."

"Why Lark?"

"They took me as a way to get under Lark's skin. He's as much a target as you and I."

"You should wait until we know what he wants. There could actually be another man named Boyd Huntington."

I gave her a dead-eyed stare.

She looked contrite. "You never know."

I grabbed her phone off the counter and handed it to her.

She called the number and put it on speaker.

"Is this Ivy?" a man's voice asked.

Ivy's face twisted with a fake smile. "Yes, sir. Is—"

"You're a hard bitch to find," he said, cutting her off.

"I'm sorry, is this Mr. Huntington?"

His mirthless chuckle spiked my anger. "Yeah, but my first name ain't Boyd."

Ivy kept her gaze pinned to the wall. "I'm sorry, may I call you Mr. Huntington?"

"You can tell me what the fuck you and that bouncer did to Campbell."

Finally she looked up at me. I shook my head. This was no time to tell him anything.

"I don't know what you're talking about," she fibbed, but it sounded believable. Maybe I was just biased to her now that we'd become more than co-hostages.

"It's bad enough you killed Boyd. If Campbell's dead too, the least you can do is tell me."

"Sir, do you have a real estate issue?"

The man emitted a low growl. "Bitch, you're the one with an issue. There's tracking on his truck. I'm gonna find it, and when I do, I'll find you."

That was an empty threat and we both knew it.

I leaned forward and whispered in Ivy's ear, "Ask if his name is Rusty."

"Should I call you Rusty, Mr. Huntington?"

"How the fuck do you know my name? Have you got Campbell with you? That must be why they said you aren't going into the office today."

Jesus. Ivy's coworkers needed to stop sharing so freely.

I reached out and tapped the red button to end the call.

"Ryan! Why'd you do that?" she asked, her eyes wide.

"First, that was a fishing expedition and I didn't want you giving anything away. Second, your damned coworkers have to stop sharing your schedule."

Her head twisted an inch to the side. "Good luck with that. It never pays to be cagey with clients."

I leaned toward her. "It never pays to tell criminals where you are or when you'll be back either."

She opened her mouth and then closed it. Except she recovered and said, "You're right, but my coworkers had no idea about my problems. I'll take care of that, now."

My hand curled around my neck to ease my building tension. "How are you gonna do that? If you tell them about the abduction, it raises the question of why you never reported it."

She put a hand on my chest and rubbed gentle circles there. "We have a system, Ry. I'll let my boss and Shayla know that this guy is a potential problem. I'm not going to pass him off to Bill or Anderson because that will only cause more issues. So, don't flip your lid when I underplay this with my boss."

"Ivy."

"Ryan. I need to play it cool at work or one of my male colleagues will horn in on what they think is a potential client. Sales is very cutthroat, and I can't have them doing that in this instance especially since this guy would love to throw me under the bus."

"I still don't like it."

She nodded. "He wants to find the truck. Is Lark planning to leave it to be found?"

I shrugged a shoulder. "I'm not sure. But now that he's made contact, I need to tell the brothers and they'll decide or call a session of church."

Her hand had paused on my chest. She put pressure there, went up on her toes, and brushed her lips against mine. "You call them while I let my boss know I followed up on a potential client."

This driving need to protect her surged through my whole body. I'd never felt like this before, and I couldn't wrap my head around it. I pulled my phone from my back pocket and acted as though I was going to make a call.

She chuckled and it sounded almost melodic. "You're not gonna call anyone until you listen in on my conversation, are you?"

I looked up from my phone to her. "What makes you think that?"

"You're not that difficult to read, mister."

"Make your call, Trouble."

She shook her head but called her office.

Whoever she spoke to took her word that this man was a problem.

I called Volt. He didn't answer and I tried Lark instead.

"Talk to me, Nickel," he answered in his gravelly voice.

"Rusty – the man Boyd and Campbell were reporting to – called Ivy through her real estate office. He wants the truck and has threatened to come after me and her once he finds it."

"Put her in a safe house and let the asshole come to us," Lark said without a moment's hesitation.

I didn't like the idea of being away from Ivy, but I knew having her around the bar wouldn't work either.

"The club doesn't have a safe house, Lark. There's navigation on that truck, why don't we go to them?"

"That's not my call, and a safe house doesn't have to be owned by the club, Nickel. Have her stay with that friend of hers – he'd do anything to help her."

I ignored his suggestion. "Do you want me at the bar earlier than normal?"

Lark hummed so low, I almost missed it. "Nah. You sound like you're ready to go off half-cocked. That won't help any of us, so get here at three."

He ended the call and I saw Ivy was on the phone again with a humongous smile on her face.

She looked up at me and her smile dimmed by a degree. "Listen, Chad, you're the one who told me I have to roll with whatever punches life throws at me. Same goes for you, so let Kristen know we aren't meeting at the bar tonight. Maybe she can meet for lunch today, even though it's Wednesday."

Shit.

Every Wednesday, Mickayla insisted on having lunch with me and Killian.

Ivy had gone quiet again while she closed her eyes and shook her head. She opened her eyes and looked at me. "Well, you're gonna have to make a table for four because I have a feeling Ryan isn't leaving my side."

The moment she ended her call, I crossed my arms on my chest. "What's going on?"

"We have a lunch date with Chad and our friend Kristen. And if it helps any, we're going to Kickback's, so at least that's something to look forward to in a couple hours."

I nodded. "We'll be a table for six because Mickayla has this standing lunch date with me and Kill. I'll text her, so she can get us a table."

CHAPTER 18

GROWING ON ME

IVY

"Do you have more than one gun?" Ryan asked.

I nodded.

He tipped his head toward my bedroom. "Get them both and make sure they're loaded."

I failed to hide my eyeroll. "An empty gun is just a paperweight."

He kept a stoic expression. "If you say so, but I want you to spend the night with Chad or your other friend – even better if your coworkers don't know about them."

I twisted my hands up in concession. "Kristen fits that bill, but she has nowhere for me to sleep because she has a one bedroom studio and her brother is currently staying on her couch."

He closed his eyes for a beat. "Then stay with Chad. If I can, I'll pick you up when I'm done."

"Why can't I stay here?"

"No gate. You own this place, right?"

I laughed. "No, I'm renting, sadly. And hypocritically, given my profession."

His lips pressed together as he contemplated my words. "That makes it harder for someone to find you in the property databases, but I'd rather not leave you alone."

A sleepover at Chad or Kristen's place would be fun, but not half as fun as staying with Ryan.

He mistook my hesitant expression. "I'll be picking you up after my shift – probably around eleven-thirty or midnight."

"You could check in with me and—"

"No." He bit out the word.

The overprotective tone was new. I hated the idea of Chad being disturbed around midnight, and his chihuahua, Ginger, would raise holy hell when Ryan came around to get me.

"What if I stayed at your place?" I asked.

Disbelief swept over his face. "You are not gonna be able to stay in my room."

I shot him some side eye. "Considering the book haul you gave me last night, I most certainly could. I just need snacks and lime juice."

He huffed out a breath mingled with a chuckle. "You aren't day drinking without me. What are you gonna do about dinner?"

I shrugged. "We're headed to Kickback's. I can order something huge and have leftover lunch for dinner."

"Are you always this..." he trailed off, searching for the right word.

"Obstinate? Headstrong?" I suggested.

"That one. Headstrong."

I grinned and nodded. "Yep. Chad got me a t-shirt to prove it."

"Fuck. Guess you only need one gun then."

I smiled. "Excellent. That leaves room for my skimpy sleep shirt."

He uncrossed his arms, stepped closer, and wrapped those bulky limbs around me. "You're in my bed, you sleep in one of my shirts."

"I thought you liked my shirt."

"I like you in my clothes even more."

Little did he know, I loved sleeping in his t-shirt, which made it a win-win all around.

Ryan kissed my forehead, then waited for me to look him in the eye. "You don't leave my room though. I didn't like the way Tic watched you Monday night."

My eyebrows furrowed. "Was he the one with the really close haircut—"

"Who looks like a bald, heavyweight boxer? Yeah."

I frowned. "I wouldn't have described him that way, but I'll be sure to avoid him."

He gave me a squeeze. "If you stay in my room, you don't have to avoid him."

"You're right, but—"

"No 'buts' Ivy. If you can't hole up in my room reading your haul, then you're hitting Chad's this afternoon. That's the deal."

I sighed and my chest pressed against his. "Fine. Do you have plans this morning? There's two hours before lunch. I wasn't sure if you work out or something in the mornings."

"Nope, but your couch is calling my name."

Heat surged through me at the memory of last night. That had been hands-down some of the best sex I'd ever had. A repeat of that? Yes, please.

I stopped dead on the sidewalk.

Kristen stood with her head tipped backward, her mouth in a huge gorgeous smile as she laughed straight from her belly. As beautiful as that might have been, my eyes were locked on her hand holding onto Ryan's bicep like he was her anchor in a sea of humor.

"What's the problem?" Ryan asked, draping his arm over my shoulders.

Shit.

It took a moment for the high tide of my jealousy to recede.

My best friend was flirting with *Killian,* not Ryan.

I should have known this would happen because I couldn't distinguish between the two of them at all. If I were lucky, with enough time, I'd figure out a way to tell them apart.

"Babe?" Ryan asked, shifting so he stood in front of me.

"It's fine. I'm fine. I just got a little confused for a moment."

He stared at me, looked over his shoulder, then turned back with a nod. "You knew I was at your side, right?"

I put both of my hands on his chest and leaned into him. "I did when we got off your bike, but that obviously fell by the wayside when I caught sight of my friend and your brother. It threw me, and the worst part was that deep down I knew something like this would happen, I just haven't had a chance to spend time with both of you which would help me figure out a tell-tale sign to distinguish you from your brother."

I listened to his low chuckle while he traced the bottom of my jaw with his index finger. "I hate to tell you this, but there really isn't one." He tilted his head then righted it. "Well, I suppose you could tell the difference when we're shirtless because our chest tattoos are different. Otherwise, you're gonna be shit out of luck until you get to know us."

I nodded. "I'm sorry. Really. I shouldn't have freaked—"

"Ivy, I'm used to it. Hell, I had the money for a kickass forearm tattoo. Killian talked me out of it because he gets off on women being confused about which one of us is which. It's one of the few things that makes me grateful Mickayla's female. If there really were three of us…there's no telling how awful we'd be on the ladies."

"What's the hold up, Nickel?" a man yelled, and I peeked around Ryan to see it was his brother.

Ryan turned around and took my hand. "Nothing, Ricochet."

Kristen saw me and dashed over to give me a hug. "Oh my God. Chad told me this morning what happened to you! Are you sure you're okay?" she asked pulling out of the hug.

I gave her hands a squeeze before letting them go. "I'm fine. Seems you met Killian, but I'd like you to meet Ryan."

Kristen and Ryan shook hands and exchanged pleasantries. He nodded at both of us and wandered over to his brother.

"Chad wasn't kidding. They are both smokin' hot," Kristen muttered under her breath.

"Right. Where is Chad by the way?"

"He got held up by a train. He'll be here soon," she said.

"I'm right here," Chad said, strolling up from behind us. His gaze shot past us to Killian and Ryan before he focused on me. "I didn't believe you when you said those two hotties were going to join us."

"Like you mind," I said.

"Well, this should be fun," Chad muttered.

"Come on, now that we're all here, they should give us our table," Kristen said.

"Where's Mickayla?" I asked.

Kristen slanted her head toward the doorway. "She went to talk to the hostess, and now she's waving us over."

As worlds colliding went, this could be deemed a success. Killian kept shooting looks at Kristen, but she was acting cooler than a cucumber. Considering her earlier laughter, I wondered if she was playing games and if so, why?

I was able to share with Chad and Kristen what happened with me and Lark.

"That is not how I expected that to go," Chad groused.

If Killian or Mickayla were eavesdropping, they hid it well.

"What did you expect, Chad?" Kristen asked.

"You aren't going to make me feel bad for wanting Ivy to get another family out of this," Chad said louder than normal.

Killian glanced our way.

Mickayla's gaze swung to me and something about the look in her eyes told me she knew.

"Mick, is there a problem?" Ryan asked, picking up on the silent interaction between us.

Before she could look to him, I guessed, "He told you."

She shook her head. "He told one of the brothers. I barged into the office for change not knowing they were having that kind of conversation."

Ryan's hand on my thigh tightened.

I leaned my shoulder into his. "It's not a big deal."

He stared at his sister.

"Don't give me that look," Mickayla said.

"Who did he tell?" Ryan asked.

"Tundra, but that hardly matters. One of your brothers isn't going to put her in danger anymore than you are," Mickayla said.

Ryan shook his head. "Why was he there last night?"

Killian tipped his soda glass at Ryan. "To fill in for your ass. If you're worried he's comin' for your job – you should be. He's got more experience and he's better than you."

Ryan narrowed his eyes at his triplet. "He's not better than me, jackass."

"No, he's better than both of you combined," Mickayla said.

"Bullshit," Ryan and Killian said at the same time.

We all laughed at that.

A few minutes later, Kristen and I went to the bathroom before our food came out.

We were washing our hands and I noticed Kristen's gaze on my reflection in the mirror. "This is going to sound crazy, but would it be weird if I gave Ricochet my number?"

"Yes," Mickayla's voice came from a closed stall. "It's weird already just hearing this conversation."

"I thought you stayed at the table! When did you come in here?" I asked on a laugh.

"Not thirty seconds after y'all left, all the coffee I had this morning caught up with me, so I came in right after you two."

I dried my hands and faced Kristen. "I thought you weren't looking for a man."

"Neither were you, as I recall," she said. "But Ricochet is not like his brother. He's a one-and-done kind of guy. that seems clear."

"Good Lord! Can you two cut a girl a break," Mickayla cried from her stall just before the toilet flushed.

I twisted my hands out at Kristen. "You're a free woman."

Mickayla wandered to the sink and aimed a look at Kristen. "Woman to woman, he's an insatiable flirt – always has been. Don't take it to heart if he never calls. He'd hate to do something to make her or Ryan feel weird long term."

"I'm surprised you'd tell me that," Kristen said.

Mickayla gave her a closed-lip smile and jerked her head toward me. "I can see how tight you and her are and something makes me think she's gonna be around for a while. Which means you'll be around, too. I'd hate it if someone didn't forewarn me if they knew someone might string me along."

Kristen nodded. "Makes sense."

Mickayla moved to the towel dispenser. "I'm sorry if I wrecked your plans with Killian."

Kristen shook her head. "Far from it. You reminded me to think of my girl first. Making things awkward works both ways, so I appreciate it."

We meandered between tables to get back to ours. Killian had a sharp focus on us the entire time, and even knowing who he was, I struggled to differentiate him from Ryan.

Killian had shaved, but I wouldn't be able to count on that all the time. The thought of Ryan with a beard appealed to me. I wondered if he'd be cool with that.

Chad looked up and grinned, prompting Ryan to turn in his chair.

Yeah, I could tell the difference in their eyes.

"As ever, you worked your magic. Our food came out a minute ago," Chad said.

I settled in my seat and Ryan leaned toward me. "Did my sister make you uncomfortable?"

I choked down my laughter. "Kristen did, but I'm used to it."

"Are you going to see Debra tonight?" Chad asked.

"Not tonight," Ryan said.

Chad's gaze shifted to me. "Ivy—"

"It's okay, Chad. I'm gonna call her when she's off work."

"One of you needs to fill me in, here. I hate being the odd one out," Killian said.

I shifted my eyes to his. "Lark is my biological dad, but I haven't told my mom that I found him."

"Or that you were still looking," Chad muttered, with more sass than necessary.

I twisted a hand up. "She knew that I might try, considering she gave me the sperm bank info ten months ago."

Killian did a spit-take, but got his napkin to his mouth in time. "Are you shitting me?" he demanded.

"You can't be surprised. He does all kinds of shit on the fly. Imagine him in his twenties," Ryan said.

Chad aimed a dramatically pointed look my way.

"I don't do anything *that* spontaneous," I said.

Kristen laughed. "Girl, if someone said, 'dance on this table,' you'd be on it in under ten seconds."

"Dance on this table," Killian said.

"Killian," Ryan growled.

I glanced between Kristen and Chad. "Dancing in public is *not* the same as donating my reproductive DNA."

"That's why it was private," Killian said in a low voice.

"Great work, Sherlock," Ryan bit out.

I rested my hand on Ryan's forearm. "It's okay, Nickel. Really."

Ryan turned his face toward me. "Yeah, but he needs to back off."

"Brother, I'm just trying to understand what's goin' down," Killian said.

"And now you do," Mickayla said.

We rode to the clubhouse on Ryan's bike. I hated being without my car, but I couldn't deny how much fun it was riding on his bike in the daytime.

He carried my duffel bag and the bag o' books to his room with me trailing behind him toting my leftovers.

I closed the door to his room while he set the bags down.

"I got a mini-fridge where you can put your leftovers," he said, gesturing to the far corner of the room.

I stashed my food in his fridge, straightened, and edged closer to him. "You make your bed every day."

He chuckled. "No. A prospect makes my bed."

"I see."

He sat down on the foot of the bed. "You gonna dance on a table for me one day?"

I laughed. "Maybe. I've calmed down a lot these days."

He pulled me on to his lap. "Are you sure Mick didn't freak you out?"

I grinned while running my fingers through the hair at the side of his head. I loved the prickly yet soft feeling. "Yeah. She's a good woman, even if she may have kept Kristen from going there with your brother."

He nodded and let his hands drift down to my tush. "I have an hour and a half before I need to leave."

"Oh. Do you need to do something before you go?"

That devilish smirk of his appeared. "Yeah, you."

Ryan grabbed his keys from a dish on his dresser and shoved them in his pocket. Then he shrugged on his leather vest.

"Do you always wear your vest?" I asked.

He looked at me. "It's a cut, and if I'm on my bike, yes."

"Even in the rain?"

"Yep. Though I put rain gear on over it – assuming I don't take a cage instead."

"A cage is a car, I take it."

"It is. Come give me a kiss before I go."

I met him at the door, snaked my arms around his neck, and kissed him. It quickly turned into a mini makeout session, even though we had spent the last hour working off lunch.

And even though I'd just had two orgasms, I felt like I could jump him again, but then he'd be running late.

I broke the kiss and exhaled hard. "What are you doing to me?" I whispered.

He rested his forehead on mine. "Been asking myself that all week, Trouble, because this is..."

"Unreal," I suggested when he trailed off.

"Something like that," he said, his arms giving me a squeeze.

He kissed me once more with a single tongue touch and stepped back. "I gotta jet. Lock the door after me. I'll see you tonight."

After I locked the door, I dug my phone out of my purse to check the time. I had a few hours to kill before Mom would be done with work. I grabbed the thick rom-com from my stack of books, climbed into Ryan's bed, and started reading.

Around four-thirty, I heard the clinking of glasses and the occasional traces of voices coming from downstairs. The extrovert in me hated being holed up in

Ryan's room, but I'd made him a promise. In a way, it reminded me of dorm life. While everyone else was partying, I had to stay in and study.

I took my phone off the nightstand and called Mom.

She answered after one ring. "Hey, Ivy-bean. It's been a while. How are you?"

"I'm good," I said, unsure of which topic to broach first.

"You don't sound like you mean that."

"Are you cooking right now?" I asked because Mom ate early and often made homemade meals for one.

"Nope. You caught me before I got up to start dinner."

I took a deep breath. "I probably should have told you this sooner, but I've been searching for my biological dad."

She kept quiet.

I opened my mouth to apologize, but then she spoke. "I suspected as much when you and Chad went up to Atlanta and made that supposed *impromptu* side-trip to Memphis."

I fought off a frown. "Chad oversold it with Graceland, didn't he?"

Mom's tone went gentle. "Chad's never been an Elvis fan, and I still don't understand why."

I chuckled. "You're right, but he loves Paul Simon."

"Seeing as you're finally telling me about your search, I'm guessing you've found him."

I took a deep breath. "Yes."

I didn't know what else to say. Part of me felt like finding Lark was a betrayal to Jeff, and that made me realize maybe Mom wouldn't want to know and probably wouldn't want to meet him.

I really should have thought longer and harder about this rather than spontaneously following my stupid heart.

This was when I needed Chad to be around. He didn't need to be there to hear Lark semi-reject me, he needed to be here now that I was navigating uncharted waters with Mom.

Actually, I wished Ryan were here more than Chad, and I wondered why I didn't do this when he was still in the room.

That brought me up short.

Chad and Kristen were my ride-or-dies. How did Ryan jump into the front seat?
I knew I could fall for him, but it struck me that I was already falling.
Crap.
"Well, what's he like?" Mom asked, dragging me from my monumental thoughts.

I stared at Ryan's dresser and blurted, "He runs a bar and he's a biker. A real one and he's a member of a club."

"A gang?" Mom asked.

"No, it's a club," I said, remembering my conversation with Alexandra and the way that she made it clear that the club was more like a family and *not* a gang.

"There's something off here. I wish you were sitting in front of me, but from your tone...What aren't you telling me?"

I wondered if there was something about being a mom that had her dialed into me and every little nuance, and even over the phone I couldn't pull anything over on her.

"Was he a jerk to you?" Mom pushed.

I shook my head. "No, no. When I first tried to see him, I wound up meeting someone."

"Okay," Mom drawled, not hiding her skepticism. "Is this person the same age as your biological dad?"

"No, but he works with Lark and he's a member of the club."

"Ivy, I don't know about this."

"Mom. Please keep an open mind. I wanted to tell you these things in person, but—"

"Then why didn't you? Come over for dinner after you get off work."

I pressed my lips together, this conversation was getting out of control. "I can't. Not tonight."

"Why? Is this new man in your life being uber controlling? I don't have to remind you of how Austin was—"

"He's *nothing* like Austin," I said, harsher than I'd intended.

"Ivy F. Brummis, watch it, young woman."

I closed my eyes and almost smiled. Only my mom would inadvertently give me a name that sounded like the very procedure that got her pregnant.

"I'm sorry, Mom. There's so much more to this story, it's not funny."

"Lay it on me anyway."

"You might want a glass of wine first."

Mom paused, then blew out a breath. "You know, I think you're right. Let me go uncork a bottle of white."

"While you do that, how are things with you?"

"From the sound of it, not nearly as fascinating as your life right now. On Saturday, there's a knitting group meeting at the library and I'm going to check it out. If you still have that purple yarn, you should join me."

In the background, I heard the glug of the wine pouring from the bottle.

I gave her another minute because I couldn't share this with her standing up.

Finally she let out a long exhale. "Okay, I'm back on the couch. Give me the whole story."

"I'm gonna tear off the Band-Aid here, Mom. We're fine. Everything is fine, but on Monday, Ryan and I were abducted at gunpoint."

"What?" Mom splutter-yelled, and I suspected she really did do a spit-take.

"It's fine, Mom."

"And you're *involved* with this man!"

"*He* didn't abduct me."

"You need to get checked out for Stockholm Syndrome."

I swallowed down a sigh. "That's when someone has feelings for the person who abducted them. Ryan didn't abduct me."

"Well, he's obviously a bad sort."

"Don't be so quick to judge before you've even met him. Chad loves him already."

"Was Chad there?" Mom asked, her voice incredulous.

Oh boy. Now I'd stepped in it.

"He showed up late, and alerted Lark to me being MIA."

"MIA. Do you hear yourself? Were you hurt?"

"They hit both of us over the head, but neither of us had concussions."

"The doctors told you that, right?"

I bit my lip, when I should have kept talking.

"You didn't go to the doctor. Ivy, why wouldn't you go to the ER?"

Yep, definitely should have done this in person.

"Mom, when people show up with head injuries nurses and doctors ask questions."

"And you have answers, young lady. Someone who abducted you, hit you over the head."

"But the authorities wouldn't be able to find them, and it—"

"Did Ryan kill them?"

I scoffed. "I didn't say anything like that."

"Then why can't you leave this to the authorities?"

"Ryan and I worked together to...get free."

"You wouldn't hurt a fly, Ivy."

I glanced down at my lap. "I've swatted many a fly, Mom. And being taken against my will brings out a whole other side of me."

"Let me get this straight. You went to speak with Lark on Monday night, got abducted along with Ryan, and that fast, you're involved with him?"

I explained about the first time I met Ryan.

"My girl, I know you're an adult, but I can't leave this unsaid. You're moving way too fast with this man. After three days, you can't know that much about him."

That made me angry even if I understood her concerns.

"It's funny you say that because I mentioned that to him, and he rattled off that he's a triplet, he's from Biloxi, a member of the club, where he works, and then he offered up his political leanings."

"That is not enough in—"

"Mom. We're getting to know each other. It's a process. I'm not betrothed to him or running off to Vegas."

Silence crept along the line. I heard her take in a breath. "You sound like you would."

She was right. I didn't understand it, so I couldn't explain it.

"He's a triplet," Mom prompted.

I grinned. "Yes. He has a brother and a sister."

"And Chad likes him."

"Yes. He said he's better than Austin by a long shot."

"I'm sorry dear, but that's not saying much."

"Please, Mom. Keep an open mind. You haven't even met him."

"I will, sweetheart. It's just hard for me to ignore that he didn't take you to a doctor, and for some reason you aren't able to come see me."

Before we went to lunch, Ryan had told me more about Blood and his wife, Abby.

"You're right, but he did call an ER nurse who's married to one of the MC brothers. Then he set an alarm to wake us up every hour."

"He slept at your townhouse?"

I explained how we wound up at his room. "As for being able to swing by for dinner, the person we assume is in charge called the office this morning and insisted I call him back. Until the threat is gone, Ryan's insistent that I be somewhere he knows is safe."

"He might be growing on me," Mom said dryly.

I chuckled. "That's good to know."

"Yes, but I'm calling Chad tonight."

"Mom."

"Oh no, dear. He should have called me the minute he knew you were missing."

"And worry you for nothing?"

"No, to worry me for everything that matters in my world."

I sighed and fought off tears. "I'm sorry. Don't beat him up about that. He doesn't need a guilt trip. Heck, before he met Lark, he wanted you to meet him after I did."

Mom laughed. "That man. Ever the matchmaker."

"I'll let you get to cooking. I love you, Mom."

"I love you, too. Bring Ryan to dinner on Thursday. I know that's short notice, but I want to meet him. You'll tell me Sunday's out, Friday and Saturday are out for me, so tomorrow night it is."

"Could you make it a brunch? He works at a bar and grille, you know."

"We both work during the day, so not likely. Figure it out, sweetie. I'm meeting him, and it's going to be sooner not later. Bye!"

CHAPTER 19

DISTRACTED ME

RYAN

"Aw, shit," Lark muttered.

I stood next to him behind the bar and let my gaze follow to where he was staring across the room.

One of the rednecks had walked inside with his eyes fixed on me and Lark. This had to be Rusty.

On the one hand, it surprised me it took this long for him to come around, on the other hand, I couldn't believe he wanted this to be public.

He stopped at the bar in front of us. "Both of you fucked up."

Lark's eyes were empty - he was a master of the dead-eyed stare. "We close in twenty minutes. If you aren't ordering a beer, then leave."

"You don't deny it?" Rusty asked, his eyes darting between us.

"Are you Rusty?" I asked.

His eyes glittered at me. "You killed my cousins."

Rusty stood at five foot, eight inches and probably weighed as much as I did which meant he was at least forty pounds overweight. He appeared to be in his mid-thirties, but he didn't have the rough demeanor Boyd and Campbell had. No wonder he left the dirty work to his cousins.

I shook my head. "I don't know what you're talking about."

"Bullshit, but Corrupt Chrome MC is gonna take care of you assholes."

Lark's head twitched. "What do they have to do with it?"

He focused on Lark. "You fucked one of their women." Rusty swung his gaze to me. "And you fucked with me when you killed Boyd."

"I haven't done shit to you," I said.

Rusty chuckled. "More bullshit."

"Corrupt Chrome doesn't have a chapter here, and you don't ride. What are you? A hang-around who can't afford his own bike?" I asked.

Rusty narrowed his eyes. "I oughta shoot you right now, but Sig told me his club's gonna take care of everything."

It was taking everything I had to ignore him and stay calm.

"Why isn't Sig here with you?" Lark asked.

"They don't do things half-assed," Rusty muttered.

Killian sidled up to Rusty. "We got a problem here?"

Tundra, who had been sitting at the far end of the bar, stood and lumbered over to Rusty's other side. "Did I hear there's a problem?"

Rusty's expression betrayed his nervousness at being outnumbered by us. He fixed his gaze on Lark. "This bar's days are numbered, asshole."

Tundra turned outraged eyes to Lark. "You gonna let that shit slide?"

"Get him out of here," Lark said, his eyes cold on Rusty.

Killian reached for Rusty, but he backed away. "I'm leaving."

Tundra and Killian followed him.

"Where's Ivy?" Lark asked.

"Clubhouse."

His eyes rounded. "Really?"

I shrugged. "You said put her in a safe house, and I can't think of anywhere safer than my room."

"Boy... Don't string her along," Lark said.

I stiffened. "I'm not a boy, and I'd never string a woman along."

"Fine. You wiped the steering wheel down the other night, right?"

It floored me that he'd talk about this when Rusty had just left.

I nodded.

"Passenger side?"

"No," I said, angry at myself.

Lark nodded. "I'll have Liar or Patch take care of it."

"Why not Adam?" I asked.

Killian and Tundra came back inside. Tundra sat on a stool close to us. Killian came behind the bar.

"Call me paranoid, but I swear someone followed me here. Any one of us is probably being followed – especially now that Rusty decided to grow a pair and confront us," Lark said.

"You should have told us about suspecting a tail," Killian said.

Lark made a show of looking around the bar. "We've been a little busy. It's not like I wouldn't have warned you before you left since I suggest you two ride back to the clubhouse together."

Killian skewered Lark with his gaze. "And what about our sister?"

"I'll be following her," Lark said.

My eyes widened. "She's been here ten hours already, and you won't be leaving for at least another two."

"I can follow her tonight," Tundra said.

Lark mulled it over, then nodded. "That works. Thanks, brother."

I stared at Tundra for a beat. His willingness bugged me; then again, everything about this situation bugged me.

I glanced back at Lark. "Even before Rusty came in here, why do you think this threat is aimed at you? Ivy mentioned that, but didn't give me specifics. Did you really hook up with a Corrupt Chrome ol' lady?"

Lark scooped ice into a cup and filled it with soda. "I figured the threat was aimed at me because there were plenty of people who pushed back at that zoning hearing last year. As for the Corrupt Chrome MC, I don't go after ol' ladies from any club… but that don't mean one of their women didn't decide to fuck around on her man and leave her property cut at home."

"But why would Rusty take me for Corrupt Chrome? That's whacked."

After he set the soda on a serving tray, Lark turned to me. "Those boys aren't the sharpest. And you said at church, Boyd thought they'd get paid no matter who they took."

Killian caught Lark's attention. "What precautions are you taking to stay safe?"

"Yeah," I muttered.

Lark shot us an incredulous look. "I've been livin' the MC life longer than you two have been alive. I know how to handle an asshole like Rusty."

A customer across the room caught my attention and I went to their table.

"This blows. I hate wearing a fuckin' helmet. To confirm: one flick is the signal," my brother said, fastening his helmet.

I nodded. "It's one flick. You're right about the helmets, but if Rusty's in a cage, my guess is he won't hesitate to run us off the road."

"Yeah. You really should have pulled your piece on those bastards."

I put on my helmet. "Can't change the past, man. If we're followed, I'm going east, you take Chaffee to the interstate."

We mounted our bikes and backed out of the parking lot. A vehicle pulled out onto US 90 behind us before we'd even gone half a mile. I forced myself to keep my eyes on the road. My side mirrors posed too much of a distraction. Halfway between the bar and Chaffee Road, the vehicle gained on us drastically.

I increased my speed and so did my brother.

We reached the turn off for Chaffee Road and Killian gave one flick along with a nod, put on his blinker, and veered into the right turn lane.

I twisted the throttle and sailed through the green light just as it tuned yellow.

The vehicle following us turned right, and I sent up a prayer that Killian was able to lose him. Deep down I knew that he could, but Rusty was unpredictable.

Now that nobody was following me, I took a direct route back to the clubhouse. I couldn't wait to get back to Ivy.

Twenty minutes later, I pulled into the forecourt of the Riot MC compound and parked my bike. While I stowed my helmet, my brother pulled in and eased his Harley next to me.

"I take it you lost him," I said after he shut down the engine.

He nodded and took off his helmet. "Yeah. Had to split lanes and piss off a truck driver, but I saw no sign of anyone following me once I got onto Wilson Boulevard."

"Good. Do you think he was actually following you? Maybe we're just being paranoid."

Killian shook his head. "No. He was so damned close to me, I'm lucky he didn't rear end me at the light. He tried to ride my ass getting on the Interstate, but he didn't expect me to ride between vehicles like I did."

I wiped a hand down my face. "Glad you lost him. Do you think Lark's taste for younger women actually got us into this mess?"

Killian shrugged. "I know shit gets crazy at biker rallies, and that Lark rarely misses one because that's his chance to seriously let loose. It would not surprise me if a woman wanted to get even with her ol' man and get herself some. Either way, we're in this shit now. We gotta deal with those assholes regardless."

"You're right. Are you getting a strange vibe off Tundra?"

He narrowed his eyes at me. "What kind of strange vibe? I overheard him flirting with your girl, but that was to get under your skin."

I hesitated. "Just between us, it seemed strange he was first to volunteer to patrol the lot. Then he was right there when Lark mentioned following Mickayla home."

Killian shook his head. "You're imagining shit, man. He's been around us since we were kids."

I slowly dipped my chin. "Yeah, and Mick always—"

He held up a hand. "She always ran to any of the Jax brothers because we only got to see them when they came to us. I'm not getting a strange vibe. I think you're seeing things."

I sighed. "You're right. Thanks for hearing me out. If I mentioned it to anyone else, they'd think I'm crazy."

He chuckled. "I still think you're crazy, but I get it. You wouldn't be able to air that shit out with another brother. It's all good. I won't say anything to anyone."

"Cool. Have a good night."

"I will, as long as you keep it down in your room," he said, giving me a sidelong glance.

I chuckled. "Whatever. You're the one going at it in the fuckin' hallway."

We started toward the clubhouse back door.

"How the fuck do you know that?" he asked.

"Ivy noticed the two of you. She didn't know *who* she saw, but I sure as fuck did. Neither one of us needs to see each other getting busy."

Killian laughed. "Sounds like that's your problem, not mine."

"Says the brother who just told me to keep it down in my own fuckin' room."

Killian opened the back door. "Damn right. Life's too short not to needle you every chance I get."

Upstairs, I opened the door to my room expecting to find Ivy asleep. Instead, she sat with her back to the headboard holding one of the paperbacks she picked out last night.

She set the book aside and I realized she was wearing my t-shirt.

"Did you shower already?" I asked.

"Um..." she hesitated.

"Fuck it, you're gonna shower again, babe."

"Ryan..." she started.

I shrugged out of my cut and hung it up.

Putting a knee to the mattress, I crawled toward her. "Babe, it's not like we have to pay the water bill."

Her expression softened and I watched her concern fade away. "This is true."

I woke up when three deep thuds sounded from the door. A flashback to my teen years hit me because that was how Dad knocked on my door.

"Is someone at the door?" Ivy asked, her voice thick with sleep.

"Yeah, I hope it's not who I think it is."

"Who?" she asked, sitting up.

I tugged on my gym shorts. "My dad."

Her eyes went huge. "I'm hitting the bathroom."

"Don't do that. It's better to get this out of the way."

"I'm in your shirt!" she hissed.

With a shrug, I went to the door. I opened it two inches.

Dad stood in the hall with his arms crossed. "Took you long enough."

"What are you doing here? No way you just rode into town because you'd have had to leave at two in the morning."

He shoved his hands in the pockets of his jeans. "Got in yesterday and stayed with Blood and Abby. I'm here because rumor has it, you got a concussion and I had to learn about that from someone else."

"It wasn't a concussion," I muttered.

Dad aimed his 'you're-full-of-it' look at me. "Why are you keeping me out of your room?"

I opened the door wider, looked over my shoulder, and saw that Ivy had gone in the bathroom.

"I should have known," Dad said.

"No, Dad. It's not what you're thinking."

"There's a stack of books and women's hair shit on that nightstand. Club bunnies don't stick around long enough to leave their hair bands. Pretty sure it's exactly what I think it is," he said, strolling into the room and closing the door behind him.

Even though the clubhouse walls were thin, he spoke low enough, I doubted Ivy heard him.

"Ivy, you can come out here," I said.

She opened the door. "Really? That was—" She came out of the bathroom still wearing my shirt and stopped short. For a second, she narrowed her eyes on me, which was cute as fuck. Then she aimed a sheepish grin at Dad and held out her hand. "Sorry, I'm Ivy Brummis. I didn't expect to meet you first thing in the morning."

Dad shook her hand with a chuckle. "Nice to meet you, Ivy, I'm Gamble."

"Did you bring Mom out too?" I asked.

Dad failed to hide his grunt. "No. If I had, we would have been at the bar last night causing all three of you problems."

"Who told you I got hurt?" I asked.

Dad shook his head. "You can't figure that out on your own?"

I shot him a dry look.

"Abby told Fiona, who let it slip to Cynic. He told me—"

"And you were able to keep it from Mom? That's impressive," I said.

Dad crossed his arms. "I try not to worry your mom if I don't have to."

"Right. Maybe Ivy and I can meet you downstairs."

Dad nodded. "Sounds like a plan." He looked to Ivy. "I promise I don't bite."

The moment Dad left, Ivy planted her hands on her hips. "Why would you make me meet your Dad in nothing but your shirt?"

I closed the distance between us. "You'll have to meet him today one way or the other. He pegged me having a woman in here immediately."

She sucked in a breath. "He thinks I'm one of—"

"No, he doesn't. A club girl wouldn't bring a pile of books with her."

That seemed to appease her. I continued, "Get dressed. We should go downstairs. I'm guessing Dad needs to ride back this afternoon."

"Mom's gonna be fit to be tied when she hears I met your dad before you met her." She locked eyes with me. "Is there any chance you can get tonight off? Mom's expecting us for dinner this evening. I meant to tell you when you got here last night, but you distracted me."

I grinned at the memory of how I distracted her.

"I'll see what I can do," I said, pulling on a t-shirt.

She grabbed her bag and went in the bathroom.

CHAPTER 20

TAKE CARE OF NUMBER ONE

IVY

AFTER I DRESSED IN a turquoise and gold paisley-patterned baby-doll dress, we went downstairs and found Gamble with Ricochet.

Gamble had his phone to his ear. "Yeah, sweetheart. I texted you, but if we're doin' breakfast, I can't let that wait until you decide to unlock your phone. I'm not sure Ivy can handle me and your brothers when we're hangry."

He paused, then said, "I met her ten minutes ago."

Another pause.

"No, we're at the clubhouse. If you can't haul ass over here, we might be able to hit a truck stop off I-10 at 301."

"No," Ryan and Ricochet said at the same time.

Gamble chuckled. "Seems that's off the table. Don't sweat it, I'll swing by your place when we're finished."

He grinned at whatever she said. "Love you, too, and I'll tell Ivy you said, 'hey.'"

Ricochet stared at Ryan. "Our own sister says 'hey' to her, but nothing for us. Can you believe this shit?"

Ryan grinned. "Yeah, 'cause she knows Ivy wants to bolt."

"I didn't say that," I muttered under my breath – even if deep down I absolutely *yearned* to bolt.

Ryan leaned toward me. "You didn't have to," he whispered.

Gamble tucked his phone away. "There's a Krispy Kreme off 103rd Street. Let's go there."

"Donuts?" Ricochet asked, his tone laced with judgment.

"Yeah, because we don't have the restaurant back in Biloxi."

Twenty minutes later, we were crowded into a small plastic booth and Gamble had put away his third donut.

He tipped his coffee cup at me. "How did you meet Nickel?"

My eyes darted to Killian, not that he could help me, and I turned to Nickel. "Doesn't he know?"

He gave me a half-frown, and looked to his dad. "You knew I had a concussion. Didn't Cynic mention how I got it?"

Gamble swallowed a sip of coffee and put his cup down. "Abby probably didn't pass that along to Fiona, so one of you needs to fill me in."

I shared about the first time I went looking for Lark, and meeting the triplets. Ryan took over to tell him about our abduction, and getting hit in the head.

Gamble shook his head as a smile spread across his face. "Never a dull moment with you three. Good to know some shit never changes."

I turned to Ryan. "You didn't tell me the bastard came to the bar last night. And that he followed you."

Ryan twisted his head to the side, as though he hadn't meant to mention it with me around.

Ricochet chuckled. "Don't worry. We left the bar together, and split up halfway to the interstate. Really, Rusty followed me, not him."

My eyes widened. "That's one time. What are you going to do the next time?"

"Calm down," Ryan muttered.

Suddenly, I didn't care that his dad was sitting across from us and I slowly turned to give him some side-eye.

"When are you gonna learn that phrase never works with women?" Gamble asked.

"Yeah," Ricochet chimed in, laughing.

"It's fine," Ryan said.

"Sure," I muttered, grabbed my coffee, and took a sip.

"Your mother's gonna love her," Gamble said.

I swallowed and put the cup down. These people were acting like we were a sure thing.

Then again, as long as Ryan didn't cast me aside, we probably were.

After donuts, Ryan and I rode back to the clubhouse. Ricochet followed his dad to Mickayla's place.

As I stood, waiting for Ryan to dismount, I said, "I'm sorry if I kept you from being with your sister and your dad."

He turned to me. "Don't sweat it. I'm around Mick and Kill all the time. Love seeing Dad and I'm glad you got to meet him, but I'm not missing anything."

He grabbed my hand and we went up to his room.

Once he shut his door, I asked, "Any chance I'm going to the office today?"

He twisted his hands up. "How's your boss going to react to Rusty coming in and accusing you of killing his cousins?"

My eyes slid to the side.

"Yeah, I didn't think so. Hate to ask you to do it, but if you got a vacation day, it'd be good to take one. Between the shit Rusty's spewing, and you having an obvious wound, your boss is going be suspicious and someone will call the cops."

"Great," I whispered. A thought struck me and I held up a finger. "I have an idea."

His eyebrows shot up. "Ivy—"

"No, really, hear me out. What if I go to the cops myself?"

He opened his mouth, but I put a finger to his lips.

"The less my boss knows, the better off I'll be. Plus, this way she isn't going to wonder why I might know something about a missing person—"

"People," he corrected.

"Right, but it'll keep my boss out of this, and maybe let us both get back to normal."

After a long moment, he nodded. "I heard what you said."

There was a difference between hearing me and listening to me, but I wasn't going to point that out since I wasn't sure where Ryan fell on that spectrum.

"Okay," I muttered.

"Have you ever been questioned by a police officer?"

I grimaced. "No."

"Are you good with answering the same question over and over and over, especially when there's little to no variation in how it gets asked?"

I gave a small shrug. "My answers won't change."

He aimed a lopsided smile at me. "You think that. The problem is the cop is going to be watching your body language, and what your eyes do when it's the fourth time he asks that question." He gave me another squeeze. "And no matter what, you're probably going to give *something* away."

I narrowed my eyes. "How would you know? Is that more info from your mom being a public defender?"

His head went to the side. "A little bit. More of it's from Dad and his Riot brothers. There's nothing like getting grilled by them, and they aren't even former cops. It's that they've sat through questionings with cops."

"But there ought to be something we can do to take control of this situation."

He stared into my eyes for a beat. "If you really want to go this route, I'll call Volt, see if we can get the club lawyer to go with you."

"Why would I need a lawyer?"

"Better to have someone there and *not* need them, than to not have them when you *need* them, babe."

"That makes sense," I murmured.

"How'd you get that black eye?" he asked, and from his tone of voice, I knew it was his attempt at a test run.

"I was in the wrong place at the wrong time," I said.

"That's a bad start already, Ivy."

"Well, I didn't want to say I walked into a door. That's ridiculous."

"Yeah, but cops are accustomed to women saying they walked into a door. You're too much of a good girl to go to the cops, honey. You're gonna be so tempted to admit that Boyd or Campbell hit you... That's going to throw into question why you wouldn't report it when it happened."

"You're right," I said with a hint of disappointment. I softened my tone. "I'm sorry I brought it up."

"Which one was it that hit you?"

"Boyd."

Ryan shook his head. "Should have stabbed him again."

I tipped my head back and laughed. "That's mean."

When I righted my head, I discovered him staring at me with a serious expression. "Nobody hurts you ever again, Trouble. Not in any form, no matter what."

"You sound like Chad."

"Yeah, because he told me not to hurt you and that hurt comes in many forms. I want you to explain that to me, but you can do that after we work off our donuts."

I grinned and ran my hand up to his neck. "Oh, and how are we going to do that?"

"A run," he said.

My face fell. "I don't run, Ryan."

"Today, you should try."

I chuckled. "No. When the zombies show up, I'll start running."

He huffed out a single laugh. "By then, it'll be too late."

"Yes, but your brains will be tastier than mine."

Ryan leveled a solemn look on me. "At some point, Rusty may come looking for you. If he isn't full of shit and he's got an in with the Corrupt Chrome MC, you might have more than one man coming after you. It'd be better if you could outrun someone for at least a fifty or hundred yard dash... That'll be enough of a start that you could hide, get to a vehicle, something."

I stepped out of his hold. "That's also a big part of why I carry a gun, keeps me from having to run."

"Ivy, I'm serious. You need to stay safe. Did you bring any gym clothes?"

My lips stretched out with my grimace. "Can't say that I did."

He eyed me up and down. "You can wear my shirt and a pair of my gym shorts – they've got a string that'll keep them from falling off."

My mouth dropped open. "You're serious about this. What about my gun? No joke, smart people stop in their tracks, and I'm pretty sure I proved that I don't have any problem hurting these assholes." I glanced to the side. "I should probably talk to someone about that, but..." I glanced back to him. "When it's me or him, I'll take care of number one, honey."

My phone rang with the ring tone I'd assigned to my boss. I dug it out of my purse and took the call.

She started speaking before I could even greet her. "Ivy! Did you call that new client yesterday?"

"I did, and I left word with Shayla that I did."

"He says you never spoke to him."

Yeah, seemed Rusty was adept at lying.

"Did Shayla make a note that I contacted him and he was threatening?" I asked.

"She did, but how threatening could he be over the phone? Take Anderson with you—"

"I'm sorry to interrupt, but Mr. Huntington didn't say *what* real estate service he needed. Buying, selling, rentals, he didn't mention any of it."

"Then why would he ask for you specifically?"

I had to come clean at least a little. "He thinks I know where a friend of his is, but I don't know Rusty or his friend."

Belinda sighed. "Okay, fine. This one sounds like a dud. What time will you be in today?"

"I'm taking another PTO day."

"Do you have closings scheduled?"

"No, ma'am. I'll follow up on some inspections and appraisals, but those are just phone calls."

"All right. Keep me posted, you're on track to hit a million in closings, I don't want you to lose any momentum."

A tentative smile curled my lips. "Neither do I."

I ended the call and saw Nickel lounging in bed. "Rusty called for you, I take it?"

I gave a bitter half chuckle. "More like he's telling my boss that I didn't do my job. Lying bastard."

Ryan nodded. "He probably expected that would force you to call him."

I nodded once. "What time do you have to leave?"

"Two-fifteen. Same as yesterday."

"Is there any chance I could go to my place?"

"Babe, I'd rather you be somewhere I know is safe."

"How about we go to Mom's? You can meet her, check out the lay of the land, and leave me there until tomorrow," I suggested.

He stared at me for a long moment. "I'll meet your mom, but I'm pretty sure you liked me coming to you last night. Damn sure seemed that way in the shower."

I felt my cheeks heat. "Well, sure and—"

"If I'm tailed, I can't lead them straight to your people or your home."

I twisted my lips to the side. "What if—"

"Trouble, come here."

Hearing him call me that gave me a bizarre thrill.

I wandered to the bed. He moved over and patted a spot next to him. Once I was situated on the bed, he pulled me close and kissed the top of my head.

"What's the problem? You did fine being here yesterday."

With my index finger, I drew circles on his abdomen. "Yes, but I got stir-crazy. I'm not sure I can deal with that today."

His chest rose with his deep inhale. He leaned toward the other nightstand and grabbed his phone. "Let me check something."

He tapped the screen a few times, then I heard the whoosh sound effect of a text being sent. "I think Tic is gone until Saturday. If so, you can hang in the common room. If you get uncomfortable, you come back up here."

I grinned up at him. "Thanks, Ryan."

That earned me a dry look. "Don't thank me. I haven't heard back yet."

"Right," I said, leaning a little more of my weight against him.

He chuckled. "You aren't fooling me, Trouble. It's time to run, and you're coming with me, so get up."

Ever so gently, he gave me a nudge and I stood.

He went to his closet and tossed a shirt and a pair of shorts on the bed. "That's for you. If you can't get the drawstring tight enough, we'll find some safety pins."

I eyed the shorts like they might bite me, then looked at Ryan. "Not that you care, but you're losing major cool points because of this."

He stalked to me. "Better to lose cool points than lose you."

I gave a short head shake. "You're way too good at being sweet."

His fingers came to my chin, he tipped my face up, and he kissed me short and...more sweet. "C'mon, it'll be good for you."

Chapter 21

All Sweet Again

Ryan

"You're worse than Coach Battle, and that is saying something, mister," Ivy said as she struggled to catch her breath.

"Sounds like my kind of coach."

"You would say that," she said, with her hands over her head and still breathing hard.

I grinned. "You did great, Trouble. Grab your clothes. We'll shower and I'll take you to lunch."

She put her hands on her hips. "We *just* worked off the donuts." She held her index finger up and wagged it in the air. "You go shower. I'm not exactly feeling the love for you after that."

Love?

I let that slide. It was a figure of speech. Still, I wanted to earn her love.

Dammit. How did we get here?

She shot me a quizzical look. "Would you have made me run if I were pregnant?"

My head reared back because the idea of her pregnant with another man's baby pissed me off... but the idea of her pregnant with *our* baby freaked me out and intrigued me at the same time.

"Ivy," I growled.

"Seriously, go shower. Then I will."

Rather than lunge at her and tug her body to me, I slowly closed the distance between us. She looked up at me, and I could practically see the objection written on her face.

I traced a finger from the top of her hairline down to her jaw. "You're even sexier when you're sweaty. Did I tell you that?"

Her eyes traveled up and to the side as though she didn't believe me. "Now, you have."

"Shower with me. It's not good if you let your muscles get stiff – especially since it's been a while since you ran."

Her lips tipped up in a ghost of a smile. "And it'll be another long while before I run again."

I lowered my face to hers and gave her a soft kiss. "Maybe. You're cute when you run."

She tipped her head back and laughed. "Now that's funny."

I kissed her neck.

Her sharp inhale spoke volumes, but her hand at my neck said it all.

"We gonna shower?" I murmured at her ear.

"Yeah," she breathed.

I pulled back. "Then you better grab your clothes, Trouble."

After we dressed, I checked my phone and saw that Tic had gone up to Memphis and wouldn't be back until the weekend. Ivy and I went down to the common room.

"What are you doing here?" I asked when I saw Mickayla sitting at the bar.

She tossed her hands out to the side. "Is that really how you greet your sister?"

"When you're sittin' in here alone, yes," I said.

"She isn't alone. I had to hit the supply closet to switch out the box of syrup on the Sprite because the prospects didn't do it," Tundra said, trudging into the room.

I shot my sister a look. "So you came here just to talk to Tundra?"

That got me her sly grin. "No, not that it's your business. Dad had to hit the road and my shift doesn't start until later. I thought I'd see what was going on here today. I'd hoped to find Alexandra here, but she responded to my text just as I pulled into the forecourt."

That reeked of bullshit, but at the same time, my sister hated being at loose ends.

Tundra filled a pint glass with ice, filled it with what appeared to be Sprite and set it in front of Mickayla. "There's your soda. I've gotta go. I'm working noon to nine tonight, and Turk's posted about it being Thirsty Thursday, which brings out all the cheap bastards. Later."

I had to be imagining it, but my sister looked put out that Tundra had left. Before I could question her about it, Ivy spoke.

"Where does he work?"

"Platinum's," I said.

"Okay," Ivy drawled.

Mickayla's eyes widened with an expectant look.

I turned to Ivy. "It's a gentlemen's club that the Riot owns."

Ivy did a slow nod, then turned her face to me. "And you didn't want to work there?"

I felt my face get warm and my mouth dropped open.

Mickayla laughed.

Ivy put her hand on my bicep. "Don't worry about it. You don't have to answer that."

"Oh no! You hold his feet to the fire, Ivy," Mickayla said, her humor fading fast.

I narrowed my eyes on Mick for a beat, then turned to Ivy. "My sister had the bright idea about opening a bar and grill, and trying to get two or three up and running in this area because of how spread out it is."

"That's not the only reason," Mickayla said.

I shook my head. "No, it isn't. Getting bankrolled by the chapter has something more to do with it, but you have a great business plan, and Killian and I liked her idea, we both wanted in on the ground floor."

Ivy nodded. "I see." Her gaze shifted to my sister and back to me. "Maybe I know the answer to this already, but why not do this out in Biloxi? You have tourists practically all year, and I'd think the chapter your dad is part of would be interested too."

I twisted my hands up and looked at Mick. "You want to address that?"

She shrugged. "You're right about the tourists, but that's also what makes it more difficult to get a solid footing. Finding a good location is critical, and there's no way we'd have the money for a space inside the tourist district. These days casinos are only interested in restaurants with celebrity chefs or some other celebrity tie-in. The number of restaurants that come and go is outrageous, on average. It'd be even more difficult in Biloxi. Plus, I didn't want to do this with Dad's help. It's probably splitting hairs because so many of the men here see me as a daughter they never had, too, but I don't feel like such a nepo baby."

Ivy nodded. "No, that makes a lot of sense."

Mickayla turned her phone over and checked something on the screen. Then she looked at me. "I'm hungry and it's nearly lunchtime. You two feel like going to the One Night Taco Stand? I'm hardly ever over here, and I'd rather not eat alone. Though for their tacos I'd make that sacrifice."

Ivy chuckled. "I love that place."

Mickayla shot me a devious grin. "Will you be able to survive my driving?"

I gave her a dry look. "The better question is will Ivy?"

Fifteen minutes later, we were waiting for the hostess inside the restaurant. The brightly colored walls were decked out with hand-painted pictures of famous professional wrestlers, along with frames and shadowboxes containing wrestling memorabilia. I had my arm wrapped around Ivy's shoulders and Mickayla stood close to my other side.

My sister leaned toward me, both of her hands wrapping around my arm. "Do you remember when Dad dressed up as Nacho Libre because you and Killian wanted to be pro wrestlers for Halloween?"

My lips split with a huge grin at the memory, but my chuckle was cut short when a man who'd been seated at a booth facing the door, slid out, and approached us.

His gaze swept over my sister, me, and then fixed on Ivy. My instincts went on high alert. I tightened my grip on Ivy when she tried to pull away from me.

"I knew you were lying," he said when he was halfway to us.

"Who is he?" I muttered out of the side of my mouth, doing my damnedest to ignore the urge to punch him.

"Bad ex-boyfriend," she murmured as he came closer.

He shifted his eyes to my sister and he looked her over from head-to-toe.

"Austin. Just leave us alone. There's no need for a confrontation," Ivy said.

His lips curled into a sneer at Ivy, and I had another urge to punch him.

"Outside," I said.

He looked at me with narrowed eyes, but I turned on my heel, turning Ivy with me, and Mick led the way out of the restaurant.

"Stick by my sister's side," I whispered in her ear.

She sidled up to Mickayla. I stood in front of both of them.

Austin stopped in front of me and stared. He was three inches shorter than me, and had the lean frame of a swimmer. I had the advantage over him, no question, which was why I wanted this to happen out on the sidewalk. He shifted to walk around me, but I shifted with him.

He sighed. "This doesn't concern you."

"The hell it doesn't," I said.

He leaned to the side and focused on a point beyond me. I assumed he'd locked eyes with Ivy. "Looks like you're down with a threesome after all, you lying bitch."

If there were cameras, I didn't care. Suddenly, all I saw was red, and I threw a quick, powerful right jab to his mouth.

"What the fuck, asshole?" he yelled, grabbing his lip.

"Apologize," I demanded.

He looked at me like I had two heads. "For what?"

"Nobody calls Ivy a bitch, and damn sure not a lying bitch. Apologize to her, *now*."

He pulled his hand away from his lip, and I was surprised at how bloody it was. "Fuck. I'm suing you."

"No. You're not. You came at her in a threatening way inside, and then you hurled insults at her. Turn around, pay your bill, go home and forget all about Ivy."

Austin narrowed his eyes again. "Man, I just want what you got. Two gorgeous women and—"

"Shut the fuck up before I bloody your nose, too."

"I'm his sister. This isn't what you think it is, but that would require you to actually think," Mickayla said and from her volume, I knew she'd stepped closer to my back.

I blew out a breath and did my best not to tell her to move backward. She'd never let me hear the end of it, and I didn't want to take my eyes off this douchebag.

His eyes lit and focused on Mickayla. "Are you free—"

"Shut your fucking mouth," I said.

"You're delusional," Mickayla said at the same time.

"This is mortifying," Ivy murmured so low, I wasn't sure anyone else heard her.

"Go home, Austin," I suggested, but it sounded like an order.

He glared at me, and since I'd become accustomed to the signs, I anticipated his next move. After a beat, his fist came toward my torso, and in the nick of time I caught it in my right hand.

I squeezed his fist hard. "You're not good at this, Austin. I deal with assholes like you nearly every day. Get the fuck outta here."

The way he silently groaned reminded me of a dog we had when we were kids. She'd give short groans to let you know how unhappy she was that you weren't doing what she wanted. Austin didn't like that I had his fist in a vice grip and he hadn't put me in my place.

Finally, after one more semi-silent groan, he pulled his fist back, I let it go and with a petulant glare he turned around to leave.

"I guess we have to find somewhere else to go," Ivy muttered.

Mickayla threw her a grin and chuckled. "I wouldn't be so sure."

A moment later, Jasmine, Rafferty's younger sister came out and approached us. She wasn't wearing her waitress apron, so I guessed she was working the bar. "I'm supposed to tell you three to leave, but screw that. It's about time someone gave him what he deserves. He's been a jerk since the first time I had to serve him."

"I told him to leave, so you might want to make sure he pays his tab."

Jasmine flung her long brown hair over her shoulder. "I'm not waiting tables on the main floor, so he won't be stiffing me. But if you need me to march him out, I'm on it. October's right around the corner."

She turned on her heel and went back inside.

"Why is she talking about October?" Ivy asked.

Before I could say I'd tell her later, Mickayla spoke. "She wrestles at Bike Week and Biketoberfest. Her mom was really good back in the day, and Jasmine's just as good, maybe better, but if you tell Trixie that, I'll deny it and throw you right under the bus."

"Okay," Ivy said.

The door swung open wildly. Austin prowled out with a sandy-brown haired woman following closely behind him. She looked our way. "Austin, tell me what's goin' on. Your lip is bleeding!" She looked me up and down. "Did he do that to you?"

"Let's go, Zoe."

She stopped and stared at us.

"I said, let's go, Zoe."

She looked back at Austin, then narrowed her eyes on us for a beat before she followed him into the parking lot.

"All right. Crisis averted. Let's get inside, because otherwise a new crisis is going to develop when I become hangry," Mickayla said. Then she hurried past me and back inside the restaurant.

"I'm so sorry," Ivy said.

I turned around. The mixture of embarrassment and shame on her face made me want to chase after Austin so I could hit him again. "Come here, babe."

"I'm right in front of you."

"I've got a loose hold on my temper right now. I'd never take it out on you, but I need you to come here."

She came to me, slow and almost skittish.

I cupped her jaw with both hands. "You have *nothing* to be sorry about. You and that jackass are done, and everything that happened is on him."

Her head tilted. "You were the one who hit him."

"Because he insulted you – and my sister – but it was mainly because of you."

She bit back her smile. "You're being all sweet again."

"There's nothing mortifying about what happened. Not for you. He's an imbecile. I'm just glad you kicked him to the curb."

She nodded.

I grabbed her hand. "Let's go get some food."

Chapter 22

Good Choices

Ivy

"I took the liberty of ordering you a gimlet. Rumor has it, you prefer vodka to tequila," Mickayla said when Ryan and I sat down.

"Why?" I asked.

She lowered her chin while giving me a pointed look. "It's always stressful to run into an ex. I can see exactly why you tossed him aside." She held up a finger toward Ryan – who didn't look too happy from what I could see from the corner of my eye. "None of what happened is a reflection on you, but I imagine you're stressed after that bullshit."

I nodded. "Thanks. That's thoughtful of you."

"Was it Tundra who told you she prefers vodka to tequila?" Ryan asked.

Mickayla smiled at him, and I admired her anew. Her smile looked exactly like Ryan's, and her eyes were downright mischievous. "I never reveal my source, and just to say, he wasn't the only man there that night."

Even though she wasn't waiting tables, Jasmine brought out our drinks along with a basket of chips and salsa. Seemed Mickayla had ordered a sweet tea for Ryan and a water for herself.

As soon we were alone again, Ryan looked up from his menu to his sister. "You're getting awful chummy with Tundra."

Mickayla set her menu down. "Seriously? I've known him – no, *we've* known him since we were kids. I wouldn't say I'm getting chummy with him, and besides, he's involved with someone."

"Could fool me," Ryan muttered.

Mickayla focused on her menu. "Not every brother makes good choices about women."

Ryan closed his menu. "How would you know he hasn't made good choices?"

Mickayla's expression fell. "He told me." She shook her head. "We're not doing this right now because there's nothing going on with me and Tundra."

This exchange made me recall one of my first impressions about Ryan: that he had an issue with women who dated older men. I wondered if this was the reason why, but I hoped it wasn't. If Mickayla was attracted to one of the other bikers, it seemed like that wouldn't be a problem regardless of age... but I had to bide my time before asking about this.

I picked up a tortilla chip. "Do the two of you get to go to Biketoberfest? Or will Lark leave you in charge of the restaurant?"

Mickayla sipped her water. "I won't be going to Daytona." She tipped her head at Ryan. "Now that he and Killian are patched members, I'm not sure if they'll have to stick around On a Lark or not."

Ryan gently bumped his shoulder into mine. "Why do you ask?"

I shrugged. "No reason, really. I was surprised that there's women wrestling there."

Mickayla laughed. "Almost anything goes at a biker rally. Pretty sure what Ryan meant to ask you is, if you want to go in October."

I shook my head. "That wasn't why I asked. After missing the last couple days of work, I'll be lucky if I'm not working every weekend in October."

I felt Ryan's eyes on me. "Why?"

After a sip of my gimlet, I said, "My boss is intent that I hit a specific milestone in sales for this month. Right now, I should be able to pull that off, but if I don't, there will be even more pressure to really ramp up in October."

"Do you think you'll hit your goal this month?" Mickayla asked.

I pressed my lips together. "Not to jinx anything, but it is dependent on meeting with new clients."

Mickayla shot a pointed look at Ryan. "How long do you think this is going to continue?"

Ryan sighed. "Hard to say. Rusty made his approach, but we don't know when the Corrupt Chrome MC will show."

Mickayla shook her head and grabbed a tortilla chip. "I don't see why the brothers need to wait on another MC to arrive before you just make Rusty go away."

I squeezed the lime wedge into my drink. "Something that's been bothering me is that Rusty knew Boyd's dead, but he didn't report it. What's up with that? You would think it would be in the news."

Ryan pulled his phone out. "You're right. And it makes me wonder what he did with Boyd because a funeral director isn't going to take a body without a death certificate or some proof shit's on the up and up."

"I guess we should have—" Ryan's finger on my lips cut me off. "Sorry," I whispered.

He gave a single nod. "You're right, we should have dealt with the other."

Mickayla grinned at us. "Look at you two... Talking about something without mentioning it."

"Whatever," Ryan muttered, focused on his phone, and sent out a text.

***

"Are you sure this is the last thing we need before another inspection?" Mr. Willamet, my client, asked.

"Yes, sir. I'll get the second inspection scheduled within the next two weeks and let you know exactly which date," I said.

My client groused a little more about the process, and once I had him appeased, I ended the call.

After lunch, Mickayla had dropped us at the clubhouse and Ryan took off for work on his bike. I came down to the vacant common room, and returned some phone calls.

A red-haired woman strolled into the room and smiled at me. "You must be Ivy."

"I am," I said.

She sat on the couch that was adjacent to mine. "I'm Abby. You're just as stunning as Blood said you are."

My eyes widened. "He said that? We only met once."

She chuckled. "Once is usually all it takes." Her focus concentrated on the side of my face. "Your black eye is healing well. If you have the right kind of concealer, you can hide it from most people."

"What kind of concealer would you recommend?"

Her eye brow ticked up and down. "The good kind. I'll see if I have some in my room."

"That's very nice of you, but I don't want to impose."

She shot me a closed lip smile. "Girlie, you're not imposing. You're part of the family now even if Nickel doesn't claim you, because I heard about your connection to Lark." Her expression turned wistful. "Blood and I were there when Zeus dared him to become a donor. It's surreal to be hanging with you now."

I closed my eyes for a beat as her words ran through my mind. "He really did that on a dare?"

She turned her hands up and spread her arms out. "I stopped trying to figure the brothers out a long time ago. They do what they do, and I just pray nobody gets arrested." She paused. "Or shot."

My eyes widened again.

She laughed. "I screwing with you. I can't remember the last time a Jacksonville brother got shot." She held up a finger, then pointed it at me. "Now, Nickel's dad is another story. Gamble got shot going after the men who hurt Nickel's mom."

"Really?" I whispered.

"Yeah. I'm not trying to freak you out. I'm saying you never know what's gonna happen around here."

I smiled. "Yeah, I've caught onto that."

The back door slammed open and closed. Volt and Cal stormed into the common room with thunderous expressions.

Abby looked at them as though nothing was amiss. "What's going on, Volt?"

Volt's anger softened slightly with his surprise. "Didn't expect to see you here."

Abby sat a little straighter and stared at Volt. "Yeah, but something's up."

Volt sighed and looked at me. "Everyone's fine. There was a drive-by shooting at the bar about fifteen minutes ago. Nobody was hit, but two of the windows are all busted to shit. The bar and grille's been closed until the cops have gathered all their evidence, and finished questioning everyone on the scene."

My stomach twisted. "You're sure nobody got hit."

Volt looked at me. "Yeah. If Nickel could call you, he would. As it stands, it's gonna be a while."

Abby aimed an expectant look at Cal. "What are you doing here? I'm guessing you're gonna get the windows handled."

Cal looked at Abby like she should know better. "Can't do shit until the investigation's done. In the meantime the prospects are gonna help out and I got to make sure they know what they're doing."

Abby turned to me. "What'd I tell you? There's no telling what's gonna happen next around here."

———

I sat at one of the picnic tables on the back patio of the clubhouse to get some fresh air. It took serious willpower not to call Ryan. I'd never considered myself to be impatient, but this was killing me.

The moment my cell rang, I snatched it up, grinning at Ryan's name on the display.

"Are you okay?" I said when the call connected.

His low chuckle came over the line. "I'm fine, Trouble."

"Yeah, Volt said you were, but... Are you really?"

"Yes, sweetheart. I'll be leaving in a few minutes. Let your mom know, we might be late."

My head tipped back and I stared at the puffy afternoon clouds. "Oh God. I forgot all about that." I righted my head. "I can just tell her we need to cancel."

"No, Ivy. If you try to reschedule, she'll want to know why and I don't want you lying."

"Fine," I said.

"Are you in my room?" he asked.

"No, I'm sitting outside on the concrete patio."

I heard him blow out a breath. "There shouldn't be anything to worry about at the clubhouse, but I'd feel better if you were inside."

My head bobbed in a small nod. "All right. I can do that."

"Good. I'll be there soon."

<hr>

After sending Mom a text letting her know we might be a little late, I spent thirty-five torturous minutes in the common room waiting. The moment I heard the engine noise of a bike pulling in, I dashed out the back door. Ryan pulled his bike into a spot, put the kickstand down, powered down the engine, and swung off.

I didn't run to him, exactly, but I performed a decent twenty-yard dash.

He watched me approach with a boyish grin on his face while he shook his head. "I told you I'm fine on the phone, Ivy."

I slid my hands along his neck. "Well, you'll have to forgive me for being worried about my man being at a drive-by today."

He kissed me fast, turned so we were side-by-side, and we headed into the clubhouse.

Volt wandered toward us from the end of the corridor. "Church first thing in the morning."

Ryan nodded, and guided me up the stairs with his hand at the small of my back.

Once we were in his room, I turned to him. "Are you sure you're okay? I mean, being shot at has to be traumatic no matter how it—"

He stepped into my space and kissed me silent. His tongue slid inside my mouth, while he wrapped one arm around my waist and the other around my shoulders. I slid my hands under his cut and up his back.

He pulled away, but kept hold of me. "No, it's no fun having my day ruined by a coward like Rusty."

I narrowed my eyes. "How do you know it was Rusty?"

His lips pressed together for a beat. "Who else would do it? The location is well away from downtown. And he was there the night before telling us the bar's days were numbered. The upside is that the bar's closed for now, and your mom's dinner isn't a problem."

My eyes darted to the side. "I'm guessing a drive-by means you're still going to keep me from going to my place, aren't you?"

He shook his head. "No, tonight we're staying at your place."

I couldn't hold back my beaming smile. "No matter how much I want to question you, I'm not going to, because I love that sound of that."

He nodded. "I'm hitting the shower."

Mom's house was in the heart of the Town of Orange Park. She lived in a ranch house built in the late seventies with a kidney bean pool in the back. The driveway was L-shaped and Ryan pulled his bike up the drive in a huge arc so it was parked parallel to the garage.

"Are you trying to block Mom in?" I asked jokingly as I got off the bike.

He swung off and smiled. "No. I'm trying to make it less obvious there's a bike in her drive."

He really wasn't fooling around about safety.

After he grabbed a bottle of wine from his saddlebag, we walked around to the front door. Mom opened it before I could dig out my keys.

"I don't mean to seem eager, but your motorcycle announces you," she said.

Ryan chuckled. "That's the idea, Mrs. Brummis." He held out a hand, introduced himself, and offered Mom the wine.

"Thank you for this, you shouldn't have. It's great to met you, Ryan. Come in."

Mom led us through the living room. "I didn't know what you like, but I went to Costco today and got their shrimp cocktail and there are spring rolls coming out of the oven soon."

Mid-way to the kitchen, I stopped, stared, and felt my heart lurch. I hadn't been to Mom's house since late August. A decorative mirror had been replaced by seven pictures printed on square canvases. All of them pictures of Mom and Jeff, and three of them from a trip the three of us took shortly after Jeff's cancer diagnosis. The images were so bright and vibrant – at once they felt like both a betrayal and a comfort.

"Mom, when did you get these printed?" I asked.

"A month ago, sweetie. Chad helped me hang them on Labor Day."

I couldn't believe Chad hadn't told me about that.

Mom's face was filled with concern. "Darlin', I loved him. I always will, and honestly, I wished I'd thought to do something like that years ago because we all need a reminder of the good times."

I nodded and fought against my tears.

"I'll give you a moment, then you two can come in the kitchen."

"You good?" Ryan murmured in my ear.

I took a deep breath. "No... I mean, yeah. I will be. It's cool. I just hadn't seen them."

We wandered into the kitchen.

Mom's eyes focused on my face. "Young lady, you said you got hit over the head, not in the face."

So much for Abby's make up techniques. Then again, I thought it was a futile endeavor, anyway.

"Mom—"

She aimed a pointed look at Ryan and then me. "You said there was more to it, but you couldn't get into it on the phone. Spill, Ivy Felicia."

My lips pursed. "I don't know why you looked at Ryan that way, but he didn't hit me."

Mom crossed her arms. "Where is the man who did, then?"

"Dead. And that's really all you need to know," I said.

She leaned against the counter. "Dead?"

"Yes, Mom. That's why we couldn't go to the cops, because there are a lot of questions we wouldn't be able to answer."

"Not willing to answer, you mean."

"Not without incriminating ourselves," Ryan said.

Mom shook her head. "I cannot believe you're hiding this from the law."

"Mrs. Brummis, if I could go to the law without Ivy finding herself in trouble, I'd do it right now. But it simply isn't feasible under the circumstances."

"Why can't you tell them what you did and leave her out of it?" she asked.

"Because we worked together," I said.

Mom aimed a stern glare my way.

"We did," I added.

"So you say," Mom said.

Ryan shrugged. "She has a way with a frying pan."

I choked on my laughter.

Mom closed her eyes and sighed, then meandered to the other side of the kitchen where her wine glass sat. She pulled down another glass and poured some pinot grigio for me and topped off her glass. "Do you drink white wine or would you prefer a Shock Top?" she asked Ryan.

"Shock Top works, thanks."

Mom grabbed a beer and handed it to him. "Are you doing anything about what happened? Are you avoiding the police in order to save your pride?"

"Mom, seriously?"

Mom turned her attention to me. "My girl, it's easy to see why he appeals to you, but murder is as serious as it gets. You could lose everything."

"It wouldn't be murder seeing as we were defending ourselves. Aggravated manslaughter - maybe, but her hitting either one with the skillet didn't kill them," Ryan said.

Mom's eyes popped with alarm. "Wait! There was more than one of them?"

"We could have taken just one of them," I said without thinking.

"Ivy!" Mom cried.

"Campbell wasn't that smart," I muttered.

"It's no reason to kill him."

"From what Boyd said, Campbell liked to... sexually assault women... so I got the impression she would have been in much more trouble if I hadn't been there."

Mom sighed and stayed focused on Ryan. "Why hasn't she been staying at her place?"

"You could ask me that," I said into my wine glass.

After a fake smile, Mom said, "I want to hear his side of it."

"I thought they'd be able to find her because I expected her to own her home. Since she doesn't, in theory it makes it a little bit harder for them to find her address. But only a little."

"First time renting has helped you," Mom said.

"But Rusty posed as a client at her office – so he knows how to get to her," Ryan said.

"For what it's worth, we're staying at my place tonight," I said.

Mom arched a brow at Ryan. "She has a gun, you could let her stay alone."

Ryan tipped his head to the side. "I could, but I got her into this mess, I'm getting her out of it."

"Um-hmm. Sounds like there's a little bit of pride here after all."

Ryan set his beer on the counter. "Perhaps, but like it or not, Ivy and I have a bond now. Everything I learn about her I like enough that I know I'd be a fool not to see what might develop between us."

Mom stared at him long and hard. "That almost sounds rehearsed."

I gasped.

Ryan laughed out loud. "It isn't. The timing is awful, but life never runs according to our own timing."

Mom dipped her head and her expression softened. "I know that's the truth."

"I would imagine so," Ryan murmured.

The oven timer went off.

"You want me to get those?" I asked.

"No, sweetie. You can get some plates down instead."

CHAPTER 23

SAVORING

RYAN

MEETING A WOMAN'S PARENTS always felt like a grind, but with Ivy's mom I enjoyed it. She cared deeply about her daughter, and I couldn't fault her for grilling me about all the shit swirling around us. By the time we finished dinner, I thought I'd won her over.

Maybe.

"How often do you visit your parents in Mississippi?" Debra asked.

"Not as often as Mom would like, but Dad came to town last night and had breakfast with me, Ivy, and my brother Killian."

No sooner were the words out of my mouth than I realized I should have kept that to myself.

Ivy's annoyed expression almost made me laugh, but I knew that would only make things worse.

Debra turned to Ivy. "You met his father already?"

"Yeah, Mom. Not much I could do about it, and it wasn't like you could drop work to come to Krispy Kreme."

Debra twisted her lips. "You're right." She focused on me again. "I'll tell you what I told her last night. This is moving awful fast in my opinion."

"It really isn't, Mom."

Debra sipped her wine. "Let me rephrase. This is more serious than I expected so soon."

I nodded. "You're right, but that's life. I won't hurt her, and Chad warned me, too. I'd never go out of my way to do her wrong. Damn sure not like that jackass we ran into today."

Debra glanced at Ivy.

"We ran into Austin at One Night Taco Stand."

"Bet that went well."

I shrugged. "He left with a bloody lip, so I'd say it did."

Debra's eyes widened. "Do you solve everything with violence?"

I chuckled. "When someone insults her or threatens her, yeah, violence is my go-to."

Debra sat back in her chair and brought both hands to her mouth, looking almost like she was praying. Finally, she dropped her hands. "I disagree with violence most of the time, but...I'm glad you're someone who isn't going to let her take any shit."

I nodded once. "That's the general idea."

She shifted her gaze to Ivy. "I see why Chad likes him so much."

"Ivy. Shit, you're killing me, woman," I groaned.

Her mass of dark curls were draped over my thigh and I gathered that hair in my hand so I could better watch her suck my cock. She looked up at me, and the sultry gleam in her striking green eyes hit me hard.

"Get up here, Ivy," I ordered.

She released my dick from her mouth, but kept pumping me with her hand while she ran her tongue around the crown. "I'm focused, Nickel," she whispered, then took me deep.

My head tilted back and a familiar sensation built low in my spine. In a few moments my balls would tighten and I refused to come down her throat.

I let go of her hair, and slid both hands under her armpits and pulled her up.

"Ryan! You had to be close," she said, trying to wriggle away from me.

Part of me wanted her to get back to sucking me off, while another part of me wanted to tussle with her because the idea of wrestling with her made me even harder.

I shifted my body weight and took her to her back. "Baby, I was damn close, but I'm not shooting down your throat tonight. Spread those gorgeous legs for me."

She opened her legs and lined up my cock with her pussy. Nothing felt better than this: the first moment I entered her sweet, wet heat. It sucked pulling out of her when things were finished which was why I was always so slow and gentle about it... because it was the last thing I wanted to do.

"What are you waiting for, Nickel?" she asked.

"Not waiting, I'm savoring, baby," I said, grabbing her thighs.

I leaned up so I could watch my cock slide inside her.

She wiggled her hips, trying to get more of me.

My eyes met hers. "No, Trouble. You take what I give you."

"Honey...please," she pleaded.

This woman. I couldn't fucking deny her.

I lifted her legs a little higher and drove inside to the hilt.

She bit one half of her lower lip, then whispered, "Yes."

"You're mine," I said on an outward stroke.

My body stilled. I'd never thought that let alone said it to a woman.

"You bet I am," she said, her gorgeous green eyes locked with mine.

Damn. Why did that hit so deep?

"Ivy," I groaned on an inward thrust.

"Yeah," she breathed.

I lowered myself down so we were almost nose to nose. "Do you mean that?"

Her eyes searched mine. "Yes. I'm yours – I wouldn't be doing this with someone else."

I cupped where our bodies connected. "I know this is mine." I dragged my hand up to her heart. "Is this mine? Are *you* really mine?"

"Yes, but—"

My eyes reflexively flared and she paused before a coy smile flitted across her face.

"But that's contingent on *you* being *mine*, too. Us only children aren't known for sharing."

I withdrew and slammed back into her on a laugh. "Yeah, Trouble. You won't have to share me. I don't pull that shit."

"Good. Now, fuck me like I'm really yours."

I leaned down and kissed her. Rather than fucking her the way she wanted, I made love to her slow and easy.

"Ryan," she whined.

"Go with it, Ivy."

"I need more."

I picked up the pace a touch and ground into her. She flexed her inner muscles, squeezing my cock and I drew in a sharp breath. Her hands gripped my ass, another sign to go harder, but I kept it at the same pace.

I palmed her breast and played with her nipple. She moaned, then she bit her lip again.

Her hips bucked to meet my thrusts and I couldn't control myself. The slow pace gave way to a much faster rhythm. I slid my hand down to her pussy and rubbed my thumb over her clit.

"Finally!" she whispered.

Her head tipped back, and she moaned as her pussy spasmed around me. My balls drew up and I heard my blood roaring in my ears when I came.

***

Ivy turned the bathroom light off and walked to the bed, naked. I loved watching her nude figure move around my room.

"The way you look at me is good for my ego, mister."

"You're gorgeous. There's no way you don't know that."

She gave me a closed-lip smile, then climbed into bed next to me. "Whether I know it or not doesn't change the fact that some men tear a girl down at a very young age."

I felt my shoulder get tense. "You need to elaborate, sweetheart."

"Before Mom met Jeff, she was with Ed. He lived with us... until she found out how terrible he was to me."

"To you?"

She nodded and put her hand on my forearm. "He's long, long gone, Ryan."

"How was he terrible to you?"

She leaned up on her elbow and twisted toward me. "Not like that. He yelled at me, like in my face yelling at me when I was six years old. It always made me cry, which only made him angrier... and yell more."

"Jesus."

Her hesitation concerned me, but I forced myself to wait her out. Finally, she said, "He'd tell me to stop crying, and that never worked. Thinking happy thoughts never worked because my tears would just flow like a faucet."

"Fucking hell," I muttered on a sigh.

"Are you angry?"

I leaned up on an elbow to look her in the eyes. "Baby, of course I'm angry, but not at you. That jackass never heard one of my favorite quotes, 'The cure for anything is salt water: sweat, tears, or the sea.'"

Her eyes got shiny and she smiled. "Oh my God. If it weren't for referencing sweat, that would be my new favorite quote, too."

I chuckled silently. "You felt better after our run, no matter what you tell me."

She shook her head. "I'll never admit that."

"Seriously, Ivy. You're gorgeous. Whatever that asshole did to tear you down, I'm gonna build you back up."

She cupped my cheek. "I'm sensing that. Seeing as we had a pretty big conversation earlier, I'm just gonna say it. I'm falling in love with you, Ryan. And that isn't the sex talking."

I pulled her closer. "Yeah, Ivy. I'm right there with you. I didn't expect you to say you were mine, but when you did it shifted the axis of my world. I love you, and if there are any more assholes like Austin out there, I have to brush up on my boxing."

She giggled. "Your boxing skills are just fine, sir."

"Are there any other ex's around?"

"No. The other one left town."

"Good. Your mom will come around, you know."

She lifted her head and looked me in the eye. "She likes you."

I arched a brow. "She was cordial, and it's fine—"

"No, she doesn't understand your way of life," she said with a head shake.

I ran my hand up and down her back. "She doesn't have to get my world, you do."

"You're right, but still, she'll come around."

My mind drifted to memories of my mom's mother. Even as a kid, I knew she didn't get the MC world. Debra didn't seem as tightly wound as Grandma Carlton, but time would tell.

Ivy grinned up at me and kissed my jaw. "Wanna go again…to make things more official? Or are you too tired?"

I flipped her to her back. "Did you say 'too tired?' Woman, you're the one who's older. You don't ever have to ask me twice about going again."

CHAPTER 24

SAY NO

IVY

FRIDAY MORNING I DECIDED to pair my vintage CBGB t-shirt with my khaki shorts when someone knocked on the door.

"Ivy! It's me, Mickayla."

I opened the door and saw Mickayla and Alexandra standing in the hall.

Alexandra gave me a little wave. "Hey, I'm here too. Not to derail her plan, but you should say no."

Mickayla pushed inside the room and shot a dirty look over her shoulder at Alexandra. "It's not a bad idea."

Alexandra followed her inside and shut the door. "It isn't a good idea either, so where does that leave us?"

Mickayla focused on me. "You still aren't going to work today, right?"

"That's right."

"I thought the three of us could go check out the house where you and Ryan were taken."

I turned my head a bit and shot her some side eye. "Why would we do that?"

"A few reasons," she said, then held up a finger. "One, we could see if they're using that house for anything else." She held up another finger. "Two, we could check on the other asshole, see if they moved the body."

"Bleh," Alexandra said.

Mickayla shook her head at Alexandra. "And three, we can find out if the other vehicle is still there or not."

Alexandra shook her head. "That doesn't even count as a reason. Like I said, you should say no."

I cocked a brow at Alexandra. "But it sounds like you're going along with it even if you don't like it."

She dipped her chin to concede the point. "I'm not going to let her run off on her own. It's bad enough they took you and Nickel."

"Speaking of him, I should tell him where I'm going."

"And he'll put the kibosh on this. The brothers are in church, it's not even ten o'clock, there's no better time to do this," Mickayla said.

"Our time would be better spent..." Alexandra trailed off at the expectant look on Mickayla's face.

"Doing what? Twiddling our thumbs? This is basically recon," Mickayla said.

"That could go bad," Alexandra muttered.

"Always so negative," Mickayla said.

"Nope. Just being real," Alexandra said.

Mickayla sighed. "We don't even have to get out of my car."

"I haven't had breakfast yet. We can leave in an hour," I suggested to buy some time.

Mickayla gave me a shrewd look. "I see what you're doing. If we run this by Ryan all the brothers are gonna lose their minds. Put on your shoes and we'll hit Wawa – you can get breakfast while I fill up my car."

Alexandra glanced at me. "I told you to just say no. There's still time to change your mind."

I pressed my lips together and thought about it. A big part of me was curious about the property. Ryan had convinced me not to go to the cops, but I hated waiting on these people to make the next move. Like Mickayla said, we wouldn't even get out of the car, so any danger was minimal – assuming we found the place.

I shrugged. "There's a really good chance we won't find the property. The sun was setting when we left, and the truck had navigation to guide us. Between the relief of leaving there and the concussion, I'm not sure I'll know where the turn off is."

"Which makes this an even bigger waste of time," Alexandra muttered.

Mickayla turned to her. "Consider it going for a ride... Just not with your old man."

Alexandra rolled her eyes. "I should have signed up for Friday classes."

<hr>

My cell rang while Mickayla hung a left-hand turn onto US90. Ryan's name lit the display.

"If that's my brother, don't answer it," Mickayla advised.

I was sitting in the backseat behind Mickayla and I locked eyes with her in the rear view mirror. "That'll really piss him off."

In the passenger seat, Alexandra turned to Mickayla. "Yeah, did you think about that? You're going to make them have their first fight."

Mickayla shook her head. "I am not. He's smitten with her."

I choked on my laughter. The notion of Ryan being smitten was ludicrous, then I hit the green icon and put the phone to my ear. "Hi, honey."

"Where are you?" he asked in a measured tone.

Too measured.

"I'm with your sister."

He blew out a breath. "That tells me *who* you're with, but not where, Ives."

"Please don't call me that."

He sighed. "I'm sorry, sweetheart, but I'm worried."

The 'sweetheart' endearment threw me, and I blurted. "We just got off I-10 at Devoe and we're headed west on US90."

Alexandra turned in her seat. "Put it on speaker," she whispered.

I did as she asked.

"Tell Mick to go to the restaurant," Ryan said.

"I'm not doing that," Mickayla said.

"Mickayla, you don't have the first fuckin' clue about what you're getting into with this shit," Ryan said.

"I have some idea since the cops questioned me yesterday, just the same as you."

"The goal is to keep Ivy out of this, Mick. Corrupt Chrome MC doesn't need to know who she is," he said.

I didn't want the two of them to bicker. "To be fair, I don't think we're going to find the right turn off, Ryan. I was unconscious when we got there, and the sun was setting when we left. This is more like a Sunday drive on a Friday morning."

"Which is why she should go to the restaurant," Ryan said.

"Ryan, it's fine," Mickayla said. "We're taking a drive, and I'll bring her back to On a Lark when we're done."

"Do you have your gun with you Ivy?" Ryan asked.

My lips twisted with my grimace. "Um..."

"Goddamn it," he bit out.

"I have mine," Mickayla said.

"And I have a knife," Alexandra muttered.

"Fuck, you got Bluff's woman in on this too," Ryan muttered.

"Yes, we need to go. Talk soon, baby brother," Mickayla said and made a cutting motion at her throat for me to hang up.

"Bye, Ryan," I said because hanging up on him was also certain to make him mad.

We rode in silence for a bit.

After we passed a distribution center not far from the bar, Mickayla said, "Once we pass On a Lark, start a timer on your phone. I heard Ryan say they took you somewhere twenty-five minutes west of the restaurant. That will help us find the turn off."

West-bound traffic was minimal at ten-thirty in the morning, and we passed the bar and grill after another five minutes.

I set the timer on my phone. "T-minus twenty-five-ish minutes."

"Cool. We can pull a U-ie in twenty-four minutes," Alexandra muttered.

"Have a more positive attitude, Lex," Mickayla said and turned the music down.

"I'm positive this should be over after twenty-five minutes. And how old are you? Eighty-six? Lowering the music volume isn't going to help us see better," Alexandra chided.

"Says the woman who wants my whole car to rattle with the bass notes," Mickayla said.

I laughed. "You two are worse than me and Chad."

Alexandra looked over her shoulder at me. "Keep it up, you're gonna be roped into this soon enough... Trouble."

I felt my eyes get wide as my jaw dropped. "How do you know—"

Mickayla's eyes met mine in the rear view mirror. "The brothers talk. More than you'd ever imagine."

After a few minutes, Alexandra sighed. "This is even more boring than driving west on I-10."

"Keep your eyes peeled. I'm looking for a dirt road, and that's about all I know," Mickayla said.

"It's only been ten minutes. We have at least another ten minutes of driving before we start getting close," I said.

We rolled through the intersection of US90 with a county road in Sanderson.

"My breakfast is fading fast, we should stop at that truck stop when we're done," Alexandra said.

"You should have gotten a Sizzli," Mickayla said.

A vague memory of Ryan driving us in the opposite direction hit me and my stomach lurched. I really hadn't expected us to be able to find the place where Ryan and I had been taken. The thought of going there wasn't sitting too well with me.

"You're remembering stuff, aren't you?" Mickayla asked and I saw she was watching me in the rear view mirror.

"Watch the road, please," I murmured.

As the counter neared the twenty-five minute mark, only dense woods lined the road.

"I'd ask if you see anything, but there's nothing to see," Alexandra said, staring out the passenger window.

I spied the outline of a mailbox in the distance and I bit my lip. "This might be it, but... maybe we should just pull that U-turn."

Mickayla turned on her blinker, slowed down, and turned onto the lane. The farther her small sedan bounced along the dirt path, the more I knew we were in the right place.

One hundred yards later the path veered to the left and I saw the ramshackle farm house. Unlike Alexandra, my breakfast hadn't faded; it threatened to make a comeback.

"We really shouldn't do this," I muttered.

My spine stiffened when I heard the roar of a motorcycle approaching from behind.

"If Ryan has come to get you, I'm going lose it," Mickayla said.

Alexandra turned in her seat. Her hazel eyes widened with a mixture of alarm and curiosity. "That isn't your brother. I can't imagine why they sent Tundra to come after us."

"Tundra?" Mickayla said, her eyes darting to her side mirror. "Shit," she whispered.

"Isn't that better than your brothers showing up?" I asked.

"No...and yes," she said.

"You're being clear as mud," Alexandra said.

"Aren't you going to stop?" I asked.

"Hell, no. We made it this far, we're going to check on that dead body that you and my brother hid."

Alexandra pointed a finger at Mickayla. "None of the brothers are talking about the specifics of what happened out here, so how did you hear about that?"

"There are instances when Lark and my brothers act like I'm invisible. Most of the time that doesn't bother me, and then there are the times I use it to my advantage. Like now," Mickayla said.

The roar of Tundra's bike got louder, then I saw him pass us and pull to a stop about twenty yards in front of the car.

"That stubborn man," Mickayla muttered as she stopped the car and put it in park.

She immediately unbuckled and exited the car. The way she stormed over to Tundra I could practically see her anger rolling off her in waves.

"That's quite the reaction," I said without thinking.

Alexandra gave a dry chuckle. "You catch on fast, Ivy."

I unbuckled my seat belt. "Well, since we're here. I guess we should take a look around."

Alexandra twisted her hands up, then unbuckled and got out of the car, too.

Tundra looked past Mickayla, shaking his head. "Get back in that car, ladies."

Mickayla glanced over her shoulder at us, then scowled at Tundra. "It won't take that long. Help us or don't, but we're doing this."

Tundra crossed his arms on his burly chest and scowled down at Mickayla. His scowl was terribly fierce and more than a wee-bit frightening.

I wandered toward the side of the house and couldn't stop myself from gazing up at the two-story structure. It had to have been beautiful back in its day. If it weren't so far from Jacksonville, it was the kind of property I'd love to buy and renovate on my own.

"You look at that house like you're remodeling it in your head," Alexandra said, walking beside me.

I shook my head and turned my focus toward the ground in front of us. There were plenty of exposed oak tree roots that could trip me. "Maybe a little, but having been inside, it'll take a crap load of money to fix it up, let alone afford the property itself, too."

"For what it's worth, Rafferty – or, I guess you were introduced to him by his road name, Bluff – he's planning to start his own general contracting business. He's remodeled the house we're living in, and I'd imagine he'd love taking on something like this."

I nodded. "If he's licensed, I'll keep him in mind as a referral for my clients."

"Oh, I didn't even think about that. Do you know where you're going?" she asked as we wandered farther away from the house.

"Yeah, as much as I thought I'd obliterated this from my memory, it seems this is something you don't forget."

"Yo! Slow down," Tundra yelled from behind us.

Alexandra and I stopped and turned half-way to watch him and Mickayla approach.

Tundra lumbered closer. "Neither of you are getting close to that body, if it's still there."

Alexandra held up a hand. "There's a reason I went into dentistry instead of becoming a doctor. I didn't want to deal with cadavers, so I'm not about to get close to a decomposing body."

Tundra tipped his head toward me. "Seeing as she helped move the body, it's her I'm concerned about."

I fought off rolling my eyes. "There wasn't much choice. They way they hit Nickel in the head, I couldn't expect him to move the body on his own."

"I'm sure. Lead the way, Ivy," Tundra said.

We trudged ahead another ten feet before we came to the gathering of trees and palmetto bushes.

I held a hand out toward the area. "This is where we left his body, but... He must have been moved, because there's no way he just disappeared."

Tundra turned to Mickayla. "Time to go. Straight to the clubhouse, Mick."

"We should check the house," Mickayla said.

Tundra's jaw clenched. "Woman, I told you why that's an even worse idea than just being here. That body isn't going to be in there. Take them back to the clubhouse."

"Not the bar?" I asked.

"No. It's more likely someone's watching the bar, and there's no decent way for her to approach from another direction."

"We have to stop at that truck stop in Sanderson because I'm hungry and I need to pee," Alexandra said.

Tundra shook his head and closed his eyes for a beat before he opened them again. "Fine. But I'm letting Bluff and Nickel know that's the plan."

Alexandra started back toward the car. I followed her as a breeze kicked up from behind me. Tundra stood rooted the spot, grabbing his phone from his back pocket.

"You need to get yourself a man who can get you in line," Tundra said in a low voice that I only heard because it carried on the wind.

"Whatever, Tun," Mickayla muttered and picked up her pace based on the increased sound of her footsteps on the fallen leaves and twigs.

Alexandra turned in her seat toward Mickayla as we bumped along the dirt lane back to the highway. "It isn't my business—"

"Then leave it alone," Mickayla muttered to the windshield.

Alexandra went quiet and I thought she was letting it drop.

Then she said, "I can't. What in the world is with you and Tundra? Was he just being—"

"He was being an overbearing biker. You know exactly how that feels, Lex, and you and I both can't stand it when the brothers get that way."

"I'm sorry. That sucks," Alexandra said.

Mickayla took a deep breath. "I'm trying to tell myself he didn't mean what he said. Otherwise, forgiving him will be a tall order."

My brows drew together. "You mean the part about getting yourself a man? His voice carried on the breeze."

Mickayla's bitter laugh filled the sedan. "No, him saying he didn't have time for 'dealing with the shit a wayward wild child pulls' with special emphasis on *child*."

Alexandra's head dipped toward her shoulder. "He probably didn't mean it like that."

"He did. It came up more than once in that conversation. We were both pissed though, so I'm trying to let it go."

Alexandra's cell rang.

"Hey, Raff—," she answered, then paused.

After a moment, Alexandra said, "You should call me after you calm down. "

Another pause. Alexandra twisted her head to aim an annoyed look at Mickayla, who chuckled quietly.

"Tundra stopped us from doing anything, not that there was anything we could do, and I know *you* know that because you're at that truck stop thanks to Tundra's text."

The next pause was much shorter.

"No, Raff, we're almost there, so please use the next fifteen minutes to cool down or we're going to have an entirely different type of problem. See you soon, babe," Alexandra said.

She tucked her phone away and looked over her shoulder at me. "Nickel is at the truck stop with Rafferty. Seems you and I are riding back on their bikes, and Mickayla has to drive back alone."

"That sucks. Even though I love being on his motorcycle," I muttered.

"Oh, boy. Sounds like you got it bad," Mickayla said.

Alexandra aimed a gentle look at Mickayla. "I hate to tell you this, Mick, but if your future man is a biker, you're gonna have it just as bad because there's a big difference between riding with my dad and riding with Rafferty."

"Yeah, yeah," Mickayla said, then twisted her head toward Alexandra. "You sure we need to stop at the truck stop?"

"I'm sure I don't want to poke the bear," Alexandra said.

CHAPTER 25

A DRESSING-DOWN

RYAN

No matter how much I tried, I couldn't help but overhear Bluff's side of the conversation with Alexandra. He sounded as pissed as I'd felt when I discovered Ivy wasn't in my room. With anyone else, I'd still be pissed, but somehow I'd calmed down after talking to Ivy. Or maybe it was that I knew how persuasive my sister could be, and I'd have been along for the ride, too.

Maybe.

Then again, I had years of experience in resisting her ideas or even diverting her attention to something completely different.

The notion of Ivy going back to that place set my teeth on edge. I hated her revisiting that trauma – especially since it was a damned fool's errand. No way Campbell's body was still where we'd left it, five days later.

Our morning session of church and information Lark shared had cast a new light on the whole situation.

"I can't believe Lark got us into this fuckin' mess," Bluff said.

I sighed. "Yeah, but he isn't gonna ask a woman if she's someone's ol' lady if it's a random hook-up and she hasn't given him reason to suspect that shit."

Bluff's eyebrows arched as he shot me a pointed look. "But it wasn't just random. He said he was with her at a rally and hooked up again back in May. Would

Ricochet have a random hook-up with a customer at On a Lark? Something tells me all of you know not to do that shit."

I wobbled my head as I thought about it. "She wandered in the first day of our soft launch four months ago. He made sure to cut her loose after that. Problem was her nephews didn't come around until two days later. I'm amazed Lark put it together."

Bluff shook his head. "Exactly. He never would have if Rusty hadn't come to y'all and run his mouth."

"Rusty and his cousins were also at the zoning hearing though, Bluff."

His head reared back. "Am I hearing you right? You've never liked that he's got a thing for younger women. If he'd kept his dick in his pants, none of this shit would have gone down."

I shrugged one shoulder. "I don't know, man. He couldn't know that at the time."

Bluff pointed a finger at me. "Your woman wouldn't be wound up in this."

"Perhaps, but if it weren't for her being cornered at gunpoint, I don't think she'd even be my woman."

"Bullshit. I saw the way you acted the first time she came in. You were going to find a way to get in there no matter what."

I shook my head. "You didn't see shit."

He chuckled. "Right. Keep telling yourself that." Staring off into the distance, he dragged his hand down his beard. "You pissed at Ivy?"

"Not any more."

He sighed. "How the hell do you do that? Just let that shit go? Lex told me we're gonna have problems if I don't calm down, but I still can't believe she joined in on this bullshit and left me a goddamn note to say so."

I grinned. "I'm used to my sister and the shit she gets up to. Hell, I should have anticipated this and warned Ivy."

In the distance, I heard the sound of a motorcycle engine. I turned to look at the main truck stop entrance and caught sight of Tundra following my sister's Corolla swinging into the parking lot.

"About fucking time they got here," Bluff muttered.

"Calm your shit, man. It's not worth it to fight over what's done," I said.

"You're right. I'm locking it down."

Mickayla pulled into a space next to us. Tundra walked his bike into a space beside her and gave me and Bluff a chin lift.

Alexandra angled out of the car, holding a finger up at Bluff. "I'm hangry and have to pee. We'll talk after I take care of that because it's not a good combo."

Ivy wandered over to me.

"Are you hangry?" I asked.

"No, but I thought I'd hit the restroom, too."

I held a hand out toward the building. "Hurry up, Trouble."

Her eyes darted toward Bluff and back to me. "I will, but don't be mad at your sister. She meant well."

"I know, and I'm not," I said with a nod.

"Good. I'll be right back."

From behind me came the sound of a car window being rolled down and I looked over to my sister, who hadn't turned off her car. "I'll be on my way now because I'm not enduring another dressing-down from either of you."

"If you got a dressing-down, maybe you deserved it," Bluff said.

Her eyes narrowed on Bluff. "Or maybe I didn't. Later, boys."

She pulled away and Tundra followed her out to the traffic light.

"Why did he get involved in this?" Bluff asked.

I clenched my teeth to get my temper under control. "I'm not sure. I'm just glad he caught them in time."

Bluff shook his head. "Yeah, he had to have been doing at least eighty-five to catch up to them like that."

Something had definitely come over Tundra when a prospect interrupted church to let us know Mickayla had left the clubhouse with Ivy and another woman. Luckily, we'd already called the meeting to a close, but he'd stormed out to his bike and took off without the first word to anyone. That kind of drive was more than friendly concern.

"Are you sure you're not angry? Because you damn sure don't look happy," Bluff pointed out.

I exhaled and forced myself to relax. "I'm good. It's been a long week."

He chuckled. "Yeah, any week that includes a drive-by is a long fuckin' week."

———

Ivy had her head resting on my shoulder and an arm draped around my stomach while we watched *Black Widow*. I loved that she was as big a fan of Marvel movies as I was, but I couldn't say I was paying much attention. She'd told me Campbell's body was gone. Even though I expected that, I had to wonder if Rusty had moved him or not. Why would he call to ask her about Campbell on Tuesday morning otherwise?

"You aren't paying any attention," Ivy said, staring up at me.

I glanced down at her. "Sorry, babe. I'm wondering about the body and other shit."

She sat up a few inches. "What's the other shit? Because I'm curious about what happened to the body, too."

"Don't worry about it, Ivy."

Her eyes widened and she sat up fully. "Oh, no. You don't get to lay there and stew about something, then tell me not to worry about it. Spill, Nickel."

I dug when she got spunky like that and I grinned. "It still bugs me that Rusty insisted on calling you about Campbell. If he moved him, why fuck with you that way? Tundra said there weren't any wild animals out there to disturb the body either."

She shook her head. "That's not necessarily true. Coyotes are turning up more and more in the suburbs. It's become a growing concern to prospective buyers. You can bet there's coyotes in a rural area."

"I didn't realize that," I muttered.

Her cell rang, she looked at it on the nightstand and frowned. "What time is it? Chad doesn't normally call me this early in the afternoon."

"Four-forty-five," I said, shocked at how much time had passed.

"Hey, Chad," she said.

Her mouth dropped open and her eyes filled with irritation. "You're kidding me! The bar isn't even open."

She paused.

Her head tipped back and I sat up. "What's wrong, Ivy?"

She leveled a look on me. "Chad is with my mom at the bar so she can meet Lark. I guess they opened up about an hour ago. Why he'd take her there is anyone's guess."

She paused, then said, "Yes, I know you're still there, but Ryan's right in front of me and concerned."

My body shook with my silent chuckle.

"Are you laughing?" she asked me.

"Do you want to head over there?" I asked.

Her gaze became unfocused for a moment, then she stared at me like I had superpowers. "Yes."

I heard the murmur of Chad's voice, but couldn't make out what he said.

"Too bad, Chadwick. You should have thought about that and called me before aiding and abetting my mom."

Her eyes widened. "It was *your* idea. What were you thinking?"

She stared up at the ceiling. "Yes, I know I said that, but then I chickened out when push came to shove, so maybe I changed my mind."

Her expression shifted and she looked almost contrite, which I didn't like. She didn't need to apologize from what I knew about the situation.

"All right, well, don't leave before we get there."

She looked at me with a remorseful expression. "I'm sorry you're going to have to ride all the way out there again, I can pay you for—"

I put a finger to her lips. "Don't even think about it, woman. If it were any other week, I'd be making that ride every day. Forget about it."

She nodded. "Cool. We should hurry. Mom sounded like she wanted to bail before I got there."

I smirked. "That isn't an elaborate excuse to ride fast, is it?"

She held up her hands. "Two things can be true, Nickel."

The crowds at On a Lark had been steadily building over the past five weeks. The drive-by threatened all of that growth. To my surprise, when we pulled up I circled the entire lot before deciding to park across the street in the lot of a business that closed at four. The owner had told us we could use their lot for overflow, for bike parking only.

"Wow, I've never seen it so crowded," Ivy said, freeing her curls from her hair tie.

I swung off my Triumph. "Yeah, hopefully that means Lark's too busy to talk to Debra."

She chuckled. "I just hope your sister and Killian are as good at keeping them away from Lark as you were with me."

"I regret doing that to you," I muttered, putting my arm around her shoulders.

She slung her arm around my waist. "Don't be. It all worked out in the end."

Tundra glowered at us while he stood behind the counter at the front door. "They told you not to come in here tonight, Nickel."

"It's my fault – or really my best friend's fault – because he brought my mom here."

Tundra narrowed his eyes in confusion.

"She doesn't want Lark forced to meet her mom, and neither of us expected Chad to pull a stunt like this," I said.

"Keep it short. Got it? We don't need any more trouble today," he muttered.

We moved into the main room.

"I can see why Mickayla was so upset with him this morning. He's good at delivering a reprimand," Ivy said.

Chad and Debra were sitting along the side of the bar closest to the entry.

Debra spun around on her stool. "Are you riding on his motorcycle without a helmet?"

Ivy ignored Debra's question and focused on Chad. "Why did you bring her here?"

"For the same reason I told you on the phone. You wanted her to meet him."

I loved it when I riled Ivy up, but seeing her get riled because of Chad hit me different.

She nodded once. "Has she met him yet?"

Chad's eyes widened. "No." He jerked his head toward me. "His triplet refuses to let Lark know we're here, but seeing as the man hasn't even come out of his office, I'm guessing he *knows* we're here and is actively avoiding us."

"Or he's trying to keep her and her mom safe," I said.

"That's craziness," Chad said.

"A man came in here and said the bar's days were numbered, and the next afternoon there was a drive-by. Another MC has it out for Lark, and if they find out she's *technically* his daughter, they won't hesitate to target her. It's far from crazy to keep Ivy and Debra out of this," I said.

Mickayla approached the bar with an empty serving tray tucked under her arm. Her gaze moved from me to Ivy. "Someone would like to talk to you in the office." She looked at me. "Only her."

"Does he know this wasn't her idea?" I asked.

Mickayla nodded. "Yes."

I tipped my head toward the office. "Don't keep him waiting."

Ivy hurried away.

Chad took a sip of his soda. "The gatekeeping is exhausting for everyone. You should let Lark know that."

I chuckled. "I'll be sure he gets the message."

"Do you have a helmet she could have worn?" Debra asked.

"Yes, but I'm not—"

"You can't control the other drivers," Debra said.

I'd heard that umpteen times before from my mom (who had no problems with Dad riding), from Grandpa Carlton, and even from Dad. All of a sudden I was glad of the many times I had to endure their lectures.

I nodded. "You're right, but I have mirrors, and I'm acutely aware of my surroundings. I don't split lanes, and I offered her my helmet. She opted not to use it. Bottom line, a car crash can be just as deadly."

Debra nodded. "Right. Her birthday is coming up, I guess I know what she's getting."

"When?" I asked, since we hadn't exchanged birth dates.

Her eyebrows rose. "If you don't know, I'm not sharing that with you."

Chad laughed. "Like Ivy would care!"

Debra swung a finger in the air toward him. "No, but he should do the work."

I nodded. "You're right. I'll put in the effort so she shares that with me."

She sighed. "I'm sorry if I'm coming across as being bitchy. I like you, but I'm worried. On top of this moving rather fast, it seems she's in danger, and I don't like it."

"Neither do I, and it's a big reason why we're trying to keep this visit short."

From the corner of my eye, I saw Ivy come out of the office and head our way. She went directly to her mom. "If you really want to meet him, you can come with me, but he's only got about five minutes to talk to you. It's a little busy tonight."

Debra opened her wallet and plucked out two twenties while shaking her head. "No, dear. Give him my apologies. Chad and I really shouldn't have done this, and I'll come back *with you* some other time when it's not so crowded."

I caught Debra's attention. "Or, maybe you can come by the clubhouse, save yourself the drive out here. He won't be distracted by customers or anything else."

Debra gave a half-nod. "That might work. I'll let you and Ivy set that up."

CHAPTER 26

RUNT

IVY

"THIS WASN'T CHAD'S IDEA, so don't be upset with him," Mom said as we walked through the restaurant parking lot to her Hyundai Sonata.

"It didn't sound that way when he called me," I said.

"He's a middle child who despises conflict, and he knew this would flip your lid. He cares so much about everyone, that he'd rather you be mad at him than me."

She was right about that.

"It was your idea then. Why? And why rope Chad into this? You had to know he'd call me."

Mom unlocked and opened the door to her car. "It was more of a spur of the moment impulse than an idea. I didn't think it through, and Chad didn't try to talk me out of it. I should have let it go. You were so shaken by the pictures of Jeff around the house, that I wanted to be sure this man, Lark, wasn't going to leave you troubled in a different way."

I shrugged. "Ryan became really protective after I first talked to Lark, like he didn't care that he was disrespecting him or about to cause a fight, when he thought Lark had hurt me. Considering that, I don't think Ryan will let that happen."

"That's good to know. I recognize you're going to be around Lark one way or the other if you two work out."

There wasn't an 'if' about that in my mind. I kept quiet.

Mom continued. "We're close and I'll have to learn to accept both of these men in your life."

I gave her a hug. "That's sweet of you, Mom. I'm not sure Lark will be around much. It's hard to say right now because of the outstanding issues."

Mom's sharp laugh ripped through the air. "That's one way to put it, my girl." She stared past me at the restaurant. "I like that he dropped everything and brought you here against their wishes. It's what Jeff would have done too."

There it was.

Certain things Ryan did reminded me of Jeff, but I hadn't seen it until Mom pointed it out.

Mom yawned. "I'm headed home. You tell Ryan to be careful taking you to his place."

"I will, Mom."

I watched her drive away, then hurried back inside.

Chad slid off his barstool when I approached him and Ryan. "I'm gonna head out."

Ryan seemed very tense from the way he held his body and his silent demeanor. I gave Chad a remorseful smile. "I'm sorry. Mom told me it was all her idea. You know you don't have to cover for her."

Chad returned my smile, but his was sheepish. "Can't help it, sweets. My mom and I used to be close like that, but after I came out—"

I put a hand on his forearm. "I know, honey. Don't go there right now. I'm just saying, I don't blame you, and hopefully Ryan doesn't either."

I looked at Ryan expectantly.

He shook his head. "I don't blame him. It's all good, and it'll be even better if he gets going because we're being watched."

Chad and I both stared at Ryan in disbelief.

He shook his head. "Don't make a scene. Rusty's here, and there's no reason to toss him out. Once Chad splits, you and I are heading out."

Chad looked around the bar.

"I'm not pointing him out to you," Ryan said in an exasperated tone.

Chad dug his keys out of his pocket. "Maybe Ivy should go home with me. What's going to stop him from following you two?"

Ryan's eyes took on a calculating gleam. "There's six other brothers here, not wearing their cuts. He makes a move right after us, they're going to slow him down."

Chad sighed. "I really hope this gets handled soon."

"From your lips to God's ears," I muttered.

Chad gave me a quick hug, cheek kiss, and wandered out of the bar.

"Now that Mom and Chad are gone, do you think Lark will come out?" I asked Ryan

"Why do you ask?"

I shot him a half-hearted scowl. "You have to stop asking questions when I ask them, honey."

He chuckled. "Are you asking because you want to talk to him again?"

I shrugged a shoulder. "No, I figured *he* would want to talk to Rusty."

"Ah," he said with a slow nod. "He left while you and your mom were out in the parking lot. Beast is managing the rest of the night."

"Is that unusual?"

"Yeah, and it almost feels like a slap in the face to me, Mick, and Ricochet."

"They don't trust one of you to run it tonight."

"Yeah, but even saying that, we only have a little over three months under our belts, so I can also see it from the club's perspective. We need more time before we run solo on a Friday night."

I stared at Ryan. He seemed antsy. "I take it we should get going."

He sighed. "Yeah. Rusty isn't focused on us. He's busy watching Mickayla."

Ricochet sauntered up behind him. "We know. Tundra's high-key pissed about it, too."

Ryan turned to his triplet. "Really?"

"Yeah, but all the brothers are pissed," Ricochet said, shrugging.

Ryan nodded. "If you need me, call. I'm gonna take her to the clubhouse. I can come back."

Ricochet shook his head. "No. Seven of us to one of him. It's all good."

We cruised through the forecourt of the Riot MC compound at a torturously slow pace. The area in front of the clubhouse had at least two dozen people milling about and the back patio was equally crowded. Ryan eased his Triumph to a stop next to a Kelly-green Harley.

"Shit," Ryan said.

"Is something wrong?" I asked and climbed off his bike.

Ryan swung off and turned to me. "That's Block's bike. I just hope like hell, he left Heidi back in Biloxi."

"Why?" I asked.

"She's my mom's best friend, and probably the biggest influence on Mickayla – though both of them would deny that."

He stared at me and put his hands on my shoulders. "Don't be freaked."

I shook my head. "I'm not freaked about meeting her. The crush of people here is surprising. I guess I didn't expect it to get so 'peopley.'"

"Thought you were an extrovert," he said.

I nodded slowly. "Yeah, but I was looking forward to getting some sleep. They're loud."

He dragged his hand down his face. "Yeah. We can head to your place."

I put my arms around his waist. "No, Ryan. This is part and parcel of your world. I'm gonna have to get used to it. No better time than the present."

He wrapped his arms around me and kissed my forehead. "Right. It doesn't look like all the Biloxi brothers are here because there's too many bikes I don't recognize, so something else is goin' on, but it's all good."

I stepped out of his hold, and he grabbed my hand. We wandered through the back lot to the patio. Most of the men wore Riot MC cuts, but there were a number of men wearing cuts that had a different club name on them. "Devil Lancers", and the bottom patch indicated they were from Augusta, Georgia.

"Hmph," Ryan said under his breath. Then he leaned toward me. "Members of another rival MC are here, but Volt's daughter is married to their president. I'm guessing they must have issues with Corrupt Chrome."

A Riot MC Biloxi member twisted on a picnic bench and grinned. "Nickel! Heard you got yourself a woman."

We came closer to the table and the man stood up. He wore a bandana around his bald head and the skin surrounding his blue eyes crinkled with his wide smile.

"Uncle Block," Nickel said, grabbing his hand and doing the man-style hug with a resounding back slap.

"Good to see ya, brother," Block said.

"Ivy, this is Block, he's the treasurer of the Biloxi chapter."

"Hi, it's nice to meet you," I said, shaking his hand.

"Did you bring Heidi with you?" Nickel asked.

Block shook his head. "Nah. All the Biloxi ol' ladies stayed home."

"Good," Nickel murmured.

"You looked freaked," Block said.

I shrugged. "It's more people than I expected so late on a Friday."

Block chuckled. "No such thing as late on the weekends, but everyone's hitting the sack soon."

"They are?" Nickel said, taking the words out of my mouth.

Block's eyes came to me for a loaded moment before sliding to Nickel. "No telling what's happening tomorrow."

"Got it," Nickel said with a slow nod. "Who else came out from Biloxi? They'll be pissed if they hear I talked to you, but not them."

Block chuckled. "Since your dad just made the trip, he isn't here and he's taking care of Har's body shop. Speaking of Har, you just missed him, Brute, Cynic, and Roman." He tipped his head to the clubhouse. "Tiny and Mensa should be in the common room."

We made our way through the throng of people on the patio and into the common room.

A tall, burly man with a silver beard and dark blue eyes stood across the room. His head twisted to a man leaned over a pool table. "Are you seeing this shit, Mensa?"

"No, and stop trying to distract me, Tiny," Mensa, the man at the pool table, said.

The cue ball glided across the felt and clacked against the two-ball, knocking it into the corner pocket.

Mensa stood, looked at Tiny, then turned to us. "About fuckin' time you showed up, runt."

My eyes went wide hearing him call my man a runt because there was *nothing* runt-like about him.

Nickel smiled, let go of my hand and slapped Mensa on the shoulder. "Didn't know all of you were headed out."

"That's by design," Tiny said. His voice was deep, but held a sharpness to it that was both appealing and frightening.

Tiny edged closer to me. "You must be Ivy. I'm Tiny." He tipped his head toward Nickel. "Don't take any shit from him. You keep him in line."

I laughed. "I'll do what I can."

Tiny nodded and wandered away.

Volt came in through the front door and gave me a chin lift. "Ivy." His gaze skated to Nickel. "You need to rest up. We have a meet with Corrupt Chrome tomorrow."

It surprised me that they would meet with another MC after everything that had happened.

"Is that why Lark left the bar earlier tonight?" Nickel asked.

"Yeah. You, me, and Lark are meeting at Platinum's with Sig, the brother who's got the beef with Lark, and Bridge, the Corrupt Chrome president." Volt paused and stared at Nickel expectantly. "You look like you want to ask me something."

Nickel dug into his pocket, and handed me his keys. "How about you go up to my room."

Volt shook his head. "Whatever you have to ask me, she doesn't need to leave."

Nickel put his keys back in his pocket. "All right. Do you expect just them to be at the bar tomorrow?"

Volt stroked his fingers along his goatee. "That's the plan, but in case they pull something we're gonna have extra brothers at Platinum's." He glanced at me and back to Nickel. "Even though we have extra brothers here, it'd be good if you had her spend the morning with Alexandra. She's free tomorrow, and Corrupt Chrome isn't likely to know anything about her."

Nickel nodded. "Done."

I couldn't help but shake my head. "Do you actually think they'll come here? This place is so far off the beaten path, and it seems very secure."

Volt leveled his brown eyes on me. "If my woman, Jackie, were involved in this, there's not a chance in hell I'd have her here. Not if there was somewhere else she could be instead. The clubhouse isn't easy to find, but it's not that hard either. And, if they don't pull something at Platinum's, this makes for the next logical target." He tilted his head back and forth once. "Or Hock's, but I'm not certain they know we own and operate that pawn shop."

Nickel swung a finger toward Volt. "You heard that Rusty was at On a Lark tonight, right?"

Volt scoffed. "Yeah. Pretty fuckin' bold of him, but he probably did that to get a rise out of us."

"The Devil Lancers...are they really here to help us?" Nickel asked.

Ever so slowly, Volt dipped his chin. "They are. It isn't a favor to me, either. Steel and his vice president, Torque, don't like what Corrupt Chrome did to them last year. Even though that was dealt with, they're feeling froggy and want to send a stronger message."

Nickel slung an arm around me. "Good. We're gonna head upstairs then. Meet you down here in the morning?"

Volt nodded. "Yeah, the meet is at eight, but I'll be here at seven. The three of us will ride over to Platinum's together." He tipped his head toward me. "Coordinate with Bluff so she gets out of here before seven."

CHAPTER 27

FULL DRIVING MISS DAISY TREATMENT

RYAN

IVY HIKED HER PURSE strap up on her shoulder as we walked out to the driveway in front of the clubhouse. "This seems like overkill, honey."

I stopped at the edge of the drive and turned to her. "Safety first, Ivy."

She took a deep breath. "Yeah, that goes triple for you." She went up on tiptoes to give me a peck. "Please stay safe."

I wrapped my arms around her waist. "We have them outnumbered, sweetheart. It'll be fine."

"Right," she breathed.

"You need to kiss me, Trouble."

She smirked and I leaned down to kiss her. Her lips parted and I slid my tongue into her mouth. She tasted like hazelnut coffee and woman. Her hands glided along my shoulders, one of them sliding into the hair at the back of my head. What should have been a single kiss turned into a make-out session until I heard the crunch of gravel and a car engine approaching.

We broke apart, and I saw Bluff driving Alexandra's Honda Accord with Alexandra in the passenger seat.

The moment the car stopped, Alexandra got out of the car and pointed at Ivy. "This may not penetrate the fog of your lip lock but learn now. These brothers give overbearing not just a new definition, but a whole other dimension to the definition."

Ivy chuckled. "And you had to get out of the car to tell me that?"

Alexandra shook her head. "No. I got out of the car because, if Rafferty's so insistent about driving, then I'm gonna sit in the back with you and get the full Driving Miss Daisy treatment."

I shot Alexandra a dry look. "Lex, you might not want to play it this way."

"I'm not going to make Ivy feel like a third wheel," Alexandra said.

Bluff leaned toward the open passenger side door. "Can y'all hurry this up? We need to get moving so I can get my bike and come back here."

Alexandra grinned at Ivy. "You're shorter than me, so you're sitting behind Rafferty."

While Alexandra got back in the car, Ivy looked up at me. "I'll see you...around noon, you think?"

"With any luck, sooner."

She went up on her toes again and kissed my cheek. "Bye, honey. I love you."

My eyes widened and my mouth went dry as thoughts whirled in my head about how to respond. Except she didn't even wait for a response, she'd scurried around the front of the Honda and climbed into the backseat.

Shit.

As they pulled away, Ivy waved at me and I waved back.

How the hell had I earned her love?

"You better not do her wrong," Lark said, trudging out from the side of the clubhouse.

"Fucking hell, how long were you hiding over there?" I asked.

He gave me a wry look. "I was out here first, for a smoke. Surprised one of you didn't smell it."

"It's not even seven o'clock, man."

"Yeah," he said coming closer to me. "Heard her say she loves you."

My jaw shifted. "Yeah. She hadn't done that before."

"That why you stood there like a dumb dope?" Lark asked.

I huffed out a chuckle and shook my head. "You could say that. It took me by surprise that's for damn sure."

"Women are good at that."

I looked into Lark's brilliant green eyes. "Yeah. I'm not gonna do her wrong... Though come to think of it, you should follow your own advice where she's concerned."

Lark's lips turned down, but it wasn't a full-on frown. "Yeah, I guess that's fair."

The sound of a motorcycle engine approaching could be heard, and moments later Volt rode through the open gates.

"You got your gun with you?" Lark asked.

"No, I'll run up to my room and take care of that right now."

I hadn't been back to Platinum's since I earned my place in the club. Even though the cleaning crew had been through this morning, the room felt heavy with the scent of smoke, hairspray, perfume, and booze. Yak led us to a back room where private parties were held.

A table and six chairs were set up, and Volt gestured for Lark and I to take a seat on one side.

"When they get here, me and Turk will pat them down the bring them in. Tundra and Punc are sticking around at the door to make sure nobody else tries to get in here. The back door's locked, but we've got Beast and Liar out there to prevent any attempted ambush," Yak said.

Volt nodded. "Good."

Yak turned to leave then looked over his shoulder at us. "If you want anything to drink, hit the bar for some soda. There's half a pot of coffee up there, too."

Twenty minutes later, Yak came back with a member of Corrupt Chrome. His cut indicated his road name was Bridge, and he was the president of the chapter. He came into the room and Yak shot Volt a concerned look.

"Just you?" Volt asked.

Bridge nodded while he took a seat across from us. "Yeah."

Lark heaved a sigh. "With all due respect, the issue Sig has with me is between him and his woman. If I'd known she wore a property patch, I wouldn't have given her the time of day."

Bridge's head moved in a couple of small nods, then he jerked his head toward me. "Why is he here?"

Volt cleared his throat. "He's the brother who tried to stop an abduction ordered by Rusty – he claims to be connected to your club and knew about Sig's woman being with Lark."

Bridge frowned. "Don't have any members named Rusty – road name or legal name."

"He had his cousins carry it out. Boyd and…" Volt trailed off looking at me.

"Campbell," I said.

Bridge's face moved a miniscule amount – I almost missed it.

We waited him out. After a long, tense moment, he said, "Two wanna-be prospects go by those names."

Volt's brows drew together. "So, they're hang-arounds."

Bridge shook his head. "No, if they'd bought bikes they'd have been prospects. Only thing holding them back, so they're a step up from hang-arounds."

"Not in most clubs," Lark muttered.

"Different club, different rules," Volt said.

"Right. They're both Sig's nephews," Bridge said.

I kept a stony face. Deep down I hated that we had *three* beefs with Sig.

"Be good if Sig were here," Volt said.

"Yeah," Bridge leaned to the side. I went tense at the movement until I saw him pull out his cell phone from his pocket.

While Bridge unlocked his phone, Volt said, "Did you or Sig know those two had come out here? They were here four months ago and came back this past Monday. If Rusty's their cousin, wouldn't Rusty be Sig's nephew too?"

"Not to my knowledge. Asked about that in my text. Along with an order to get his ass over here."

Something about this felt wrong. My gut expected Bridge to brush this off as a misunderstanding. On the surface that would work, but I couldn't see any biker letting all three issues go.

If anything it would make us more vulnerable. What better way to fuck with Lark than to frame him for a double homicide.

Lark shook his head. "Is Sig that close?"

Bridge shrugged one shoulder. "He isn't too far."

We sat in silence for a few minutes.

The door opened and Yak stuck his head inside. "Biker named Sig is at the door."

"Pat him down and send him back," Volt said.

"Always so cautious," Bridge muttered.

"Caution prevents an ambush – most of the time," Volt said.

Sig entered the room reeking of cigarette smoke. His dark hair hung down past his shoulders and looked unhealthy and greasy. His eyes narrowed on Lark. "You're the motherfucker who fucked my woman."

"He didn't know. Sit down, Sig," Bridge said in a firm tone.

Sig took a seat next to Bridge.

Once Sig settled, Bridge spoke, "You and Tori have had problems off and on for years."

"Yeah because she steps out on me, but he should have—"

"She wasn't wearing a property cut," Lark said.

"So you say," Sig retorted.

"She caught you cheating back in April," Bridge said.

"That don't—"

Bridge hit the table with his fist. "It's a problem between you and her. The club isn't taking on the Riot MC because you got problems with Tori."

Sig tipped his head toward me. "That asshole killed my nephews who were set to be Chrome prospects."

Bridge turned his eyes to Sig. "They acted on their own. Or did you know they were targeting that bar?"

Sig frowned and it deepened the wrinkles lining his face. "I knew they'd gone looking for the asshole Tori cheated with, but I didn't know they'd found him."

I struggled to keep my reactions in check. The conversation I'd overheard on Monday wasn't something I'd forget.

"Boyd said they'd get money no matter who they took. Why would he be so certain of that if he hadn't told you his plans?" I asked.

Sig leaned forward over the table. "I said I didn't know they found anybody."

"Is Rusty related to you?" Volt asked.

Sig sat back and ignored the question.

"Answer him," Bridge ordered.

Sig's eyes slid toward Bridge, then slid back to Volt. "No. He's their cousin on their daddy's side of the family."

Volt's eyes narrowed. "Then why would Rusty give a shit?"

Sig twisted his hands up. "Fuck if I know. I got a grieving sister and I have to help her bury both her boys."

I took all my willpower to stay quiet.

"Does that mean Rusty found Campbell's body?" Volt asked, as though he read my mind.

Sig stared at Volt.

"Answer him," Bridge said.

"I suppose. Rusty had both bodies by the time he called me to tell me my nephews were dead," Sig said, shooting me a glance like he wanted to tear me limb from limb.

"What'd you tell your sister?" Volt asked.

Sig rolled his eyes. "That her boys are dead."

Volt sighed. "Your nephews wanted to be prospects. Did you tell her their deaths were club related? I can't imagine any parents not reporting their kids being murdered. Are they calling the police?"

Bridge shot Sig a sidelong glance. "Sig, this is not the time to get cagey."

"No. I told her not to go to the cops."

Volt turned his attention to Bridge. "Does your club have an issue with us about Boyd and Campbell?"

"Yeah, we do," Sig blurted.

Bridge closed his eyes for a beat then shot side-eye at Sig before focusing on Volt. "No. We don't." He turned to Sig. "You got that, brother? They went off half-cocked and didn't even tell you or any club officer what the fuck they were doing."

Sig's brown eyes widened. "My nephews deserve—"

"Your nephews got what they deserved," Volt said. "That's harsh, but you know damn well if someone took you and your woman against your will, you'd end them in order to get free. That's what Nickel did."

Sig stayed silent.

"You convince your president to push this, it's not going to go well."

"Empty threats," Sig said.

"Shut it, Sig," Bridge said.

Sig turned to Bridge. "What? They're totally empty."

Bridge gave a beleaguered sigh. "There were three Devil Lancers at our hotel, and two different Devil Lancers followed me to the gas station before I got here. You can't be that obtuse."

If he came from the same gene pool as Campbell, there was every chance he was just that obtuse, but I kept that to myself.

"They weren't real Devil Lancers," Sig muttered.

Bridge jerked his head toward Volt. "His daughter married the president of the mother chapter. Our Augusta chapter fucked with them, and our brothers paid the price. I'm not putting the rest of our chapter through anything like that. Open your fuckin' eyes."

Sig stared at Volt, then shifted his gaze to Lark.

"Your issues with your woman are yours, Sig. I cut her loose months ago," Lark said.

"Are you cool with the Riot MC?" Bridge asked.

Sig closed his eyes for a moment and let out a sigh. He opened his eyes and looked to Bridge. "Yeah. I'm cool."

"You mean it?" Bridge asked.

"Mean it," Sig said.

Bridge turned back to Volt. "I'll have Sig introduce me to Rusty. I'll make sure he backs off. None of this shit should have happened. Will that make us square?"

"Tell me if Rusty refuses to see logic. He comes around any of the brothers, he's going to feel their wrath."

"Understood," Bridge said.

Bridge and Sig stood. Volt took to his feet, and Lark and I followed suit. Bridge shook hands with Volt, and the two men left.

Lark crossed to the door and shut it. He turned around. "I don't trust that bastard."

Volt tugged at his goatee. "I don't either, but I'm gonna follow up with Bridge later. In the meantime, I've got someone looking into Sig and his sister. If she's really going to bury her sons, then those bodies have to be at a funeral home or something."

"You really think Rusty won't be a loose cannon out there?" I asked.

Volt quirked his lips to the side with skepticism. "I can only take another club president at their word, but he and Sig know we aren't going easy any longer."

Lark's lips tipped up. "Good."

CHAPTER 28

GREAT PICTURE

IVY

ALEXANDRA AND I WERE standing around her Keurig waiting for my chai latte to brew.

"I can't wait for this to be done and over," I said.

She nodded. "Yeah, I can relate. Some crap went down with me back in late April, early May, and waiting for shit to get sorted sucks."

The Keurig finished, and we took our tea to the living room.

Alexandra sat down with one leg folded under her. "I don't know if anyone mentioned it, but if things go smooth at this meet, the brothers are going to have a blow-out party tonight."

My brows drew together. "I thought that happened last night."

She chuckled. "Oh no. Tonight, they'll be partying until at least two in the morning."

"As fun as that sounds, I was kind of looking forward to sleeping in my own bed tonight."

She grinned. "No you're not. You want to go tonight. It's what makes it all worth it."

"I'll have to take your word for it," I said.

"Have I steered you wrong yet?" she asked.

I thought about it for a beat. "No, you haven't. And I'm so glad you warned me about Ryan picking the locks because that would have freaked me out huge."

An hour later I heard the sound of a motorcycle. The living room had beautiful picture windows that looked out to the street and since the drapes were opened wide, I spied Ryan walking his bike to a stop.

I dashed out the door, down the front walk, jumped up and nearly tackled him. He caught me, wrapped his arms around my waist with his hands at my ass, and he went back on a foot, but steadied himself.

"Jesus, Trouble. You're gonna send us both to the ER."

I leaned back and cupped his cheeks. "Not a chance, my man."

His lips quirked. "You hurried off earlier, but I love you, too. Don't think that was lost on me."

My eyes widened. "Oh my God. We're gonna get arrested for indecency if you don't hush."

"Why?" he asked on a laugh.

"Because I want to jump you right now."

He squeezed my ass. "Hop down, sweetheart."

"Well, that's a great picture," Alexandra said from behind me.

I dropped my legs and turned to face her. "What are you talking about?"

She turned her phone to me. On the screen was a fantastic picture from a side angle of Ryan holding me and me cupping his cheeks. My mind filled with visions of canvas pictures in Mom's living room and I knew I wanted to get that shot printed.

"You have to send that to me," I said.

"Consider it done," Alexandra said.

I shifted so I could see Alexandra and Ryan. "Speaking of 'done', is the situation handled?"

His eyes darted to Alexandra and back to me. "Tentatively, yes. I hate to leave so soon, Lex, but she and I should go."

Alexandra shook her head and swatted a hand out at us. "No worries. I get it. Ride safe."

"Thanks for the tea," I said, and followed Ryan to his bike.

I led Ryan into my townhouse. The moment Ryan closed and locked the door, he stalked to me and kissed me hard.

His hands were roving my body with clear intentions, but I broke the kiss. "What's the story? Are we staying here tonight?"

He pressed his lips together for a moment. "I hate to tell you this, but we're going back to the clubhouse this afternoon."

I stepped back, out of his hold. "What? Why? I thought the threat was dealt with now."

He sighed. "In theory, but none of us trust it yet. Besides, you need to meet the rest of the Biloxi brothers you missed last night. Seeing as you love me."

I shot him a small smile. "Okay. But how long before we know everything's over?"

His chest rose with his deep inhale. "Tonight, sweetheart. Volt's gonna call Bridge and we're verifying some of what Sig said. He's Boyd and Campbell's uncle."

"All right. Do I need to bring anything for this party?"

He grinned. "No. The club has it handled."

"Really? From what Alexandra said, it's supposed to be a blow-out party."

He bent and took off his boots. "It probably will be, Trouble, but you don't need to worry about it. Speaking of that, the way you flew out of Bluff's house, were you really that worried about me?"

My eyes slid to the side.

He sauntered to me and pulled me into his arms. "It's all right to say so, baby."

"I was worried, but seeing you pull up to their house made me rather—"

"Excited," he said.

I smirked and ran my hands up his abdomen along his chest to his shoulders. "Relieved, is more like it."

He leaned down and nipped my earlobe. "Glad to be of service."

I leaned back and gave him a questioning glance. "Of service?"

He nodded. "Pretty sure you could return the favor... be of service and give me some relief."

I dipped my chin. "Are you hinting at me going down on you?"

"I love having your mouth on me, Ivy."

"Pretty sure that makes two of us, honey."

He cocked a brow at me.

I arched both my brows. "Let's do this in my bedroom."

———

When we rode into the Riot MC compound at a quarter after six, I sat snug to Ryan's back on his bike with my arms wrapped around his waist.

If I'd thought there were a lot of bikers here last night, this proved me wrong.

From what Ryan had mentioned when we ate lunch, there were four Biloxi brothers I hadn't met last night, but from the lengthy line-up of motorcycles parked behind the clubhouse, there had to be over two dozen more bikers here than last night.

"That's a lot of bikes," I said, as Ryan powered off the engine.

"It's Saturday. More brothers are free today than on a weekday, and all the Devil Lancers are here, now that they don't have to follow Bridge and Sig."

He led me across the backyard to where some men were gathered around a large pot drinking beer.

One of the men turned his head to us. He had hair that was an attractive light brown with a heavy hint of red. In profile, he had a well-defined jaw, and a goatee surrounding his lips. A calculating gleam hit his eyes as he watched us approach.

Ryan slung an arm around my shoulders. "Har. Sorry we missed you last night."

Har turned to us fully. I saw his cut had a patch beneath his road name that indicated he was a chapter president.

"Nickel, it's been too damn long," Har said, reaching a hand out toward Ryan.

Ryan let go of me to shake Har's hand, and get a loud back-clap from Har.

Another man stood close by who was about two inches taller than Har. He had dark hair, but it was shot through with hints of gray. This man had bulk to spare, and that alone made him intimidating.

Ryan stepped away from Har and looked at the other man. "Brute, it's good to see you."

"Gamble wasn't kidding," Brute said, his eyes fixed on me.

Ryan turned his head to me and back to Brute. "What do you mean?"

A mischievous smile curled Brute's lips and he shook his head. "You'll have to ask Gamble." He stepped toward me with a hand outstretched. "I'm Brute. It's great to meet you, Ivy."

I shook his hand and was pleasantly surprised at his grip – not too firm, but not limp either. "It's nice to meet you, too."

Ryan introduced me to Cynic and Roman.

The group went silent and the men exchanged glances.

Cynic dragged his thumb and forefinger along his goatee. "Do you run, Ivy?"

My smile faltered and I turned a questioning look to Ryan before meeting Cynic's gaze. "Not if I can help it. Why?"

Cynic's deep chuckled filled the air. "Just curious."

The others were grinning and I turned to Ryan. "What am I missing?"

Ryan gave a slow head shake. "Mom likes to run. Some people say it's part of how she and Dad met." His eyes cut through the group. "But I say that's bullshit. Her being a lawyer had everything to do with it."

There was movement on the concrete patio and I saw Alexandra heading our way. "I told you they were here," she called over her shoulder to Bluff.

She hurried to us and grabbed my hand, but looked at the Biloxi brothers. "Sorry, but I'm stealing her. She has lots of people to meet, and not a lot of time before people are too blotto."

"Or high, if you're taking her to meet any Devil Lancers," Cynic muttered.

Alexandra shifted her gaze to Ryan. "Nickel, we'll be in the common room. Don't worry."

My man locked eyes with me. "Stick by her side, babe."

I nodded and Alexandra tugged me away.

"First, what are you drinking? Wine or beer?"

"I'm thinking beer," I said.

Alexandra nodded. "Cool. We'll get you set up first, but you have to meet Rainey and Vamp. She's in charge of mortgage lending at one of the credit unions and she's got a close friend who's in real estate too."

Within an hour, I'd met close to twenty people. If it weren't for the unique road names, I wasn't sure I'd remember them all.

I was sitting on a couch in the common room sipping my second beer watching Simone, Volt's daughter, rocking her one-year-old daughter to sleep. It would be a while before I'd be ready for that...but at the same time I was envious of that connection. For that matter, I couldn't imagine how her little girl was able to fall asleep in a room with so much noise. The music wasn't overly loud, but it felt like the people talking were growing louder by the minute.

"You can hold her," Simone said, looking at me.

I held up my beer and my other hand in front of me. "Oh, I don't want her to wake up."

Simone smiled. "She's out, and it's almost impossible to wake her once she falls asleep."

Alexandra turned her face to me. "That's the truth. I wish I could sleep that deeply."

I set my drink down and took little Felicity into my arms. Like Simone said, she didn't wake at all. I got her situated against my shoulder, and marveled at her soft skin and her immense body heat. There was something soothing about holding a sleeping child.

Ryan and his brother wandered into the common room, but only Ryan stopped short with his eyes fixed on me. From the struck look on his face, I wasn't sure if he liked what he saw or wanted to bolt for the hills – not that there were many hills around here.

Simone looked over her shoulder and saw Ryan staring. "Oh, that's my cue to get her into her Pack-n-Play."

Ryan blinked then came closer. "No, Simone, it's fine."

Simone lifted both hands and pointed her index fingers at him at an angle. "No, Nickel, things are about to get wilder around here, and I want Felicity in her own space."

I stood and carefully handed Felicity over to Simone.

"You want another?" Alexandra asked, grabbing my empty cup before she stood.

"We're not drinking beer," Ryan said.

"I see." Alexandra turned to me. "Have fun. I'm going to find Bluff."

I slowly stepped closer to him. "Are you upset?"

He took a deep breath. "No. That would never upset me, Ivy."

"But you were shocked," I said, not sure why I couldn't let this go.

He paused. "I'm not ready for a family—"

"Neither am I," I blurted.

With a grin, he nodded once. "Yeah, but I like seeing you holding a baby. A lot fuckin' more than I probably should."

I leaned toward him and put a hand on his chest. "Don't tell me your biological clock's ticking."

His eyes went up and to the side for a beat. "How many beers have you had?"

I laughed. "Two. But I haven't had any food."

He nodded. "That's why I came in here. If you like crab legs, the low-country boil is done. If you want something else, there's burgers, dogs, brats, and pulled pork out there, too."

"I've never had a low-country boil, so lead the way."

Two hours later, it struck me that Simone had called it. The party had become increasingly wilder. It also didn't take me long to see the difference between the Devil Lancers and the Riot MC. There were plenty of people getting their drink on, and some were smoking weed, but the moment a Devil Lancer brought out harder drugs, the air went tense. The Devil Lancer with the drug wandered off the patio and out to the farthest edge of the backyard, three of the others following.

The vibe quickly went back to the raucous party mood. My gaze darted around the backyard and I saw Jasmine talking to a Devil Lancer with corkscrew curls similar to mine. He nodded at her, then hurried away, but he didn't go in the direction of the Devil Lancers who were hitting harder drugs.

Music was blaring from speakers set up on stands. Somehow, a Bruno Mars song came on after an alternative rock tune and Alexandra raced to me.

"We should dance!" she declared.

Ricochet was siting close by and grinned at me. "Dance on the table! Let's see how much you're really like Lark. I dare you!"

Nickel turned venomous eyes to his brother who shrugged and smiled bigger.

"Don't look at me like that, bro. Her friends say she's impulsive, I wanna test that."

I glanced at the table. "People's plates are on the table," I said.

Alexandra pointed at a table across from us. "That one's empty. Let's go!"

Next thing I knew, Alexandra and I were dancing on the table to 'I Just Might.'

Over the music, I heard a man yell, "I'm not watching Cal's little girl dance like that! This'll get them to stop."

I made big eyes at Alexandra, but she wiggled her hips even more. In seconds, the song switched to 'The Twist' by Chubby Checker. We laughed our asses off at the attempt to make us stop, and we proceeded to do the twist until Bluff and Nickel were forced to make us get down.

I pointed a finger up in the air at him. "I never pegged you for being a party-pooper."

Ryan lowered his face toward mine. "Tic is watching you like you're his next meal. We call him Tic, but it's short for Lunatic. Until you wear my property patch, I don't trust him and I don't want you provoking him."

My eyes darted to the side and I recognized Tic from the first night I was at the clubhouse. "I didn't realize—"

Ryan kissed my temple and straightened. "I know, babe. You want dessert? I want to see if Block needs help with the beignets."

My eyes went wide. "You know how to make beignets?"

He laughed. "Yeah. It's not that hard, Trouble."

"Baloney! If it weren't that hard, more donut shops would carry them."

He slung his arm around me. "Let's go get you some dessert."

"And another gimlet," I said.

"After that, you're cut off."

I looked up at him. "I thought this was a party."

"It is, but we're taking this party to my room, and I want you tipsy, not sloshed when we go upstairs."

I wrapped my wet hair up in a towel after I dried off from my shower on Sunday morning. Once I was dressed and the steam cleared from the mirror, I examined the skin surrounding my eye. It was a garish shade of yellow-green, but it had faded. After learning a few tricks from Abby, I knew I could hide it from my coworkers tomorrow.

Ryan had dropped me off at my townhouse half an hour ago to work a six-hour shift at the bar. They offered Sunday brunch, which they hadn't promoted yet because Lark was still perfecting his menu options.

I had to go grocery shopping because Kristen and Chad were swinging by for Sunday dinner. Bonus, Ryan would be back in time for the fun. I hadn't looked forward to one of our Sunday cooking sessions this much in a very long time.

My phone rang and I saw it was Chad.

"Hey!" I answered.

"Hey, yourself. You are very chipper this morning."

I glanced at the clock on the stove. "It's almost noon, so the morning's nearly over. What's going on?" I paused. "You don't have to cancel do you?"

He chuckled. "Not a chance. I wanted to know if things are handled yet...or should I be on the lookout for an angry man who's searching for you or your new beau?"

I grinned. "That's why I sound chipper. Yesterday, things got sorted. Tomorrow I get to go back to work, and things will get back to normal."

"Well, hot damn! That's the best news I've had all week."

The doorbell rang while I was washing the romaine lettuce. "Can you get that? I'm sure it's Chad, but you can check the doorbell app on my phone if you want."

"I got it, babe," Ryan said, sauntering to the door.

A moment later, I heard people moving into the townhouse and I looked toward the foyer.

"Okay," Chad said, sailing into the kitchen with a bottle of wine. "Your man says he's helping. How is he doing that?"

"He's helping by manning the grill and the deep fryer."

"Come again? He should not be taking care of two tasks. Is his brother coming?" Kristen asked, perching on a stool at the breakfast bar.

"You wish his brother was here," Chad muttered under his breath.

"Zip it, Chadwick," Kristen said with a saucy smile.

"No, we're grilling shrimp so it's not even that much work. For dessert, we're having beignets – hence the deep fryer," I said.

Kristen smiled. "Awesome! Are we having Cajun sides?"

I shrugged a shoulder at her. "We could, but I picked up Boursin so you could make your uber-rich mashed potatoes."

Chad held up a bottle of wine. "I brought two bottles of wine tonight." He looked to Ryan. "Do you drink wine?"

Ryan smiled. "I do, but I made a pitcher of gimlets if either you want one."

"Mm, gimlets. Is Ivy taking another day off tomorrow?" Kristen asked.

I beamed at her. "No. Yesterday, Ryan, Lark, and Volt took care of everything. I'm headed back to the office and I have two closings tomorrow."

"That's outstanding news," Kristen said.

"My sentiments exactly," Chad chimed in, then looked at Ryan. "I definitely like you now."

"Good to know, but I had plenty of help from the other brothers," Ryan said while pouring four cocktails.

"I thought there were some missing people involved here. How is this over so fast – not that I'm complaining," Kristen said.

Ryan filled them in on the connection to Corrupt Chrome MC and what was going on with the bodies.

"What a wicked web," Chad said, sipping his gimlet.

"Are we doing lunch on Wednesday?" Kristen asked.

"That's not a good idea," Ryan said.

She aimed a confused look at him. "Why?" Her expression shifted to realization "Oh, I was talking to Ivy. I didn't mean for us to horn in on your lunch with your brother and sister."

"Let's do Thursday. I have a staff meeting on Wednesday," Chad said looking at his phone.

From behind me, Ryan wrapped an arm around my waist, pulling my back to his front. I felt his whiskers tickle the shell of my ear. "You're coming to lunch with me, Kill, and Mick on Wednesday," he whispered.

I smiled.

Chad stared at us. "As thrilled as I am for you, girlie, you two are making me feel ill."

Kristen laughed and so did I.

"Don't worry. I got potatoes to peel," I said, breaking free from Ryan's hold.

"I'll help you with that," Chad said, grabbing the peeler from the drawer.

"Why are you called Nickel? If you don't mind me asking," Kristen said, sipping her cocktail.

"The brothers make the prospects do all kinds of arbitrary shit before they earn their patch and road name. We had to go out and shoot at various targets. One of them was a nickel. My brother's shot ricocheted every time he tried, and he gave it five tries. I was the only one who hit it and put a hole in the coin."

I turned wide eyes to him. "Are you serious?"

"Yeah. They named my brother first. My name really stuck when Liar pointed out the shortened versions our names would rhyme. Nick and Rick."

Chad's face twisted with outrage. "There's no way those bikers are that corny."

Ryan grinned. "I wouldn't tell Liar he's corny if I were you."

CHAPTER 29

ROB HER

RYAN

I WOKE UP BEFORE Ivy. She'd rolled away from me during the night, but she hadn't stolen the sheets. A digital alarm clock sat on the nightstand, I lifted my head to peek at the time. Six forty-five. Before we turned the lights out, she'd mentioned her alarm would go off at ten after seven.

It wasn't cool to rob her of sleep...but I figured a couple of orgasms would more than make up for it.

I slid the sheets off me, turned to my side, then carefully tugged the covers off my woman. She'd gone to bed naked. Maybe that was why I woke up so determined to have her.

She rolled to her back with a heavy sigh. Her eyes weren't open. For some reason that made me grin. I dragged her leg to the side, moved so I was between her legs, and lowered my face to kiss her upper thigh. The rhythm of her breathing changed, but glancing up her body, I saw she still wasn't awake.

My grin became a smile just before I flicked her clit with my tongue. Her hips shifted, I licked rapidly and repeatedly.

Her sharp inhale cut through the silent room. I stared up her body.

She'd leaned up on her elbows. "What's goin' on?" she whispered.

I smirked for a split second. Rather than tell her, I showed her what was going on by sucking on her clit.

The bed jostled when she fell back, but those hands drove into my hair and I loved feeling her fingernails scraping along my scalp. I slid two fingers inside her pussy.

"Yes," she breathed.

I lapped and sucked at her clit while sliding my fingers in and out of her wet pussy. She pushed against me, her hips undulating. The moment she began to ride my face I sucked even harder.

"Ryan. Oh God, don't stop."

That was an order I'd follow gladly. I curled my fingers and felt her muscles tighten.

"I'm so close," she moaned.

I replaced my fingers with my tongue because nothing was better than tasting her release. With my finger I rubbed her clit. A moment later she came with a long moan.

I rose to my knees, gave my cock a tug, then lined up and drove inside her. Her pussy clenching around my cock felt like heaven. I withdrew and slammed back inside.

Her hands went to my ass and squeezed. "Yes, honey."

I pulled her legs up and pistoned my hips.

"Fuck, Ivy. You feel as good as you taste."

She ground her hips against me on every inward thrust. "I love you," she whispered.

I leaned forward and kissed her. When I pulled away, I looked into her green eyes. "I love you, too, Trouble."

She rose up and kissed my collarbone. Then I felt her sucking on my skin there.

"Trouble," I growled.

"Yes," she said, dragging her lips down to my pectoral.

I kept pounding into her. Sweat beaded along the small of my back. I felt my balls growing tight.

She dragged my nipple through her teeth.

"Oh, shit. You're gonna send me over the edge," I whispered.

She reached between us and rubbed her clit.

As much as I wanted her to come twice, I couldn't stop my release. I groaned and just as I thrust one last time, I felt her pussy spasm around me.

I thought I would collapse, so I wrapped my arms around her and flipped us so I was on the bottom. Somehow, we stayed connected.

After our breathing evened out, Ivy lifted her head. "That's a great way to start a Monday."

I chuckled. "I'm glad you liked it."

Her alarm went off. She reached out and smacked the clock into silence.

She cocked a brow at me. "You going to shower with me, or did you wear yourself out?"

I wheezed out a laugh. "I'll let you shower alone since you're headed back to work today."

Lark had assigned me the early shift today. I'd expected him to make me pull a double considering all the time I'd missed over the past several days. I wandered in at eleven o'clock and saw Beast go into the office and shut the door.

Mickayla was taking chairs off the tables and getting the floor set up. I joined her at one of the tables and set a chair on the floor. "What's the deal? Do we need Beast here today?"

My sister didn't exactly frown, but she had a similar expression as me when I wasn't pleased. "I'm not sure. I know he has experience managing a dance club and bar at one of the Biloxi casinos, but that was over a decade ago. I can't imagine he wants to work here." She shrugged. "I don't know. Maybe Lark's been more stressed than he let on over the past ten days."

I nodded. "You need me to do anything more strenuous? Do we need kegs moved?"

She shook her head. "Nope. That was handled last night. You can see if Adam and our new cook need anything."

There wasn't much I could do in the kitchen, and I went behind the bar.

Beast and Lark came out of the office.

Lark leaned against the bar. "I know you think you're ready to run this place on your own, but I'm not gonna be comfortable with that until we all spend some time training with Beast first."

Mickayla nodded, but I could see she wasn't pleased.

"How long is 'some time' going to last?" I asked.

"As long as we say," Lark said.

I shook my head. "Most businesses give employees – especially managerial employees – an idea of how long their training will last. We've been doing the work for over four months now." I tilted a hand toward my sister. "She's got a business degree. Asking how long it will be before the brothers have confidence in the three of us isn't an unreasonable question, Lark."

Beast twisted his hands out in acknowledgment. "It isn't a lack of confidence in any of you three, Nickel. I'm going to share efficiency strategies. We should have done it back in May, but Volt sent me and Tundra out to Gainesville and then other crap was going down. There's been steady growth, so it needs to happen sooner rather than later."

Mickayla nodded. "That's understandable. Can we get started now before we get the lunch rush?"

"Absolutely," Beast muttered.

The next six and a half hours went by faster than usual – likely because when I wasn't serving or making drinks, Beast was training us. I was more than ready to call it a day. Ivy had texted to let me know that she was coming by the bar after a showing on the North side.

My hunch was that she wanted to hang at the bar to eat, and maybe shoot the breeze with Lark. He hadn't been at the party on Saturday night, and I suspected she'd been disappointed. If connecting with Lark was what she wanted, I'd spend an extra hour here.

Killian came behind the bar and went to the trashcan. "You're out of here soon, right?"

"Yeah. Why do you ask?"

He took the lid off the can and pulled the bag out. "I'm gonna take this out while you're still here."

I nodded, and reached under the bar for a trash bag. "Thanks. I could have done that."

Kill shook his head. "I need to see the sun before it sets."

I put the bag in and replaced the lid.

Mickayla breezed past me to the register to update a customer's tab.

I glanced out the new front windows and saw Ivy drive by and park her car.

"You are so smitten," Mickayla said.

"Shut it, Mick," I muttered.

She giggled. "Nope. It's not that busy. Go out there and greet her so the rest of us don't have to watch you pine after her and be so damn sappy."

Part of me wanted to force her to watch me be sappy, but I took her up on the offer and went out to see Ivy.

I nodded at Adam as I walked out the front doors. The moment I stepped outside, alarm swept through me. Ivy stood on the sidewalk half way between her car and the doors to the restaurant on the sidewalk. She was facing me, but two men were blocking her path.

My gut said it was Sig and Rusty, but that couldn't be right. Sig had agreed to letting this shit go. If it was him, he wasn't wearing his MC cut. The man on the right had the same build as Rusty.

"Rusty," I called out to test him.

When he turned, I noticed he held a gun in his hand. The other man shifted, and my stomach soured as Sig stared at me.

"I knew she'd draw you out," Rusty said.

The sour in my stomach began to roil when I saw Killian saunter around the corner of the building, a good fifteen feet behind Ivy.

"Yo, numbnuts, I'm the one you want," he called out. He'd pitched his voice lower, and he only did that when he was trying to act like me.

Goddammit! This really wasn't the time for my brother to pull a switch.

"Fuck, I didn't know they were identical," Sig said in a voice so low, I almost missed it.

"Which one do want me to shoot first?" Rusty asked.

"The one who killed my nephews, dumbass," Sig said.

"The two of you got no fuckin' business here. Cops are on the way," Lark said, walking up beside me and cocking a rifle.

With anyone else, that warning would have encouraged them to leave. But Rusty was a different level of stupid.

"You said you were cool. Does Bridge know you're here?" I asked, trying to stall.

Sig's eyes narrowed. "I lied."

Rusty stared over his shoulder at me and Lark. I forced myself to stay focused on him because I'd noticed Killian inching closer to Ivy. No way did I want to inadvertently communicate that to these two. My brother wasn't directly behind her, rather he was two feet away and off to the side just a touch.

"They'll suffer either way," Rusty muttered.

I expected him to shoot me, but he twisted and without taking aim, he fired at Ivy.

The blast of his gun was loud. The boom of Lark's rifle was even louder.

My ears were ringing. I saw Ivy jerk and twist to one side before she slumped to the ground holding her shoulder.

As I rushed to her, the scene came clearer. The bullet went through Ivy and hit Killian.

I heard someone roaring, "No."

That someone was me.

Sig lunged toward me holding a hunting knife. I veered to the left and vaguely registered the sound of Lark cocking the rifle again.

Another blast cracked the air and Sig went down.

I didn't know who to run to first. I tore my shirt over my head, balled it up and put it on Ivy's wound.

She was still conscious.

I grabbed her hand and put it over the shirt. "Hold that there for me. Can you do that, baby?"

"Yeah," she whispered.

Mickayla was crouched next to Killian with her phone in her hand. "He's been shot in the chest. The bullet went through someone else first."

Adam came out with a stack of t-shirts we usually sold at the front of the store. He put two shirts on Killian's chest.

I grabbed one from him and placed it behind Ivy's shoulder. The faint sound of a siren could be heard. Lark tucked his phone away and set the rifle on the ground near the place where we'd been standing earlier.

He came to me. "Keep applying pressure. Club lawyer's on the way. If the police want to question you, make sure a lawyer is present."

A fire truck and an ambulance pulled to a stop in the parking lot. Two EMTs rushed out from the front of the ambulance, moments later another two came out from the back pushing a stretcher.

"Sir, we'll take it from here," one of them said.

I stood, but kept eye contact with my woman. "I love you, Ivy."

Her lips curled just a little. "I love you, too, Ry."

A Jacksonville Sheriff's officer sped down the side street and came to an abrupt halt in front of the scene.

I twisted toward Killian. Rescue workers were moving him to the stretcher. Mickayla had tears streaming down her cheeks. She rushed to me and I wrapped my arms around her.

"He's my triplet, and she's my girlfriend. Where are you going to take them?" I asked, my voice raw.

"The trauma center downtown for both of them," one of the firefighters said.

Another JSO cruiser had parked along the street, and the first deputy was taping off the area.

"Ryan, tell me he's gonna be okay," Mickayla whispered.

I gave her a squeeze. "He's gonna be okay," I muttered, but it sounded hollow.

"We gotta call Mom," Mick said.

I shook my head. "Not yet."

She leaned back. "It's seven hours—"

"Lark called the club. Volt or Blood will call Dad. He and Mom will be on the road in no time."

She exhaled hard. "You're right."

"If we don't have to stick around here for the cops, I'll drive you in your car down to the hospital," I said.

She hugged me. "Okay. I love you, Ryan."

"Yeah. I love you, too, sis."

———

When Mickayla and I arrived at UF Health in downtown, half the club was in the ER waiting room.

Abby rushed over to us, with Blood following close behind. "I fibbed and told them I'm you're aunt."

"That's not a fib," Mickayla blurted.

Abby aimed a wan smile at her and continued. "Killian's been rushed to surgery. None of the nurses are willing to give us an estimate on how long that might take."

"Every patient is different," Blood muttered.

"As for Ivy, I don't know her last name which means nobody is giving me bupkis. I don't work at this hospital, but my guess is that she'll be done before your brother gets out of surgery," Abby said.

Someone grabbed my bicep. I turned to see Debra staring up at me. "Is Ryan in surgery?"

I put my hand over hers. "Killian, my brother, is in surgery, Ms. Brummis."

She dropped her hand. "For heaven's sake, Ryan, you can call me Debra. How on earth is your brother the one in surgery?"

"It's a long story. Let's tell the nurse who you are. You'll get more information on Ivy since you're family, and they'll probably let you go see her," I said.

I stepped forward, then felt my sister link her arm through mine on my other side. My head turned to her.

Mickayla looked up at me. "I care about her, too, Ry."

The three of us went to the nurse's desk. The nurse told us Ivy was in surgery, also, and directed us to a waiting room on the second floor.

Mickayla shook her head. "My brother was brought in at the same time as her and he's in surgery, too. Should we be waiting upstairs for him?"

After the nurse asked for our name, she checked her computer and shook her head. "No, he's on the first floor."

We turned away from the desk. I stopped and looked at Debra. "I'll come with you to the second floor."

She grabbed my hand and gave it a squeeze. "No, you can't be in two places at once, Ryan. You need to find out about your brother. It's written all over you that you're concerned about both of them, but I'll come get you when Ivy's awake. No matter what, Ryan."

I nodded. "Thank you, Debra."

I guided my sister to a pair of empty seats next to Volt. He shifted to one of the empty seats, and Mickayla sat between him and his wife, Jackie, who held an arm out. Once my sister sat, Jackie wrapped her arm around Mick's shoulders.

I sat on the other side of Volt, doing my damnedest to keep my mind calm.

"Lark called a moment ago. The police finished questioning him ten minutes ago. They're sending an officer down here to talk to you. Maybe Ivy as well if she's able to answer questions by then," Volt said in a low voice.

My head moved in a slow nod. "Do you want me to wait for the club lawyer to get here?"

Volt shook his head. "Not necessary. Sig and Rusty didn't make it."

I twisted my head to look at Volt. "I didn't think the second shot was fatal."

Volt frowned. "Lark shot Rusty in the head because Rusty was aiming at Ivy. He'd hadn't meant to kill Sig, but the EMTs said he was dead at the scene."

"Did you or Blood call Dad?"

Volt nodded once. "Blood did. They're on their way out."

A clock on the wall indicated it was seven-forty-five. If my parents were already enroute, with good traffic, they'd get here around two-thirty in the morning.

"Dad'll be lucky if he doesn't get a speeding ticket," Mickayla said, leaning forward to look at me.

I gave her a half-hearted smile.

Volt shook his head. "Gamble isn't driving. He and Victoria are riding out with Block and Heidi in their Tahoe."

It hadn't occurred to me that this was so bad, Dad wouldn't be able to drive out here. I tilted my head back, fighting against my swirling emotions. Rage that Killian put himself in that position, helplessness, and a desperate, clawing desire that he survive.

"Garrison family," a male doctor wearing surgical scrubs said from the front desk.

Mickayla and I surged toward the desk.

"That's us. We're his siblings," Mickayla said.

The doctor's eyes darted past us. I looked over my shoulder and saw all my MC brothers standing at my back.

"They're with us," I murmured.

"I'm Dr. Ieverson. We removed the bullet from your brother's lung. He's on a ventilator and he's been moved to ICU. The next twenty-four hours are crucial. Our primary concerns are infection and blood clots. We'll be monitoring him for both. He's young and appears to be in good shape, so the goal is to wean him from the ventilator within thirty-six to forty-eight hours. After that, he'll likely be moved to a regular hospital room."

"But he's going to be okay?" Mickayla asked.

Dr. Ieverson turned compassionate eyes to my sister. "I'm sorry. All I can tell you is that the next twenty-four hours are the determining factor."

Mickayla's inhale mingled with a sob, and I put my arm around her shoulders.

"Can we see him?" I asked.

"One at a time, yes. I'll send a nurse out."

CHAPTER 30

THROUGH-AND-THROUGH

IVY

My hand tickled when I woke up. I thought it was just the IV line moving, since I'd woken up earlier and Mom had told me I'd had surgery. Ryan came to see me, but the nurses put more drugs in my IV bag, and our visit was cut short since I couldn't stay awake.

I opened my eyes and saw Ryan was holding my hand. He was drawing circles on my palm and he had his head bent to my hand, like he was studying it.

"Hey," I croaked.

His head jerked up. "Ivy."

I felt my lips tip up. "How're you doing?"

His eyes widened. "I'm supposed to be asking you that."

"I'm awake, so that's a good sign, right? But how's your brother?"

He turned his head to the side and exhaled, then he turned back to me. "He's out of surgery. And, I guess we have another twelve hours to go before we know if there's another hurdle for him."

I squeezed his hand, but it wasn't very strong.

He shook his head. "Save your energy, Trouble."

"Where's Mom? She was here the last time I woke up."

He lifted my hand and kissed it. "She went to get coffee. Are you hungry? I'll see if they can get you some food."

I shook my head. "I'm not hungry, but some water might be good."

A tall, slim woman with brown hair strode into the room. "It's a good thing I bought three water bottles instead of just one, then."

She wore shorts and a T-shirt promoting the band Slightly Stoopid. Something in her facial features told me she was Ryan's mom. This was confirmed when Gamble came in behind her.

"Ivy, it's good to see you're awake," Gamble said.

"Hi," I squeaked out.

"Did I hear you say she's awake?" Mom asked as she hurried into the room.

My eyes widened and darted between Gamble and his wife. "You two met my mom."

Ryan gave me a small smile. "It was bound to happen, Ivy."

"I'm Victoria, Ryan's mom, and your mother is lovely," Victoria said, fiddling with the wrapper covering the sport cap of a water bottle.

"Kitten, let me do that before you drop it," Gamble said, taking the bottle from her, undoing the cellophane, and handing it to me.

I realized she was as nervous as I was – probably more – since one of her sons was fighting for his life.

"It's nice to meet you, Mrs. Garrison."

She aimed a stern look at me. "Victoria. It's nice to meet you, too, but I would have preferred much different circumstances."

My mom wandered around to Ryan, holding out a to-go cup of coffee. "Here you are. Black with four sugars. You might want to cut back on that, young man."

I looked at Ryan, hoping my eyes conveyed my apology.

He grinned at me, then looked at Mom. "Thanks, Debra."

As I sipped some water, I struggled with guilt.

"What is it, Ivy?" Ryan asked.

I glanced between all the people in the room. "It's just that I'm all right, but... I feel guilty keeping you from—"

Ryan grabbed my hand while he rose to prop a hip on the side of my bed. "Stop, babe. Only one person at a time can be with Killian, and he's not conscious."

Victoria stood on the other side of my bed, and she rested a hip on my bed too. "My best friend Heidi has always called these three hers, even after she had her own kids. She's with Killian right now. Her husband, Block, is going to spend some time with him when she's done."

I recalled meeting Block. Then I had to fight off my emotions as it became clear how serious things were. "He's a nice man," I whispered.

Gamble smirked. It was diabolical – much like Killian's the first time I met him. "Block is anything but nice, but he'll like knowing you said that."

By lunchtime I had no idea when I'd get out of the hospital. My room had turned into a revolving door of visitors...which was both comforting and surprising. I had no idea so many people cared about me after only being around me once or twice.

Alexandra hurried into my room not long after Gamble and Victoria went back downstairs to get an update from the doctor and to see Killian. Kristen came in right behind Alexandra, and I did introductions.

Chad bustled in not three minutes after them. He looked disheveled.

"What happened to you?" I asked.

Chad rolled his eyes. "One of my best friends got shot is what happened to me!"

"It was a through-and-through, Chad," I muttered, never in my life thinking those words would leave my mouth.

Chad turned his outraged expression to Kristen. "Do you hear her? Where is Ryan?" He looked at Alexandra. "I'm sorry, you don't know me, but—"

Alexandra grinned. "It's all right. I get it, but be thankful she's awake and on this floor. If she were downstairs, things would be far worse."

Chad took a deep breath. "Right." He looked at Kristen. "Did you try to see Ricochet?"

Kristen shook her head. "It isn't like that, and he has family who should be there. Not me."

My mind wandered while the three of them became better acquainted. It really had been a close call, and I prayed Killian would be taken off the ventilator.

Ryan and Mickayla wandered in a couple minutes later. Mickayla gave me a feeble hug since I had one arm in a sling. Kristen crossed the room to her and gave her a better hug than I could.

"How is he?" Kristen asked.

Mickayla twisted her hands up. "No changes, but supposedly that's good. A nurse pointed out that he's not going to be able to navigate stairs for a few weeks if he recovers because of his lung needs to heal. That means he can't stay at the clubhouse."

I cleared my throat to get her attention. "He's welcome to stay at my place. The master bedroom is on the first floor. He wouldn't have to climb any stairs."

"Trouble," Ryan muttered.

I shook my head. "I could stay with you for a few weeks, since I *can* climb stairs."

"He won't want to put you out of your home," Ryan said.

Chad waved at Ryan. "I'm also in a first-floor condo, and he's more than welcome to stay at my place." His eyes darted to me and back to Ryan. "My bathroom is better than hers, not that I'm biased."

I gave a silent chuckle, then stopped because that movement made my shoulder hurt.

Ryan's eyes widened with concern.

"I'm fine," I said.

He looked at Chad. "That's incredibly nice of you, man. He's got a best friend from back home who's in the military and stationed at NAS Jax. His house isn't far from the clubhouse, and he's offered, too. Pretty sure Killian will take him up on that. Plus, Colton's going on deployment soon, and Killian and I were already on board to do weekly check-ins on the house. Now, it won't be an issue."

Chad nodded. "Good to hear. Just know, it's a standing offer in case something falls through."

A doctor knocked on the open door. "Ms. Brummis?"

I nodded. "That's me. Are you here to tell me I can go home?"

He chuckled. "If your exam is good, that will happen very soon."

Everyone but Ryan murmured their good-byes and moved toward the door.

After the doctor was done (I had the all clear to go home), a police officer sauntered into my room.

He nodded at Ryan, and I realized they'd already met. I spent close to half an hour answering his questions about what had happened.

Once he left, Ryan and I finally had a moment alone. I waited a couple minutes to be sure the officer wasn't within earshot.

I grabbed Ryan's hand. "What happened to Rusty and Sig? It all happened so fast, and the officer didn't really say."

Ryan inhaled through his nose and tipped his head back a touch. "Both of them were dead at the scene."

I squeezed his hand. "You almost sound disappointed."

He leveled his ocean blue eyes on me, and I saw his pain. "That bastard could have killed you, and if shit goes south, my brother might not make it. Things are looking good right now, but it's gonna be a long road before he's breathing on his own and back to normal."

"It doesn't say good things about me, but I'm glad they're dead."

The pain in my man's eyes morphed into an angry gleam. "Death is way too fuckin' kind for those assholes. *This* doesn't say good things about me, but I'd rather see them suffer worse than Killian is right now."

My head tilted. "No honey. That says very good things about you because that vengeance is driven by the enormous amount of love you have for your triplet."

His lips pressed together and I noticed his whiskers were thicker. "And the enormous amount of love I have for you, Ivy."

I smiled. "There you go being too darn sweet to me."

A nurse came in with a wheelchair. "Got your discharge papers here. If you have some clothes to change into, I'll wheel you downstairs when you're ready."

EPILOGUE

HAVE A SNACK

Ivy

A year later...

"I've got a surprise for you," Ryan said, coming into the kitchen where I was chopping an onion.

I put the knife down and faced him. "I love surprises."

He tipped his head to the cutting board. "Can you put that in a container? The surprise isn't here."

"Aren't we having dinner in tonight?" I asked.

He grinned. "I changed my mind."

I twisted my lips to the side and shrugged. "All right, but just to let you know, I'm starving."

"Then have a snack, Trouble."

I almost rolled my eyes at the nickname. In the past year, we hadn't had one bit of trouble, and I liked it like that. Killian had been released from the hospital after five days in ICU, and another day in a regular room. Like Ryan had predicted, his triplet refused my offer to stay in my townhouse. When Chad shared his offer to use his condo for a convalescing stay, Killian had looked flabbergasted before he chuckled.

"Man, I would cramp your style. I'm not gay, but I'm a man, and men get jealous. You bring someone home with you, they are *not* gonna believe that I'm just 'convalescing' as you put it. Besides, Colton has a walk-in shower at his place and a seventy-inch flat screen."

Ryan handed me a granola bar and pulled me out of my memories. "When you're finished with that, put your hair up. We're riding somewhere."

"Do I need to wear my cut?" I asked. Ryan had given me a leather cut that had a patch on the back that declared me to be 'Property of Nickel.' The feminist in me didn't care for it, but after spending time in the biker world, I loved that everyone knew I was his.

His head wobbled as he considered it. "We're hitting the Interstate, but you don't need your cut tonight."

Forty-five minutes later, we rode along an exit ramp off I-10 in Sanderson.

"What are we doing?" I called over Ryan's shoulder.

"Don't worry about it," he yelled back.

I turned my head to hide my irritation.

"Don't be cute, Trouble," he said, and I noticed him watching me in the mirror.

When the light changed at the off-ramp, we rode north, and then Ryan turned left onto US 90. Five minutes later, he slowed and hung a right onto a dirt lane I hadn't thought I'd see again for the rest of my life.

If it hadn't been for a conversation we'd had a few months ago, I'd think this was outlandish. But, I'd seen a listing come across the database that stood out not just because it looked familiar, but also because of the dilapidated nature of the house. Someone had listed the run-down home Ryan and I had been taken to, and when he got home from the bar that night, I'd said I wished I could buy it.

It was crazy for so many reasons. The house was forty-five minutes away from my office, and that assumed *no* traffic. Every morning there was traffic headed into town on I-10, so the idea of living out here meant I'd be committing to sitting in my car a lot more than I did already. A year ago, we'd only been in part of the house. The pictures on the listing showed *every* room needed major repairs. Some of them massive. It would be a money pit...and we weren't likely to recoup that money because of the location being so remote.

Ryan brought his bike to a stop, put down the kickstand, and powered off the engine.

I scrambled off the motorcycle and crossed my arms as I stared at the house.

It wasn't quite so run-down any more. At least, not from what I saw on the outside. A new roof had been installed and the siding had been replaced. The house had been painted a crisp yellow, like a sunflower.

I glanced up at Ryan. "Somebody bought it."

He sidled up beside me. "Yeah. Me."

My head turned with my sidelong glare. "Are you crazy?"

He grinned. "I'm crazy about you. My goal is to give you anything you want, Trouble. You mentioned it—"

I dropped my arms and turned to him. "Yes, and you told me I was nuts."

His hands came up and cupped my cheeks. "Then I thought about it, looked into the listing, it was priced way too high."

My eyes closed. He was right. It was the thing that caused us both to dismiss it – or so I thought.

I opened my eyes. "But you *bought* it, and you didn't hire me as your realtor!"

He chuckled.

"This is not funny, big guy."

He wrapped his arms around my shoulders. "I wasn't sure I'd qualify for financing."

I shook my head and tried to wave an arm at the house. "Half the reason I wanted it was to be the one who remodeled it."

He nodded. "I know, and you still can. The only things I had done are the things you weren't going to do yourself anyway – insulation, new roof, and the siding."

I stepped out of his hold. "But that had to set you back even more."

He shook his head. "Not really. Bluff did the insulation and siding for the cost of supplies. The roof was done by the sellers because the bank wouldn't finance otherwise."

My eyes darted to the house. "Do you like that shade of yellow?"

"Your eyes light up at every yellow house you see. And as Bluff pointed out, there aren't any trees close to the house so the sun's gonna beat on this place all year. That means it'll fade faster than you'd probably like."

I put my hands on top of my head as everything sunk in, then I bit my lip. "This is a long way from On a Lark."

He shook his head. "It's twenty-five minutes on US 90. Your place or the clubhouse is twenty minutes most days even if it isn't the same mileage."

"Wow," I murmured.

"On the one hand, it's a trek to your mom's, but on the other hand Lark's place is fifteen minutes away. You two aren't that close, but I've noticed he's reaching out to you more and more."

"Yeah," I said while nodding slowly. After the shooting, Lark and I had carved out some time every other week to get to know each other. It was slow going, but I was hopeful we would at least be friends, even if he'd never be a father-figure to me.

"Baby, do you still want it? It's okay if you don't. I'm gonna fix it up with Bluff's help regardless. You're gonna be in on that, and if you don't want to live in it, then I'll sell it. We can use that money for a down payment on a different place."

"How long does Bluff think this will take?" I asked, turning to face the house.

"Depends. There's a lot of square footage here, so probably a year if everything goes well. Most likely eighteen months."

I leaned toward him. "Do you *really* want to live in the house where we ki—"

He put his finger to my lips. "I'm going to live wherever you are, Ivy. What happened is over, and I don't believe in ghosts. When this place is finished, it's gonna be fuckin' gorgeous –almost as gorgeous as you. And when we're ready to have kids, there's plenty of fuckin' room for them."

I took a deep breath. "I'm gonna need a new car."

He grabbed my hands and turned me toward him. "That's another thing. You aren't happy with your firm. Haven't been for a while now."

"Yeah, but—"

He leaned toward me. "There are no 'buts' when it comes to your happiness, Ivy. You could get hired by a different realty firm, one that's closer. I know that's easy for me to say, but I've been biting my tongue for a while. I'm going to do everything I can to make sure you're happy. So, keep that in mind."

I wandered closer to the house and in the direction of where we'd taken Campbell's body.

Ryan chuckled as he followed me. "We dug out those palmetto bushes, and cut down one of the trees. That area doesn't look the same any more because I knew you'd be superstitious."

I turned around. "I'm not superstitious."

He jerked his head toward the house. "Let's take a look."

We wandered up the steps to the wrap-around porch. I noticed that down the far side, a porch swing had been hung with two wicker chairs sitting beside it. A small table sat between the chairs with a tall vase of sunflowers on top.

"What on earth?" I asked in a low voice.

"Go take a look at that," Ryan encouraged.

I crept down the porch and heard Ryan's footsteps behind me, until I didn't. When I turned around, I saw he was crouched on one knee.

My eyes widened. "You cannot be—"

He held out a hand with a small velvet box sitting in his palm. My hands went to my mouth as I gasped. His other hand shook while he opened the box. "Ivy, my troublesome woman, I love you and want to spend the rest of my life with you. Will you marry me?"

I put my left hand out. "Like you even have to ask! Of course!"

He slid the ring with a huge square-cut diamond onto my finger and stood. I wrapped my arms around his neck, went up on my toes, and kissed him as hard as I could.

Ryan

"She said yes," I murmured into my cell phone while I sat on my bed.

"Of course she did," Mom said. "Congratulations, honey. I can't wait to see you get married."

"I was wrong," I blurted.

Shit. I hadn't meant to say that and I couldn't think of a decent fib to lie my way out of it.

"Wrong about what?" Mom asked.

I sighed. "I told myself I'd never find what you and Dad have."

"Sweetheart," she started.

"No, it was more than that, Mom. I figured it wasn't worth the trouble either. Hearing from the other brothers what you and Dad went through. I never wanted that."

"I see," she murmured.

I took a deep breath. "But I was wrong because it wasn't up to me."

"This is true, but there's a reason I love the nickname you gave her. You said 'it wasn't worth the trouble,' but you were wrong about that."

I huffed out a quiet chuckle. "Yeah. She's trouble and she's completely worth it."

Movement in the dresser mirror caught my eye and I looked over my shoulder. Ivy stood there, eavesdropping shamelessly with glossy eyes.

"I gotta go, Mom, but I wanted to pass on the great news."

"I love you, sweetie. We'll talk soon," Mom said.

"Love you, too, Ma," I said and ended the call.

"How much of that did you hear," I asked while I leaned over to put my cell on the nightstand.

"Most of it," she said, coming to the bed and climbing on my lap.

I put my arms around her. "I love you, Ivy."

"I love you, too, but you should understand something," she said.

"What's that?"

"You're the one who's trouble around here, but I'm crazy in love with your brand of trouble. When we start a family...in a couple years or so, our kiddos are gonna be *full* of trouble."

I laughed and leaned back on the bed. "And I can't fuckin' wait."

Thank you for reading.
If you want more of Ryan and Ivy, use your smartphone to scan the QR code below.

The link takes you to a sign up page for the Karen Renee Newsletter and you'll receive Ryan and Ivy's Bonus Epilogue.

The Riot MC Next Generation Series continues with
Make or Break
Mickayla and Tundra's story.

OTHER BOOKS BY KAREN RENEE

Please visit your favorite retailer to discover other books by Karen Renee:

The Riot MC Series
Unforeseen Riot
Inciting a Riot
Into the Riot
Calming the Riot
Foolish Riot
Respectable Riot
Starting the Riot
Rough Riot
Fighting a Riot
Wicked Riot

The Riot MC Box Set Series
The Riot MC Box Set #1 (Books 0.5, 1, 2, & 3)
The Riot MC Box Set #2 (Books 4, 5, & 6)

Standalones
Beta Test

The O-Town Series

Relentless Habit

Wild Forces

Abrupt Changes

O-Town Series Complete Box Set

Riot MC Biloxi Chapter Series

Harm's Way

Brute's Strength

Roman's War

Cynic's Stance

Gamble's Risk

Block's Road

Tiny Problem

Finn's Fury

Mensa's Match

The Riot MC Next Generation

Break Out

Break Away

Break Inside

Make or Break

ACKNOWLEDGMENTS

First and foremost, thank *you* for reading. I'm always grateful you choose to spend your time reading my words.

Thank you to Barbara J. Bailey for your incredible attention to detail when editing my work.

Thank you to Draven and CJC Photography for such a fabulous cover image. Thank you to Bee at Bitter Sage Designs for another stellar cover and teaser graphics.

Thank you to the members of my reader group. Your feedback and support helps more than you can imagine. I know it's been a little quiet over there. I'm humbled that you dig my work as much as you do.

Thank you to Enticing Journey and the bloggers and influencers who help get the word out about my books. I'm grateful for all the work you do!

Thanks to my family and friends for your support.

Special thanks to my family and friends for your continued love and support!

ABOUT KAREN RENEE

KAREN RENEE IS THE award-winning author of the Riot MC, Riot MC Biloxi, Beta, and O-Town series of books. She once crunched Nielsen ratings data but these days she brings her imagination to life by writing books. She has wanted to be a writer since she was very young, but it's taken the time for her to amass enough courage and overall life experience to bring that dream to life. Some of those life experiences came from the wonderful world of advertising, banking, and local television media research. She is a proud wife and mother, and a Jacksonville native. When she's not out and about with her family, you can find her at her local library, the grocery store, in her car jamming out to some tunes, or hibernating while she writes and/or reads books.